Fleeing the Shadows

Floy Braun

Contents

Chapter 1

I lay here staring at the ominous sky thinking about her...

Some people wonder what their purpose is. They question their dreams—the desire in their heart. Not me. I've always known. I've known from the first time I saw her magnetic, emerald stare. The questioning gaze of the female made of my soul.

I ache for her touch, one not masked by the dreams I visit her in.

Nearly eight new moons have passed since I've visited her dreams. Not seeing her has only made the dreams of our past lives more vivid. The universe along with this creator-forsaken dimension is yearning for me to bring my queen home. Waiting for us to rule a golden age.

Foreboding surrounds the palace.

My mother hasn't looked me in the eye for days, my father is anxious. Donalt, the most powerful ruler I've ever met, the only one in this dimension, is constantly preaching his prophecies about my life. He told me that I'd succeed him. His throne will be mine...when I have her, not a moment before.

I doubt him.

He's a demon, one who has ruled for over four million years. He'll never fall. He has a sinister plan. I can feel it. Sometimes, I swear, I hear him in my mind telling me what to do, what to say.

I fight him with the thought of her.

Those eyes...

With her at my side, we've fought and died together in more lives than I can discern. This life will be different. I refuse to let anything or anyone stop us from being together for eternity—immortality.

The Blue Moon that falls on her eighteenth year is when this pain and anger of not having her near me will end. That is when the power will belong to us.

We will be unstoppable.

~Willow Haywood~

I was terrified...

Humid summer air blew through my open window as I tossed and turned in my sweat soaked sheets. I was trapped in a nightmare. The ruthless dreams where I couldn't sense the people around me, at least, I couldn't sense their emotions—I knew they were there. I could see them.

Nightmares like this had haunted me since I was a kid. The dense weight on my chest was unbearable. I couldn't breathe. Adrenaline hissing through my body gave way to hair-raising chills. Hot. Cold. Holding my breath. Panting. My anxious mind was in control. No matter how many times I told myself to chill, I only became worse.

Going unnoticed by the people in this dream place was normal. They were lost in their own personal hell. Lines gave definition to their troubled expressions. The world around them was as gray as a building summer storm. To lift the weight from my chest and wake,

I'd have to find the one who'd called me here, the only one I could sense. If I could feel their emotions, I knew my touch could help.

I pushed my way through the disconsolate streets crowded with souls draped in disdain. I could hear the sound of arguing growing louder. It had to be my way out. The weight on my chest grew stronger, telling me I was right. My fear was near blinding. I kept telling myself no one could see me.

I was a ghost to them.

I was the one who should be feared. I could help or leave them.

At least, I assumed I could leave them. I'd never tried. Help and get out had always been my game plan when I awoke here.

Small windows lined the tall gray hand laid stonewalls. Darkness lingered behind most, while soft orbs of light illuminated others. There was no grass, trees, or sign of birds or any other life beyond the hopeless people all dressed in long black cloaks. Everything was controlled and uniform. The absence of color, music, and laughter was almost as petrifying as the emptiness in their dark eyes.

I walked closer. The weight was reaching a degree of unbearable pain. The one who had called me was close.

Why did it have to hurt? I tried to push away the invisible force that was torturing me, but my efforts were in vain, just as they always have been.

The arguing was coming from one of the small windows on the first level. A man was yelling as a woman cried out. On the front steps, I saw a little boy. He looked to be five or six. He was the first one I'd seen here that gave me pause, a sense a familiarity. It was his eyes—they were blue, almost clear.

He stared blankly into the darkness, but I was almost sure I saw the tiniest grin touch the edge of his lips, as if he sensed me, and knew it was going be all right now.

His hair was long and messy. The clothes he was wearing were tattered and dirty. Every instinct I had told me to grab him and run—wake us both up in my safe world. But that was nothing short of impossible. Putting my resentment for this dream, and how helpless it made me feel, I sat down next to him and placed my hand on the small of his back.

I had no idea how I did what I did. It was like breathing, letting my heartbeat; I was born with an extra sense that I constantly struggled to fit into my life. It wasn't fun feeling emotions of others. To know that even if I was having the best day in the world, one sad person in my path could pull me into their world of darkness. It made me feel out of control, like I didn't have permission to be my own person.

It was different in dreams like these.

Here, I only felt one, and it was one that a single touch and focused thought, wrapped in emotion, could help. I could make them feel like I did. I could change the course for us both.

There was no way I was going to let this little boy feel any of the terror I was wrangling with as I searched for him.

Instead, I thought of how happy he could be if he were only given some sense of being loved. How abundant he would feel if he could be the center of some lucky parents' world. The little boy dropped his eyes as he felt me. Oddly, his emotion shifted to regret and sorrow. Not understanding, I focused on peace. His emotion slowly gave in to mine, bringing a sense of tranquility into him. I wanted to give him happiness, but my time there was coming to an end.

Silence came.

The little boy vanished, as the people on the street did. The wind whistled through the barren, cold walls. Now, I could only hear my violent heartbeat.

I stood, bracing myself for what I knew would happen.

A tall, dark figure emerged from the shadows, his contemptuous laugh echoing through the darkness.

He's been in every nightmare I've ever had, taunting me, trying to force me to succumb to him. His face is always hidden by the darkness. The dragon tattooed on the inside of his arm told me he was the same one. This figure was once a child, but now, both teens, we played the game that brought only him pleasure.

He crept closer to me, laughing under his breath. He then reached for me. I knew from my previous nightmares that a burning white light was about to push right through me. I crossed my hands in front of my face, blocking the surge of light.

When the light didn't come, I slowly lowered my hands. The figure was standing just in front of me. I still couldn't see his face, but I could feel his eyes searching over me. He grasped my wrist, where I have a tattoo of an Ankh, a beautiful cross that opens at the top with a loop. My instinct was to pull away, but I could not make my mind and body agree. With his touch, I felt a hypnotizing, warm sensation that eased through my wrist, up my arm, and circled through my body taking the weight off my chest. His thumb traced over the cross.

I sensed him smirk.

"This is true...I will find you now," he said in a deep, meticulous voice. He pressed his thumb in the center of the loop. The warm sensation turned into a scorching burn. I screamed through the pain as I thrashed and fought to get away.

In the next beat of my heart my eyes flew open—I'd made it back to reality.

My screams brought my father into my room. He's always the first person to respond when I wake in the night.

I've never told my parents the details of the nightmares. Telling my parents how afraid I was would only force me to know if should or should not be—I'd feel my answer in their emotions. Something's, I'd rather not know.

"Willow, wake up," my father said in the same serene tone that never let me feel fear for long.

It's hard to categorize emotions simply. I'd learned like many traits people carry around with them, they have a signature to their emotions. A baseline they clung to when life gave them no reason to shift drastically to one emotion or another.

My fathers had always been soothing. Hardly anything would rattle his cage.

Hastily I sat up and grabbed my wrist. I could still feel the pain of the burn.

"You haven't had one of those dreams in a while," my father said, turning on the lamp.

The last one I'd had came on the eve of my eighteenth birthday in November. It was now August. I seriously had hoped I'd grown out of them.

"I don't understand. The new moon was two days ago," my father said to himself.

As a kid, I had nightmares with each new moon. Knowing when they were coming didn't make them any easier to face them.

"I'm all right, Dad. Really."

Fear spiked in his emotion. I glanced to him; his hazel eyes had turned to a shade of brown. They tend to shift when he's concerned about something.

"Let me see your wrist," he said reverently.

My father, Dr. Jason Haywood, has always seemed to know if I'm hurting more than I let on. I've never been able to fake myself well, or sick, for that matter.

When I got the tattoo of the ankh, my mother, Grace, was furious. She grounded me for the first time in my life. My father simply asked why I'd chosen this symbol. I didn't know. The symbol stood for eternal life, something I've always found fascinating. I always thought if people really believed in such a thing, then they wouldn't be afraid. If they were not afraid then I wouldn't have to feel their fear.

I gently uncovered my wrist, expecting to see a burn. Instead, inside the loop at the top of the ankh was a small star. I felt my father's shock, fear, and disbelief. My heart hammered in my chest as I tried to understand how that dream chased me into the sanctuary of my life. In a panic I pushed past my father.

"Where are you going?" he asked, standing to follow me.

"I just want to wash my face, Dad. I'm fine. Go back to bed," I threw over my shoulder as I charged into the bathroom was next and closed the door behind me. I rushed to the sink, and tried to scrub away the star. I couldn't comprehend it. I didn't understand what I'd done to deserve this.

Why do I have to be so freaking different?

Feeling emotions of others isn't my only freak trait. I see images of the people who are not here. They're not dead, I don't think, at least. They're just not here, in my world.

They need my help, just like the soul who calls out to me in my nightmare. What's different when I'm awake is that each touch takes me to wherever they are. When I release them, I'm pulled back into my reality. It's not fun. What happens if one day I don't come back?

Not helping isn't an option. I mean, I don't feel the weight on my chest like when I dream or anything. I just can't deal. I can't watch and feel someone suffer and do nothing—especially if I know I can do something.

When the nightmares stopped a few months back, the images seemed to be few and far between as well.

I missed them for selfish reasons.

I'm an artist, or something like that. I channel what I go through by sketching. I guess on some level, I think if capture the emotions I'd changed I can focus on the good that came of it, and not how unstable the entire ordeal felt.

The good gave me the will to endure this cruel fate.

I haven't so much as doodled on a napkin lately. No images, no nightmares—no muse.

My mother believes I have a creative block. She's an artist, too, and sees my painting as a rare talent. I never had the nerve to tell her that it was simply a crutch I used to cope with the wicked war my soul fights with each breath I take.

In a couple weeks, she is sending me to an art school in New York. The thought of having a nightmare so far from home is mortifying. Fear swelled in my chest as random, unlikely scenarios played out in my mind. What made it all worse was I didn't want to go to art school. This was my moms dream, not mine.

My wrist was red and raw before I gave up. The star was still there. I splashed water on my face then stared into the mirror, trying to look past my haunted green gaze. I wanted to see the answers somewhere inside of me. All I saw was a girl trying to get from one breath to the next. I hated that. I should be stronger than this.

An instinct I hated to listen to, but knew was rarely wrong, told me that the time for me to hide from this was ending. There's nothing worse than knowing that hell is charging toward you and there's nothing you can do to stop it.

I sensed the warring emotions of my parents downstairs. Urgency. Panic. I'd done this to them. I'd spotlighted a weakness that made me self-conscious as hell.

I took a deep breath, wishing that I could change the emotions of the ones around me instead of images that take me worlds away. If I could, I would go down there and move them back to the peace and excitement that belonged to them.

I dried my face off and put lotion on my tattoo, trying to ease the burn. I turned off the light and opened the door, just wanting to go to my room and hide. I heard my parents whispering at the bottom of the stairs. I looked over the banister to see my father fully dressed. He was trying to calm my mother down, but he was having little success. He grabbed his keys and kissed her before opening the front door to leave.

My own confusion outweighed the stunned emotion my mother was feeling as she stared at the closed door.

"Mom?" I said with a crack in my voice as I slowly walked to the stairs.

I startled her.

She jumped as she glanced up at me. With a fake smile filling her face, she tried to find the familiar excitement that her emotion usually carried. She reached back and pulled down her long dark hair, trying to hide the red blemish that always surfaces on her chest when she's hiding something.

"Where's Dad going?"

She glanced down then up at me, searching for words that would not be a complete lie.

"Um, he...well, you see, he had to go meet someone. At the, at the hospital."

"It's, like, two in the morning," I protested, halting halfway down the stairs.

My mother's eyes fell to my tattoo. I felt a surge of fear as she saw the new addition. Not feeling like trying to explain it, I casually moved my arm behind my back.

"You know how good a doctor he is. They just need him. It's nothing really," she said, clearly trying to convince herself.

My father is an amazing doctor. He never really prescribes medicine or has to run painful tests to find a cure. He just seems to know what's wrong and how to heal it. People come from every state to see him. So, I almost believed her until I felt a dread rise inside her.

Before I could bother to push her for the truth, I heard my baby sister's bedroom door open at the other end of the hall. Only six, Libby is a lot like my mother. They both live with a constant child-like excitement rushing through them. Squinting her dark eyes in the light of the hall, Libby pushed her long, dark, tangled hair out of her face.

"Is it time to get up?" she asked me.

Seeing her way out of having to answer any more of my questions, my mother climbed the stairs.

"No, baby girl, Daddy just had to go help someone," she answered in the sweet tone she always used with Libby.

I felt Libby's confusion. Even she knew this was odd.

My mother reached Libby and took her hand. "Come on, sweetie, I'll lay with you."

Libby glanced back at me. I shrugged my shoulders, letting her know that I didn't understand either.

I stood in sleepy confusion for a moment before going back to my room. Leaving the light, on I climbed under my covers. Immediately my mind went back to the words that the figure had said: "I will find you now."

I'd never wanted to find a way to tell my parents, at least my dad, about all the weird things I can do until now. This was the first time I truly felt vulnerable in my real life.

Nightmares came with a new moon, but every single night I dreamt of another place. There I always found the same person. I cannot recall a single day of my life that I have not seen him.

This intoxicating soul mesmerized me with his intense blue eyes, which give way to perfect lips highlighted by sensual dimples that come to life when he smiles at me. His tall frame and broad shoulders leading to a lean, sleek toned body was what eye-candy was made of. His entire demeanor was playful but stoic at the same time. I had alto of friends, good ones, but this boy knew me better than all of them. This one saw what I hid from everyone, even myself.

I took in a deep breath and closed my eyes, holding his image in my mind, hoping this time that I'd find him instead of unexpected horror.

Deep breathes later I slowly opened my eyes to a bright sunlit field. I wished every second of every day for this dream to come to life.

A smile beamed across my face as I started to search for him.

It felt like I belonged in this dream world, like it belonged to me. There was only one flaw—utter silence. I had never heard his voice.

Everything seemed pure, innocent. A small creek led into a larger waterway that fell into a beautiful, gentle waterfall. He was there, watching the water, waiting patiently for me. Feeling my approach, he turned and grinned as he brushed his dark, wavy hair out of his eyes. I felt the air leave my lungs as I took him in, a life force. It didn't matter how many times I'd seen him butterflies still filled my stomach. My heart still beat a little bit faster, my soul hummed.

When my nightmare came before our dream he could see it in my face. His unease and anger for whoever had hurt me would wave down his body. Stepping closer to me, he read my eyes again. Instantly his smile faded. I glanced away, ashamed that I let the nightmare win—I let it follow me into the heavens my life had given me.

He held out his arms and I fell into his embrace. Those strong hands eased down my back as he pressed us together and swayed. His lips landed on the crest of my brow; the sensation sent a quake through my entire body. I craved this boy. I needed him to be real.

I know it's crazy, but I loved him so much that it hurt. His absence from my waking life was agony. I felt out of place with my world by not my family and friends. I wanted to take all the best things and put them in one place. I wanted to bury my hells. All the insane things that happened to me would be worth it if only he were real.

The sound of lawnmowers woke me before I had a chance to say goodbye to my blue-eyed boy. I looked down to see the star still resting inside my ankh.

No way...

I couldn't lie still for another moment. One way or another I was going to outrun this weirdness.

On my bedside table, there was a note from my mother. Libby is playing with Abby today. Abby's grandmother is taking them to a movie this afternoon. Can you meet them at the theater at four? Meet me at the gallery, we'll get dinner.

Love Mom

My mother owns an art gallery at the corner of Main Street. She has a big showing this week. Most of the paintings are mine. She assumes that if I see the reaction of the public I'll be inspired to paint again.

Now that the nightmares were back, I was positive I'd see an image today. Dark inspiration was whispering my name...

I'd just finished getting dressed when I heard a knock on the front door. From the top of the stairs, I could see my friend, Dane, through the glass window that surrounded the door.

I've known Dane my entire life; he's like a brother I got to pick.

The seriousness in his dark eyes would easily let you believe he's older than he is. His athletic build, and rep for being the captain of whatever team he signed on to backed up the command I felt in his vibe. The safety.

We both felt out of place in the southern life we were raised. All my friends joked about breaking out, not following the footsteps our parents laid out for us, but I don't think anyone was a serious about it as Dane. He'd been ready to run sincc hc discovered where the county lines were.

Walking down the steps, I inhaled his vibe. I made his steady flow my own. I wasn't cured from my twisted night, but was well on my way now.

I opened the door and met him with a wry grin, but his smile faded when he saw me.

"Rough night?" he asked, as that all too serious stare rained down on me.

I rolled my eyes and waved him in. He followed me to the patio that lined the back of the house. I sat down on the swing that faced the yard. Dane sat beside me and stretched his long arm out behind me.

"You okay, Willow?" he asked, knowing the answer was no.

I canted my head just so, staring into the distance.

"Nightmares come back?"

I glanced up at him, not surprised he had guessed. All my friends knew I was violent sleeper.

"Do you want to talk about it?"

"No, I'd rather just forget," I groused.

I could sense his frustration as he tried to think of a way to help me. "Was it a new moon last night?" Dane asked. He moved his fingers together as if he were counting the days that had gone by.

I shook my head no.

"I wonder why this one was different," he said faintly.

All at once I felt a gentle pull on me, the way I always did when an image would emerge, looking for my help.

I stood slowly, hearing Dane sigh before he stood to follow me wherever I chose to go. A gust of summer air rustled through the trees, causing one of the branches to scrape against the roof of the patio. I grinned, feeling a sudden fear shoot through Dane before he had a chance to process what the noise was.

"Maybe you just have nightmares because of this house," he said, blushing a little.

My house is over a hundred years old and has always been in my family. It is the most historic and admired home in the town of Franklin, but for some strange reason, Dane has never been completely comfortable here.

I didn't bother to tease him.

In the center of my yard a young woman appeared. A sinking feeling quickly absorbed me. I blinked to make sure I was not imagining her. She was on her knees, wearing a long black coat, holding a letter in her hands, crying breathlessly.

I stepped off the patio and walked slowly in her direction with Dane following right behind me. It wouldn't be the first time he had watched me help an image. In fact, I was sure I had lost count of how many times he had actually come. He never asked any questions or even spoke about it. Each time, he would just act like nothing had happened.

My eyes searched over the woman, trying to understand if the sorrow I felt coming from her was grief or loneliness. After a moment, I knelt in front of her, reached out with my hands and touched her shoulders.

With my touch, the gentle pull grew into a force that moved me forward. A tingling sensation bolted through me. The air around me shifted to freezing. It was dark. Snow fell softly through the air. The woman never raised her eyes to meet mine—the images never do. I tried to remember an emotion of absolute bliss, the way I always felt in my good dreams. I could feel her emotion shifting to the same pleasure. Her tears began to dry. A small smile came to the corners of her lips. I let go, slowly taking in her details, knowing that she would be my next sketch.

The same force that pulled me in pushed me away. I took in the tingle as it passed again. It didn't matter how many times I went through something like that, it always left me enchanted with this seemingly mystical power that was calling my name.

I was back in my yard in the small town of Franklin on a warm summer day.

Dane was standing behind me, calm as ever. When we were kids, this was terrifying to him. His emotion was powerful enough to make me question why I had no fear of this dance with the unknown. Or at least not enough fear to stop me from reaching out again and again.

Now, it's as common to him as a simple conversation.

I took a deep breath before I turned and walked back to the patio. Dane followed me. As I sat back down in the swing, he passed me and went into the house. I stared blankly at the door, trying to figure out what he was doing. He returned abruptly with a sketchbook and stick of charcoal, then walked over and handed them to me before taking a seat.

I leaned back in the swing, pulling my legs to me to balance the pad. My hand then flew across the page as I outlined the woman. As she came to life on the pad, I realized how observant Dane really is. He understood the significance of my art. Why I sketched. That it had nothing to do with a raw unclaimed talent, but that it was my grip on sanity.

When it was done, he smiled and shook his head. "Well, the rebellion thing didn't work. Maybe we should play up the nightmares," he teased.

He and my best friend, Olivia, tried to help me come up with excuses for not going away to school. I would never leave Franklin if it were up to me. I knew everyone here. Their emotions were familiar and I knew how to block them if I wanted to. The thought of being in a huge city filled with millions of emotions was exhausting. I seriously contemplated Dane's words before we both broke into laughter.

"What time is it?" I asked.

He looked at his watch. "Three thirty," he answered, a little shocked by how quickly time had passed.

"I have to walk down and get Libby for Mom," I said, standing and folding the sketchpad closed.

"I'll walk with you. I have to work tonight," Dane said, stretching before he stood. His mother, Gina, owned a small diner in town named, appropriately enough, Gina's. Dane seemed slated to run it one day, but that was a fate he would never choose for himself.

My house sat just one block from Main Street, the heart of town. I slipped on my sandals and walked side by side with Dane. Almost everyone we passed waved, followed by a Tell your dad I said hello.

Dane swayed his head. "Your dad should, like, run for president. He would so win," he said, nodding as someone else said Say hello to your dad to me again.

"You're probably right," I muttered, suddenly remembering him leaving last night and the way my mother was acting.

Olivia was working at the theater for the summer. Her passions are movies and books, so it's a fitting job for her. She's one of those people that I like being around because words are not always needed. We are the two girls who sit on the sidelines, watching others in our class. Because Olivia is small and has the same olive skin and long dark hair as I do, teachers often mistake one of us for the other. Our eyes are similar, too, but I've always thought that mine were stranger than hers. When she saw Dane and me coming up the sidewalk, a smile absorbed her bored face.

"What have you guys been up to today?" Olivia asked.

"Sketching," Dane answered all too cynically.

Olivia's smile fell. "Man, I really thought that one would have worked." She was sincerely trying to help me stay here. I had to love her for that.

"Wait," Dane said, raising his hands to make his words have more of an effect. "I have good news—the nightmares are back."

I elbowed him to tell him to chill on the negative energy he was spouting off. I was fine. I was making it from one minute to the next just like I always had.

"Really?" Olivia gasped. "Do you guys have any good news for me?" she asked as her concerned gaze melted over me.

"Afraid not," Dane said quickly. "Hey, I gotta go. If your lights are on when I get done tonight, I'll stop by," he said to me.

I nodded and watched him go.

"I don't think I will ever figure the two of you out," Olivia said under her breath.

I tossed a dirty glance in her direction. I was always teased about not dating Dane, or anyone, for that matter.

"Just kidding," Olivia said, smiling and raising her hands defensively.

The doors to the theater opened. I could see Libby coming up the aisle with her friend and her grandmother.

"Hey, let's do something tomorrow," Olivia said as I moved so Libby could see me. I nodded and grinned at Libby.

When she saw me, she ran in my direction, her emotions, as always were drenched in excitement.

"Oh, that was the best movie ever! The princess had green eyes like you!"

"Are you sure? I thought only witches had green eyes?" I teased.

Not finding it very amusing, her wide smile lessened. I waved goodbye to Olivia, and Libby told her friend goodbye. She must have known I was supposed to take her to Mom's gallery because she turned in that direction as we left the theater and all but pulled me down the sidewalk.

"Willow, why are you walking so slow? I want to see Mom. Which pieces of yours are in the show?"

Libby never had just one question.

"It's just nice out. I want to enjoy it."

"What pictures of yours are in the show?" she asked again.

She knew I was avoiding the answer.

"I don't know. Mom didn't ask me."

Libby started going on about which ones were her favorite. I listened half-heartedly as I scanned the crowd, looking for another image. The woman wearing a black coat had left me with a craving to help someone else.

People were rushing in and out of the doors of the gallery when we arrived. We didn't see Mom at first, but Libby spotted her as the people scurried around us.

"There she is."

I waved at Mom to let her know we were there. Libby then took my hand and said, "Let's find yours."

It wasn't hard. One of the first ones in the presentation was mine. It was of a little boy in a field, surrounded by wildflowers. I had painted it almost a year ago. The emotion was happy in this painting. He was so sweet, but when I first saw him he was filled with sorrow, he had lost something. I only tried to give him patience. Just as I was to leave him, I saw what he had lost come back to him.

It was his best friend, a yellow lab. It made me smile to remember him. That was the upside to this odd trait of mine: helping.

"Who did you draw?" Libby asked.

"It was just someone I thought of..."

"There are my two angels," I heard my mother say.

Libby was in her arms before I could turn to her voice.

"Did you like your movie?" she asked Libby

The energy that those two put off was unbelievable. Libby nodded and went into a full recount of the movie. My mother's eyes met mine as Libby spoke. Wanting to avoid her stare, I began to walk down the hall in the gallery and look at all the paintings. The emotion of the artwork, not just mine, was powerful. The most amazing part was feeling the emotions of the people who gazed at them. If they understand the painting, they feel it. Seeing the silent connection from the creator to the observer was breathtaking. It always gave me the reassurance that we're not alone, that somewhere someone is feeling, or has felt, what you're going through. They obviously survived it, so no doubt you would, too.

My mother caught up with me. "How did your day go? Did you sleep in?" she asked, trying to catch my gaze.

"Yeah, I'm good."

"We're going to meet your Dad at Antoine's for dinner," she said with a sigh of relief.

"Speaking of sleep, I bet he's tired since he had to work last night."

A surge of suspense rushed through her. She stood speechless before turning and trying to look busy, talking to the lighting crew.

Antoine's was busy, which wasn't surprising, as nice as it is. Dad managed to get us a table out on the street. He seemed lost in his thoughts, which was odd because he is usually very attentive to us. I melted into my seat, keeping my eyes down and tracing my forbidden tattoo, as well as the new addition—the small star—now there. It's now a part of me. Great.

I listened as Mom and Dad went over their days with each other. They were interrupted often as people would pass by and stop to talk to them. I added in a laugh or "yes" or "no" when the questions would come my way. My attention was on the people all around us. I hadn't given up my search for another image.

I could feel my father watching me, following my gaze. When he exchanged glances with my mother, I could sense his concern. What is it with him lately?

As dinner ended, I felt a familiar pull on me, so I hastily searched the crowd for anyone out of place. Across the street, I saw three girls walking toward the direction of our home. They looked wet and were huddled closely together, trying to calm each other. I looked at my mother and saw her sketching something on a napkin.

"Mom, do you care if I go by the art store before I come home?" I asked, needing an excuse for the detour that I was planning.

"That's fine with me. I'm surprised you haven't made any plans for tonight. Hannah and Jessica stopped by the shop today looking for you."

Jessica and Hannah were friends of mine and big fans of my mother. My father seemed to grow a little tense, his emotion shifted to concern.

He spoke before I had the chance to respond. "What could you possibly need at the store? Between you and your mother, you could open a store on your own."

"I just want to see if they have anything new. I think Monica is working anyway," I responded, a bit defensive.

My mother reached out and put her hand on my father's hand. Bringing his attention to her big brown eyes, she spoke softly, almost imploring him to listen to her. "Jason, let her go."

He started to say something, but she put her fingers to his lips, and with their eyes locked, she seemed to reassure him. Taking advantage of the distraction she had given me, I stood quickly.

"I won't be out late," I promised. "Hey, Libby, give me a hug."

"Can I go with you?" Libby asked, dancing in her seat. It was obvious she just didn't want to sit there anymore.

"Young lady, it's close to your bedtime. Give your sister some space," Mom ordered, putting her sketch in her purse.

I shouted, "Love you guys," over my shoulder as I walked toward the art store.

Unfortunately, the images were walking in the opposite direction of the art store, toward where my parents were sure to be walking shortly. The art store was just a few spaces down from the restaurant, so I wasn't too far off track. Going inside would give them time to leave. Monica was sitting behind the counter scrolling through her phone.

"Hey, Willow," she said absentmindedly as she looked up.

"Hey," I said, staring out the storefront.

Monica is honest with her emotions. Sometimes too honest, but she always seemed to lighten any mood I was drowning in.

"What are you looking for?"

"Nothing, really. I was just getting some space between me and my parents."

"Willow Haywood, why on earth would you ever want to do that?" she asked sarcastically. "Wait, don't tell me you're sneaking off to meet one of your many admirers. Who's the lucky guy? Dane? Josh, maybe?"

I grimaced as she said the names, which only made her laugh.

"Hey, go to the lake with me tomorrow. Hannah and Jessica are going," Monica pleaded, walking toward me and trying to see what I was looking at outside the store.

"Yeah, I guess. I'll see if Olivia wants to go, too."

"There's a new guy in town, by the way. Chase has been showing him around. Drop dead gorgeous."

She had always been a bit boy crazy, not a good trait to have in a small town. There are not a lot of them to go around.

"Who is he?" I asked not really caring.

"His name is Drake. Chase met him this morning. He's renting out the studio at Chase's house. He's going to the lake tomorrow, too," she continued.

"Monica—"

"I'll pick you up at noon," Monica asserted.

I let out a deep sigh. "Fine. Look, I gotta go. I'll see you tomorrow."

"Love ya," Monica yelled as I walked out.

Waving goodbye and walking back onto the street, I glanced back toward Antoine's. My family had left. The streets were clearing out. I could see Mom and Libby almost a block ahead of me. Wondering where my father went, my eyes searched for the group of three as I started to walk in the direction I'd seen them before.

My house was only a block away now. Just as I was thinking of turning back I felt the pull again.

I saw them a few feet in front of me: three girls, young. I wasn't sure what was wrong. There was utter silence all around them. My stomach dropped, and I felt a little sick. I always felt this way just before I got in trouble. If I had any sense I would see this as a sign to turn around and go home, but my curiosity won over my anxiety.

I stepped closer.

The night air seemed to chill as a breeze swept through the trees. I could feel emotions all around me. Beyond my images was one full of anguish. I glanced back but all I could see were the people in the distant lights of the streets. Not sure where the anguish was coming from, I ignored it and decided to help the images before me.

Breathing in, I looked at the girls and reached out for the one closest to me. Instantly, the pull and the tingling sensation absorbed me once again. I smiled as I relished in the feeling.

The night became darker. I felt the cold rain. The girls trembled as they walked. Their exhaustion was evident. They were finding their way back. I was sure they'd been lost for some time. They just needed one little push to find their second wind.

I let Libby's face flash through my memory—the warmth and energy that came off her. I then placed my other hand on the girl to the far right. Noticing that the two girls on the outside were clearly stronger, I took my right hand and placed it on the girl in the middle. I watched as determination crossed her face. I could see a house with all the lights on inside. The girls could see it, too. I let go and a force pulled me back into reality.

I stood still, trying to hold on to the tingling sensation I felt, wondering once again what force that sensation belonged to, how I managed to use it in the first place.

"Ahem..."

Hearing someone clear their throat, I turned slowly and right behind me was my father.

"Hey, Dad," I said anxiously feeling my skin blush and my heart pound.

"Willow, do you want to tell me something?" he asked in a placid tone that I had never heard him use before.

My stomach turned. Did he see me disappear—or did he see me reappear?

"About...?" I answered shyly.

My father closed his eyes and raised his head to the night sky. He was really upset, more so now than he had been at dinner.

"Do you realize how far you went that time?" he asked, lowering his head and looking carefully at me.

"Um..."

"Do you even know what you are doing?"

"Do you?" I retorted.

My father cleared his throat again and hesitated as an older couple walked by. "Willow, we need to talk. I need to explain something to you."

I swallowed hard, not sure that I wanted to know what he thought he knew.

Chapter 2

My father put his arm around my shoulder and we began to walk in the direction of our house. His mood was shifting. He wasn't as uptight as he was before. It was almost like I felt surrender in him. He'd decided dreading whatever was bothering wasn't going to stop it, facing it head on would save him the misery.

"Willow...you're a gifted child, and I'm not talking about your creativity," he began.

My body tensed. I'd rehearsed exactly how I'd tell my parents about my weirdness, but I always chickened out before I said a word. It wasn't cool knowing I'd stressed about something for no reason. Did they really know?

"The gifts you have come, in part, from me," he said in his familiar peaceful tone.

I slowly glanced up and noticed the proud grin he saved just for me hugging the edge of his lips.

"Which ones?" I asked warily.

"Well, I cannot feel the soul of others, if that's what you're asking."

My stomach dropped. Did everyone know? Feel the soul of others, his rendition of what I did seemed more poetic.

"There are many empaths, Willow. You should never feel alone." His arm tightened a bit around me. "Here, I'll admit, I doubt many come close to the clarity of your ability. It's time for you to be proud of this, to stop managing your symptoms and take control of how divinely you're made.

Once home, Dad led me around the side of the house through the back gate. As we passed by he knocked on the kitchen window to get my mother's attention. Her excitement and anticipation rattled me. Rarely was I as eager about something I was signed up for as she was.

All kinds of scenarios were clamoring in my mind. Everything from being signed up for some ghost hunt to being tested in a special ability hospital—forever erased from my life.

My heart hammered as I sat down in a patio chair and swore to myself that my parents loved me too much to send me away—or unveil me and my weirdness to the world at large. I could believe this all I wanted, under it all I knew an awakening was about to slam into me. I'd expected it near daily when I was little, right when I figured out how different I was. The day never came, no one said a word, but I never let the fear go that one day 'a talk' would come.

I knew my mental freak out was causing me to feel things that were not real, but right then I'd swear the star on my wrist was burning my flesh as the largest spotlight in existence focused on it.

No nightmare, no star, no talk.

That freaking demon was about to turn my life upside down. He'd successfully broken into my reality.

Mom made her way out to the patio with three glasses of tea and set them around the table. She then ran back inside and returned with her phone, iPad, and laptop. I kept my eyes down, waiting for her to settle. When she did, Dad continued.

"Do you want to what I can do?" he asked, settling in next to my mother,

I met his stare, silently answering.

"I can see what is wrong inside the body."

"Anything?"

A shallow nod.

"You're a really good doctor."

Maybe this was a college talk? A course change? No New York? I could use this empath trait in a career choice like he did with his 'gift'?

"Do you have a weird gift, Mom?"

"Oh, no, I wish. I'm from this dimension," she said innocently.

My father closed his eyes.

"Um...do what?"

I wasn't totally freaked yet. Mom liked to talk about breaking into a zone when she found a creative flow. For all I knew she was calling it a dimension these days—I avoided all 'creative' conversations with her like they were the plague. It was the way she said it, and how I watched my father tense like he was expecting an explosion of emotion, that had me even more on guard.

"Grace...we haven't gotten that far yet," Dad said under his breath.

Mom's eyes widened, as her anxiety built.

I sat forward in my seat. "You mean an actual 'dimension' not a state of mind? What are you trying to say? I'm part—alien? Seriously, you guys better be messing with me."

Nope, this was not 'the talk' I'd imagined. I expected weird, but not this weird.

Dad leaned forward and put his hand on my knee.

"Willow. Listen, you're not an alien. This is your plane of existence." His grin was pained. "You're blood is from a different part of it, that's all."

That's all? No. This was not real. Wake me up!

I squinted my eyes closed willing myself to shoot up in my bed. Maybe that was it? I never woke up this morning. I was still having a wicked night of dreams. My mind was trying to reason why the nightmares were back. That's all.

Dad patted my knee to get my attention, shattering the dream hope I was pushing. "Listen, when you do what you did tonight, you're using a string, and those strings connect other dimensions. I'm from a different one."

"String—?"

He cleared his throat. "This is a lot. I get it. It's fine to be disturbed, but it's not okay to deny you didn't sense how different you are from others. How aware you are."

A not so comfortable silence fell over us. Dad had a way of making crazy not seem crazy. He called it as it was. When what was bothering me was right there in black and white I knew I was never far from reaching a balance. Getting the issue in black and white was the hard part.

"Ready?" he asked when he saw me relax a bit. I was overdue to get me right. I was over outrunning myself.

I must've nodded or something because he said. "The string is like a hallway that leads to other doors, and behind those doors are dimensions much different from this one. Honestly, I do not completely understand the way you've taught yourself, but you do pass through the string." His eyes raced across my confused expression trying to gauge how I was grasping this revelation.

I went to speak a few times before the words finally came. "Those—those people I help are normal. They don't look any different than we do," I claimed. I was only half lying. They may look as human as the next person, but I never got what culture they came from. Some seemed futuristic, others like they were in the past. Hardly any fit the world I knew.

I couldn't breathe.

"These dimensions are only different because of the choices made as a whole," Dad assured.

"Wh—why are you telling me this now?" I asked unconsciously rubbing my wrist.

Dad glanced at Mom, then back to me. "It is time to go home," he said quietly.

"What? This is home. This town is perfect, safe, and beautiful."

No. No. No. I was not leaving my safe zone. Not until I had a chance to absorb this reality check.

"My dimension would make this world humble in its beauty."

"Why are we here? Why have you had us live a lie? Why have you not told me that I'm not crazy for all these things that I can do?" I stood up and shifted my weight back and forth. Mature thoughts were no longer holding back the rightful reaction anyone would have when they were about to be ripped away from all the knew.

Dad shifted in his seat and looked at Mom. She smiled, encouraging him to go on. My father then stood and put his hands on my shoulders, forcing me to look at him. His hazel eyes had shifted to a light green, which matched the tranquility I felt coming from him now. He smiled faintly, "My dimension, Chara, has a trait: we all leave to find our soul mates. We are driven by a feeling deep inside."

Oh dear God, the only thing I could think about when he said that was my blue-eyed boy. Every part of me seemed to become aware at once. What if I could find him? What if he was real? A wave of heat washed over me—my body was humming. I was more willing then than ever to hear Dad out. My blue-eyed boy got me in a silent world. I knew he could get me anywhere. I needed that right now. I needed to feel like I wasn't alone. Like I could handle anything.

Dad grinned when he saw my eyes light up, he let his hands fall from my shoulders.

"I left at twenty to find your mother. When she decided she would rather live in my dimension, I went to find another traveler to help me lead her home. The storms inside the string closed my passage. I found other passages over time, but by then you were born. It was safer to stay."

I knew this man. He was holding something back. Like details. "Storms," I repeated, still not understanding what a 'string' was.

"Not like rain and thunder. The string is made of energy; it flows, sometimes too aggressively. We always guide a new person home with the help of a seasoned traveler. If our dimension is not in your blood, all you will see is darkness. It can be frightening," he said, glancing back at my mother, trying to warn her of what she would have to face.

"So, is the storm over now?"

"Not really. We just think it's time," he said as I sensed dread saturate his emotion. He wanted to go home, but he wanted to go on his own terms. Something had pushed him. Me, it had to be me.

"If you couldn't get Mom there, then how are you going to get us all there?"

"I met a friend of mine, Ashten, last night. He's on his way home to get his family. They'll help us all get there."

Shifting my eyes between my mother and father, I tried to imagine what they were not saying. I didn't trust my imagination right about then.

"What's your plan? For us to just vanish? I have friends here. I have a life here. We all do."

"Willow, trust me," Dad said in the same fatherly tone that had always pushed me to do something I was terrified of.

"What are you not telling me? You didn't just wake up this morning and say, 'Gee, I think I'm going to tell Willow that we're from another dimension, ha ha, she will love that,' did you?"

My mother stood and put herself between my father and me.

"We've been thinking about it for a while. Libby is already six. We want her to grow up there."

"Why didn't you want me to grow up there?" I asked sarcastically.

"It was just different then," Dad said.

"Sure." I breathed, pointing out how unbelievable that response was. "Same storms, storms bad enough that you need an entire family to help us abandon our lives. But now is better than then. It was better for me—," my voice became thick with emotion as my eyes filled with tears I wasn't going to let fall. "—it was better for me to bring people in my life. Love them. Better for me grieve for them as I deal with this bombshell." I swayed my head. "There's no reason you could have worth the pain I'm about to go through."

I expected shame, perspective—something to flash into their emotions. The unwavering course they remained on promised me whatever their reason was, my pain was worth it. A necessary sacrifice.

"Listen," Dad said as gently as he could across his firm tone, "We were told someone very dark was in the string. It wasn't safe for you then or now," a sea of deep emotions swarmed through him. "If I have one chance to take you to dimension in your blood, I'm going to take it. You need this, Willow. More than I'm ready to tell you."

He dropped his head; the regret for how this was all playing out was obvious in the expression of his body. "I wanted you to have all the time you could in this part of your life. You deserved to understand the human condition the way this dimension teaches it."

"Teaches," I repeated.

He lifted his eyes. "The youth of this dimension displays elements you will find in each you visit. You were safe, learning an unspoken lesson."

"I'm happy," I pointed out through emotion that was threatening to flood me.

"You will be happy and safe where we are going."

"If we get there, right? Gotta make it past the darkness and storms in some passageway full of energy. We gotta get Libby through that, she'll never understand what's happening. I can't even make it click.

"Ashten has very strong boys. They are the elite of the travelers from Chara. They'll make sure we weather the storms and make it home safely."

Mom wrapped her arm around my shoulder. "Willow, tomorrow we're going to tie up some loose ends, then the next day we're going to go home where we belong."

"Are we never going to come back?" I felt the tears burning, begging to fall.

"We'll come back to visit, but we belong there," Dad said.

"What am I supposed to tell my friends? I have known them my whole life. You want me just to disappear, like they mean nothing to me?"

As I spoke, both of them were shaking their heads no.

"I've called all of their parents tonight," Mom said. "I told them you were accepted to a school in Paris. They're happy for you."

The phone rang, and my mother reached to answer it. When the person on the other end of the line spoke, I heard her begin a well-practiced goodbye speech.

Too stunned and angry to ask any more questions, I rolled my eyes, then turned and stormed into the house before running to my room.

I pulled myself into a ball on my bed and swayed back and forth. I thought everyone I knew, how they got me through things without even knowing they had. I thought so long and so hard my head hurt and somewhere in the middle of it the tears fell as I started to mourn a life I wasn't ready to let go of.

I heard something hit my window not long after I found dazed quiet with my thoughts.

Knowing it was Dane; I wiped my eyes as I walked to the window. I quietly opened it and climbed out onto the rooftop. Having done it more times than I could remember, I grabbed the branch of a large oak tree by my window and made my way down, feeling Dane's anxiety as he braced himself to catch me if I fell. Once on the ground, we walked quietly to the edge of the yard where we sat on a small bench. Dane's pained emotion grew heavier. I knew then my mother had already called his.

"You know, you were supposed to use the nightmares to keep you from going to New York, not send yourself to another continent," Dane whispered.

"I don't think we're going to find an excuse to keep me here," I uttered, covering my face with my hands, trying to hide my raging emotions.

"You're eighteen, you could just tell them no."

"Yep, and you could tell your mom that you don't want to have anything to do with that diner."

It wasn't that we were afraid to go our own way; it was just that we had no idea what we were supposed to be doing. Until that moment came, we would listen and follow.

"What am I going to do without you, Willow?"

"I don't know. Maybe if you're not hanging around me so much you might find a girlfriend," I teased.

Dane crossly glanced my way.

"What? I know Monica still has a crush on you," I said, trying not to laugh out loud.

"Monica likes everybody," Dane bit out, rolling his eyes.

"Hey!" I said in her defense, even though it was true.

"I didn't mean it in a mean way. She's not what I'm looking for," he said as he leaned forward.

"You'll find her," I promised, rubbing his back.

"I'm going to tell you something weird, Willow," he said letting his gaze meet mine.

I wasn't sure how much more "weird" I could take tonight. "I've never seen you as more than a friend," he said with a ghostly smile that held volumes of memories of the two of us. "But, I get this feeling that if I stay close to you, I'll find what I'm looking for."

We sat in silence for a while, staring at the night sky.

"Dane, will you do me a favor?"

He glanced at me, surprised that I had to ask.

"Will you watch out for Olivia while I'm gone?"

Dane nodded, understanding why I was so concerned. Olivia had lost her parents when she was only ten. She now lived with her cousin Hannah. Those two could not be more different. I think I'm the only one that understands Olivia and that's only because I can still feel her grief and loneliness.

"You're coming to the lake tomorrow, right?" I asked.

"I have to work most of the day, but I'll meet you guys out there after my shift."

"They said we were staying that long?" I thought we were just going to get some sun and go home, but I hadn't read a text in hours. The plans could've changed a hundred times. Monica's planning skills were erratic and always evolving.

"Yeah, they're supposed to build a bonfire. I think a lot of them are camping out. It's supposed to be a big farewell thing for you."

"You know I love you guys, but I'm not sleeping out there," I teased, elbowing him.

"Ahh, come on. You're not scared, are you?"

Just then, the back porch light kicked on and my father opened the door. I felt a little anxiety rise inside of Dane. My Dad stared in our direction. A surge of confusion came from him. Dane stood with me, reaching for my hand as he walked me to the patio. He hugged me then politely nodded to my father before he left.

I kept my eyes down and passed by Dad. I made it halfway up the stairs before he said anything.

"Willow."

I stopped mid-stride, then turned to look at him standing at the bottom of the stairs. I couldn't understand what he was so confused about.

"You can feel the way I feel about your mother and the way she feels about me, right?"

I lifted a brow to point out the obvious yes to that question.

"Do you feel that way about Dane?"

"Yeah, right, not even close, Dad," I said as I started to climb the stairs again.

"Are you sure? If you did, that would change everything," he said, climbing the stairs after me.

I froze and looked down. It would be so easy to lie right now and say that I did, but would they let me stay here, where I knew it was safe?

"How?"

"I told you that our dimension believes you are supposed to be with your soul mate. If you feel that way about Dane, then he's your soul mate, and we were wrong about you," he explained.

I sat down on the step where I was standing. The emotion between my parents is beautiful. It's a love that's unconditional. I felt that way about the blue-eyed boy I'd dreamed of. I couldn't remember ever not loving him. I would even say that I loved him more, but then I realized that my father had let something slip.

"Who was wrong about me? What am I?" I demanded as my body tensed.

Dad sighed, as he climbed the few steps between us and sat down next to me.

"I'm going to tell you a story," he said.

Trepidation washed over him.

"Every dimension has different beliefs, rulers, and ways of living. There's one dimension, Esterious, which is very dark."

My heart began to hammer as my nightmares flashed in my thoughts.

"This entire dimension is ruled by the Blakeshire empire. The ruler of the empire is a man named Donalt. He has ruled that dimension for longer than anyone can remember.

"When I was young, I was a traveler. We had taken numerous people to that dimension." His eyes drifted to distant memories. "It always felt like a rescue mission rather than a love story."

He paused and looked over at me, grief echoed in his emotion.

"We had never brought home someone who lived in the palace—a single noble, but a good friend of mine, Justus, came to me and told me it was his time. He wanted my help to bring his soul mate home, so I went with him. Esterious didn't unnerve me, it was the approach to the palace."

Dad's eyes turned green as he smiled, remembering his friend.

"Justus walked to the gate of the palace, like he didn't have a fear in the universe. There, on the inside walking by, was a young, beautiful girl. Justus looked at me and said 'That's her...'"

He paused.

"Long story short, she came home with Justus. Her name was Adonia, and her father was Alamos, Donalt's highest and most trusted priest. The rulers regent, second most powerful being."

My father stared down at his wedding band.

"Shortly after this I left to find your mother. What I know was told to me by Ashten Chambers. The story is every time Adonia would go home to see her father, they would ask her and Justus questions about our blood lines—how we traveled, where we went, things like that. Justus became convinced that old lore about Donalt was surfacing as truth. That Donalt was more than a man but a powerful evil intent to overcome other dimensions as richly as he had taken Esterious. Alamos was in his employ. Until Justus could understand the threat, he forbade Adonia from going home again. She missed her father, she kept dreaming he was hurt...she convinced another traveler, Livingston, to take her home. When Adonia arrived she was held captive. Livingston rushed home to tell Justus, and Justus, Livingston, and Beth, Livingston's soul mate went to bring Adonia home."

His sorrow intensified. He stared at the floor as he continued, "When it was over, Livingston carried Justus's body home. No one really knows what happened to Adonia or Beth. Ashten said that it's been very difficult for Livingston since that day."

Dad paused swimming in a burdened guilt as he thought back over another life he had.

"Years later, a little boy was seen alone in the strings. Livingston warned the people in Chara that Donalt and Alamos were controlling this child. I assume the little boy was Justus'. I don't know any other way he'd be able to travel the strings."

Dad glanced to me, his eyes searched over my face carefully. "Livingston told Ashten that the child was looking for a girl that was born in the eleventh month and could feel the souls of others."

With those last words, my heart thudded deep and slow in my chest. I was born in November, and I guess you could say that I could feel the souls of others. As his eyes continued to search over my expression, it was easy to see that he was looking at his little girl, not the young woman that I'd become.

"Over time, Ashten managed to learn how to navigate through the storms. He found your mother and me just after your sixth birthday. We knew that you were a powerful empath. We were living in one of the largest dimensions in the smallest town, hundreds of miles from any real doorway. We thought if we stayed here, you'd never be found by anyone from Esterious."

My mind replayed the last nightmare I had; the memory of the suffocating pain on my chest and the burn made itself known in the tense stance my body took. It was easy for me to see this evil world my father spoke of. I was easy because I was sure I'd been there, often.

"Willow, are you okay?"

"I don't understand...why was some kid in another dimension looking for me?"

"You're a direct descendant of the first recorded people in our dimension. Livingston believes they're trying to control a prophecy first made millions of years ago."

"What prophecy?" I asked with wide eyes, wanting to know what they were protecting me from.

"Don't worry about it," he said quietly. I could feel him struggling with a mix of emotions. Fear was there, and that was not helping me feel reassured at all.

"Then why are you worried about it?"

He grimaced. "You have to understand, they not only predicted your birth month they predicted the day, hour, and the very minute."

I continued to stare forward. My stomach was turning. The thought that I'd have to face that figure in real life one day was petrifying. I didn't understand what I had done to deserve this.

"Willow, the stars can be read a million different ways. They do not state our lives. I wanted to shield you from this in order for you to live a normal life."

Did he really think I had a normal life?

"You could've at least told me I wasn't insane. Do you know how hard it is for me to be in a large room with everyone's emotions hitting me like a ton of bricks? Try and imagine puberty with my friends. That was not awesome. Not to mention the fact that people would appear out of nowhere, needing my help. Do you know I was convinced they were ghosts until I was like eleven?"

"You hid the struggle well," he said remorsefully.

I closed my eyes. I knew it didn't matter how angry I was. It wouldn't change the past.

That was the one good thing about this sixth sense of mine. I always knew where someone was coming from. I knew if they meant to hurt me or not.

"My nightmare is the reason you're telling me this, isn't it?" I stated, looking down at my tattoo with the star inside the loop of the Ankh.

Dad reached over and gently grasped my wrist, looking intently at the star as he spoke. "It was predicted that on the Blue Moon of your eighteenth birth year, all those who seek you would find you."

"All?"

He gently moved his finger across the star.

"I assumed the prediction meant your gift would be magnified and you'd be able to help more people. When I saw this mark, I realized that the prediction meant that the child would finally find you."

" 'Blue Moon'?" I asked wondering when that was and how I could outrun it.

He let go of my wrist and looked me in the eye.

"A Blue Moon is the second full moon in a month. It's not very common." He glanced down as his anxiety grew. "We only have eleven days remaining until the Blue Moon will rise. I want you safe in Chara when that night comes."

Eleven days.

As far as I knew I had eleven days to live. That was enough to kick me into shock. "What if I didn't have that nightmare?" How long could I have hidden from that demon in my dreams?

"At twenty it would've been time for you to find your soul mate. I'm sure one way or another, nature would've showed you what you are cable of, even if I wasn't ready for you to know."

"Why is twenty the magic number?" I was not a fan of uniformity, in any form. This rule sucked. It meant another two years before I'd find my blue-eyed boy, if he were even real. I had every reason to believe I would not be here then. I couldn't see past the next eleven days.

On one hand, I could be happy I knew him in my dreams. On the other—the one my emotions were clinging too out of self-defense—it would've been easier to make it through this not mourning him too. The boy gave new definition to unfinished business.

"No one made a rule. That's just when most get this urge. It's undeniable...it's all you think about," he said, leaning back and smiling.

"How do you know where to go? People can't find each other in one dimension, much less several."

He stretched his legs out on the steps and looked at me.

"Travelers can see several passages, but the others who don't travel on a daily basis can only see one. The passage they see leads them to their soul mate. Once in the passage, they follow a feeling—whispers of the universe. The other person is usually looking for them as well. It really is a beautiful thing to witness."

"So how does a traveler know if they can see more than one passage?"

"For travelers, their passage is always brighter in their eyes, like a beacon."

"So when I go into the string, I will see a beacon leading me to my soul mate?"

Dad's smile lessened a little. "The 'beacon' will shine when it's supposed to."

"Okay, then tell me what the string looks like to begin with." If there was a chance I could find my blue-eyed boy I was going to take it.

He tilted his head and gave me a shy smile. "Well, it's like standing in the center of a bright light. You feel surrounded by it. As you walk, you see hazes of different colors, they are the doorways to other dimensions."

"Is it big? I mean, how do you know where to go?" I asked. Details, Dad, I need details.

His eyes danced over my face as his smile widened. "There are three traits that define a 'traveler'," he said. "Seeing the passages is only one. Another is that travelers have the ability to feel their way home. Everyone has their own way of using that feeling to navigate.

For me, I would picture my dimension in my mind, then visualize the paths to where I needed to go."

I looked at him like he was crazy. That didn't make any sense. I knew where my house was, but that didn't mean I'd always be able to find my way home.

"You'll see," he said, laughing at my incredulous expression.

"What is the third trait?" I asked hungry to know everything.

"It's the ability to understand every language."

"All of them?" I asked, astonished. That would have made the three foreign language classes I'd taken easier. Not that they were all that hard in the first place. I just hated all the rules in the written part of it.

He nodded. "That one is very important. You see, travelers do more than just pass through the string. We also learn about all the cultures and help the person who is searching to abide by them."

"What do you mean?"

He laughed at the eagerness in my voice. "If you take someone to a dimension, they have to understand what is customary for the time that they live there. We teach them everything they need to know, then get them settled."

"Settled? You don't just leave when they find someone?" I asked. That revelation was not helping my short window of time.

"It just depends. In some dimensions, a fast courtship is customary. In others, it could last years. When I knew I was coming to this dimension, Infante, I planned to stay for at least a year, and if your mother had not wanted to leave, I would've stayed here for the rest of my life."

"So you would've left everything and everyone you loved?"

"When you find your soul mate, you find the person that completes you. They are everything and everyone you love." He paused. "I'm eager for you to meet your grandparents, though."

My mouth dropped open. I didn't know I had any living grandparents. My mother's parents had died before I was born, and my father had told me that his parents were in a beautiful place. I had taken that as Heaven, not another dimension.

"Why have I not met them before?"

"My mother, Rose, feared that if she came to Infante, your hiding spot would be revealed. She and my father, Karsten, just wanted you safe."

My father glanced down at my tattoo, then back at me.

"You've never told me what your nightmares involve," he said softly.

I traced the star with my finger. "I help someone, then I see a dark figure."

"Every time?" he asked. I nodded. "Is this figure the only one you dream of?"

I took my time answering, some secrets I needed to keep—I needed to believe they were a possibility. "I dream good dreams every night."

He didn't push me to elaborate.

"Are you sure you can get Libby to Chara safely?" I asked. "I don't want her in danger because of me."

"Ashten said that they'd discovered new passages the storms have made. They're trying to find a way home without passing the Esterious dimension."

I took in his confidence and let it calm me.

"Do you want to ask me anything else?" he asked clearly wondering why I was being so agreeable now. It was the shock, but I wasn't going to tell him that. He already looked too worried.

"So, Chara is only different because of the culture? Do I need to learn anything before I go there?" Seemed like an obvious question.

He beamed with pride. "Different cultures have come together as soul mates, leaving a perfect blend of harmony in their wake." He stared at me for a second, then went on. "We have a simple faith. Life itself is a gift from above, and love is the most powerful thing in the universe."

"It sounds too perfect," I said, trying to see it in my mind. The evil place in my nightmares would not let me hold any serene image.

"You'll be happy there. I promise," my father said quietly. He looked so tired. "Tomorrow, just have fun with your friends. It may be a few months before I feel safe enough for you to come visit," he said as he stood and began to walk back down the stairs.

Months. Good. He planned to get me past this Blue Moon.

He glanced up at me. I smiled then stood to climb the stairs, trying not to think about leaving my friends. Right now, I just needed to make sure that my family got to Chara safely. If evil was coming for me I didn't want them in the crossfire.

Chapter 3

This dream was different.

It wasn't the sweet place, or even the nightmare. I was standing next to a large white windmill in the middle of a field. In the distance, I could see a beautiful home. There were gorgeous flowers of every color throughout the field. I knelt down to get a closer look and saw that the petals on the flowers were all different. Some looked like roses, others looked like daisies...it was as if they coexisted, but had no knowledge of one another. Ironic.

Next to me, I found a flower more unique than the others. The petals were deep blue with emerald green tracing through the center. The colors were separate, yet one. I stared in awe as I glanced across the field at the other flowers; they began to sway with a breeze that brushed through the field.

I stood slowly, wanting to explore, when all at once I felt a pull from behind me, the same way I felt when I touched one of my images.

A rush of love, passion, and excitement absorbed my soul.

Nervously I glanced over my shoulder, and there behind me, my blue-eyed boy stood. As I looked in his eyes, I could feel his disbelief. He stepped closer to me and reached his arms out.

I lost my focus and woke without warning.

I cursed under my breath as soon as I figured out I was pulled away from him.

I laid in my bed, trying to find my way back to my dream, but my effort was hopeless. The daylight peered through my open drapes. I sat up and grabbed my sketchpad out of the tote bag beside my bed, then turned to a clean sheet and began to sketch as quickly as I could. I was afraid my memory would leave me before I could call back the details. I sketched the I field and the flowers, highlighting the blue and green ones, by making it larger than the others.

My mind drifted to my blue-eyed boy. I wanted him to have a name, to hear his voice. Most of all, I wanted to find him. For the first time I sketched his addictive image.

I relaxed as I gazed into the sketch that was coming to life. I didn't want to wait two years to find him. I didn't want to face what was in front of me without him. I feared that if I didn't sleep right here in this bed that I would never dream of him again. That hurt.

I could hear my sister and mother giggling in the bathroom next to my room, so I placed my sketchbook in my tote bag and pulled my robe on as I walked to the bathroom.

"What's so funny this early in the morning?"

"Look at this bathing suit I found for Libby," Mom answered.

It was bright yellow with a big smiley face on the front and a sad face on the back.

"It makes sense: happy to see you come, sad to see ya go," I teased.

"I get to go swimming today, Willow!" Libby exclaimed.

"You do? Where?"

"I'm going over to Abby's grandmother's house again."

"I assume you're still going to the lake with everyone today?" Mom said as she tired to gauge where I was with life in general.

"Yeah," I said absently. I wasn't ready to accept I was really saying goodbye today.

"I told everyone we were just taking a trip to Paris to see the school and look for a place. They think we'll be back in a few weeks," mom said.

I glanced to Libby.

"Libby is very excited about our trip," Mom said. As she finished pulling her hair back into a ponytail, Libby smiled up at me, then left the bathroom and went to her room to get her sandals.

"Willow, I promise...we didn't keep this from you to be spiteful."

I didn't show any expression. The whole thing had left me confused and exhausted. Libby charged back into the bathroom, dancing in place while waiting for my mother.

"Come here, munchkin, and give me a hug. I love you. Have lots of fun," I said, holding her a bit tighter.

Libby wrapped her arms around my waist. "Miss you," she whispered.

I went back into my room and closed the door behind me. All I wanted to do was go back to sleep, but I knew I'd have to find a way to wear myself down in order for that to happen. Packing, sorting out a life that was not longer mine was my go to distraction.

Monica called, saying she would be there around eleven instead of noon. We were going to pick up Hannah, Jessica, and Olivia. After packing my bags, I dressed for the lake, covering my burgundy bikini with a black sundress.

Dad's study is by the front door. I could sense him in there as I climbed down the stairs. He was nervous. At first, I didn't realize he was on the phone, but as I landed on the bottom step I heard him say, "I agree, we'll take those precautions. I'll head out first thing in the morning."

I leaned in the threshold of the study, wondering what had upset him. When he saw me, he said, "Okay, Ashten, I have to go. Willow is on her way out for the day...yeah...no...okay... tomorrow."

"What's going on?" I asked when he hung up but never looked my way.

"Nothing...um, we're just going to alter our story a little bit."

"Why?"

"It's nothing. I'm going to leave in the morning and tell everyone that I'm going to Washington to help an old colleague. Then we'll tell them that you guys are going to wait for me in New York."

"Why? Where are we leaving from anyway?"

"We're going to leave from Montana...look, Willow, we're about to disappear, we kind of need to confuse our path so no one will worry. Just don't be very conversational about what we're doing. Let them assume."

I grinned dryly. I've never been conversational. I liked being mysterious.

"Yeah, that shouldn't be too hard for you," he said quietly.

Hearing Monica honk her horn outside, I pulled my big, dark sunglasses over my eyes. "Let the mystery begin," I said. When he hugged me goodbye, he seemed to ease up on his mood, but he was still nervous.

Monica was shaking her head at me as I climbed into her car. She loved to wear vibrant colors, and today she was wearing a bright yellow dress and make up. My darkness was clashing with her vibe. "Ya know we're going to the lake, not a funeral."

"You like me to stay here?"

"Yeah, right, this is your last day. You're not sulking. I knew you were good, but Paris—geeze. I bet you never come back from there."

I was glad I was wearing my sunglasses, even if I had no expression at all, my eyes told everyone where I stood with most things. They needed to think this was good thing. Normal.

We picked up Hannah and Olivia first. Olivia climbed into the back seat with a huge book in her hand. I had to grin. Monica and Hannah looked at each other and rolled their eyes. Secretly, Olivia and I loved to drive them crazy by being unconventional.

We picked up Jessica next. It wasn't hard to see she was upset about me leaving, but I felt it raw. I stepped out to hug her.

"Can we please cry later? We're burning daylight here," Monica yelled through the window.

The lake was only thirty minutes from Jessica's house. Once we were on the highway, Monica turned down the radio and said, "Okay, ladies, I really think this new guy is the one."

Everyone laughed out loud.

"Stop! I'm serious. Wait til' you meet him. He, like, has a magnetic force of his own," Monica continued.

She was serious, but there was no way Olivia, Hannah, or Jessica would be convinced she was sincere. All guys Monica liked had something she found alluring about them, something the rest of us could never clearly see.

Monica pulled up in front of one of the trucks that lined the shoreline. I could see Josh and Chase unloading their jet skis. Everyone but Olivia and I rushed to claim a spot on one of the tailgates. I leaned on the side of the car and watched all my friends, trying to burn the memory of their faces and emotions inside me. Olivia leaned up against the car beside me and opened her book to a marked page.

"Good book?"

"It's better than those three," she said. "It's going to be a blast when you're gone."

"What do you want me to do, stuff you in my suitcase?" I asked, halfway considering asking my Dad if that were a possibility. It felt so wrong to leave her behind. She may've had a good home with Hannah's family, but family isn't always blood. Olivia didn't deserve to lose anyone else.

A rather large, nice red Jeep pulled up to where the other trucks were parked. Chase jumped on the bed of his truck, waving the Jeep in.

"That must be the new guy. Looks like he has money. Hot, too," Olivia commented in her trademark I'm not impressed tone.

I didn't answer her, simply because I was perplexed. I couldn't feel a single thing coming from the Jeep. It was a void, like it was driving itself. I squinted my eyes to get a closer look.

I drew a short breath as he stepped out of his jeep and sunlight hit his face. He was extremely hot, tall, and lean built. His dark brown hair was swooshed back out of his face, and his eyes were as black as coal. His best feature was his dominant profile. In real life I'd never met someone as sure of himself as he seemed to be.

Drake walked over to Josh and Chase. Monica peeked through the cab of the truck where she was to gauge my expression. I quickly changed it from perplexed to boredom. She grinned and turned forward, stretching out and posing, as Drake got closer to her. Through my dark glasses, I followed Drake as he walked, checking my senses with each person that he passed. With him, it was empty. First time for everything I guess.

"What do you suppose he did to his arm?" Olivia asked.

I hadn't noticed the white brace on his right arm. He was wearing a black sleeveless shirt and white swim trunks. He looked so strong, so... so familiar.

"Come on, let's go watch Monica make a fool of herself," Olivia whispered.

"No, I want to stay here."

"What's wrong?"

"Nothing, I just...I don't know." My stomach was tying itself in knots. I had never felt so uneasy around anyone.

"Okay, I can look mysterious, too," Olivia said as she pulled down her sunglasses, opening her book again.

Chase and Josh were very different from Dane. They were teenage boys who were only interested in one thing. When Dane was around, Chase behaved, but when he wasn't, Chase took every opportunity to annoy me.

Chase stood on his tailgate, looked me up and down, and yelled in my direction, "Willow, baby, would you like to join us sometime today?"

I was glad I couldn't read minds. His was sure to make me sick to my stomach. Olivia rolled her eyes and threw her book through the open window of the car. She knew she'd have to play Dane's part until he got there.

"So, have you talked to Dane since they told you that you were leaving?" Olivia asked with a hint of disdain in her voice.

"Yeah, he'll be all right. And so will you," I said, still staring at the void Drake was.

"Come on, one day you might miss being annoyed by Chase," Olivia said, pulling my arm toward the others.

Chase whispered something to Drake as I walked closer. Drake just stared at me as if the others had disappeared. I felt my heart beating through my chest. I could barely breathe. The gift that had brought me so much grief was instantly missed around this guy. I felt blind. Not a good feeling to have. Not at this point in my life.

"Baby, this is Drake," Chase said as he put his arm around me.

I pulled my sunglasses on top of my head so Chase would get the full effect of my glare. I heard the girls giggle. Chase let his arm drop and looked at Drake.

"I told you she was feisty, didn't I?" Chase said to Drake.

Drake walked over to me, and I questioned his every step. He stopped inches from me and stared into my eyes. Monica was right—he was magnetic, though I didn't find it appealing the same way she did. This was not a boy. This was a man. A man who knew what he wanted and how he was going to get it, I better not be on that list of wants. I didn't have time for this.

"The good doctor's daughter. We meet at last," Drake said smoothly.

"Seems you aren't having any trouble making friends here." I didn't really care for the fact that he and Chase had been talking about me.

Drake didn't say anything. He just stared at me with his dark eyes, pulling me in and smiling confidently. This boy was dangerous. He had a warning label tattooed all over his soul. I'd also bet every sketch I'd made that this boy knew the effect he had on girls and played it to his advantage.

"That's a new approach. I don't think any of us have ever tried staring her down," Chase said sarcastically.

Everyone laughed. I took advantage of the distraction and broke eye contact, then slid by him onto the tailgate next to Monica and Jessica.

Josh called Drake and Chase out to the jet skis. Drake glanced back at me as he walked away, smiling cunningly.

"When do you leave again?" Monica asked, teasing me.

I rolled my eyes and pulled my sunglasses down. Monica hopped down and walked over to where Drake was, flirtatious as ever. She managed to talk Drake into taking her out on the Jet Ski. The further he was the better I was. I was downright counting on Monica disappearing with him.

I leaned back next to Jessica, who was lost in in her phone. "Hey, when did you get that done?" she asked. Out of the corner of her eye she'd spotted the star inside my ankh.

"The other day. No big deal. I went alone."

I lay down and drifted into a peaceful afternoon nap as the sun warmed my face. Dreaming always came quickly to me.

That was a gift.

I opened my eyes in the field again. This time, I was closer to the home that I'd seen in the distance before. It was a rustic red brick with white porches that wrapped around both levels of the house. When I reached the porch, I followed it around to see where it led, as I did I stopped in my tracks. Just inches in front of me, he was there. My soul seized with anticipation. I didn't understand why the routines of our dreams were altering, but I wasn't complaining, they were shaping him into something real, tangible.

A warm rush absorbed my soul as my heart pounded, deep and slow.

When I gazed into his eyes I lost all feeling. They were so blue, so mesmerizing. He was smiling down at me, staring, questioning why I was there. Carefully he eased closer to me, exploring every part of my entranced expression. His fingertips reached for the side of my face, ghostly tracing every feature, when they touched my lips he outlined each, leaning forward ever so slightly.

My entire body was numb, but I felt my soul pulse with raw expectation.

My eyes fluttered closed. I felt his lips feather across my brow, then my cheekbone. I opened my eyes finding his stare melting into mine.

Time stopped.

He brushed the flesh of his lips against mine.

A quiver rippled through me. I gasped, that slight part of my lips invited him in. The innocent brush of his lips elevated to an entirely new level when I felt his tongue glide against mine, a slow sensual caress.

A lover's touch.

Though the heat of his body was absent, I felt myself melt from the inside out. My head spun wildly. I was sure I was going to faint. Is that possible? Can you faint in a dream?

Thinking it was a dream gave me more courage than real life would've afforded. My hands slowly slid up his chest as his hands gripped my waist and pressed me against his body. I gasped between the movements of his lips. I couldn't get enough. I wanted to kiss him deeper, longer.

We had seen each other every night, but this was our first kiss, and it seemed so overdue.

He had ignited me.

That's when I woke up.

That's when someone cruelly called my name and took me from a record breaking first kiss.

My chest was rising and falling rapidly as the rush of my dream subsided. Dazed, I pulled myself up and pushed my sunglasses to my head. Ready to kill whoever had woken me.

"Willow, I said what's your sign? I want to read your horoscope," Jessica asked, shaking her phone like the open app was about to vanish. I didn't answer; her words were lost in the background. I deeply considered going home and trying to fall asleep again. Figuring this boy out was exactly what I needed right now. It was more than a distraction. It was infusing hope, an unbreakable will to survive anything, inside of my reality beaten soul.

"Scorpio," I heard a smooth, deep voice say. I looked to the void from where it had come, Drake. He was right. How did he guess that?

"Is that right?" Jessica asked, still trying to find my birthday in one of the signs.

"How did you know that?" I asked Drake coldly.

His smile was ironic, like I was missing a punch line. He moved to where I was sitting. In front of me he paused, like he owned the world and all the time in it, then reached for my face, cradling it in his hand and tracing the base of my eyes with his thumb.

His touch moved me, literally.

I felt my skin hum under his. My stomach dropped...I had felt that way before—just before that evil person had burned me in my dream. I held my breath.

"Only a Scorpio could have those eyes," Drake whispered.

Monica's jealously slapped me into a stronger defensive stance. I glanced at his arm, expecting to see a tattoo of a dragon, but I only found the cast that Olivia had spotted earlier. I looked back into his eyes. He winked at me, turned, and walked toward the lake.

"Okay, so that was weird," Jessica said under her breath.

Stunned, I tried to remember a single time that I'd seen the figure's face in my nightmare. I'd always imagined it as a gruesome devilish person, not tall, hot, and human. Then I realized that I'd never felt the emotion of the figure either. If this were the guy in my nightmares, would that not make him the kid that was looking for me? I swayed my head arguing with myself. If this were him, he wouldn't hang out at a lake. He would have, like, tried to kidnap me or something.

I told myself my imagination was running away with me. Its not like I could count on normal anymore. Everything was off track. When I glanced to the water's edge Drake winked seductively at me.

Monica saw the exchange and stepped in front of me, blocking my view. "Let's get the coolers out. They're going to start the fire soon."

I managed to avoid Drake for the last two hours. I sat down on the opposite side of the fire from him when I was forced to be in the same area. Every once in a while, I'd glance in his direction, only to find him staring at me through the flames. They seemed to accentuate his defined features. I didn't see how he could be this evil person that my father had feared...he seemed too...addictive. Enchanting.

"So, are you ready for Paris?" Josh asked me, settling next to Jessica, who was beside me.

I shrugged my shoulders.

"Paris..." Drake repeated, leaning forward and taking the opening in the conversation. "That's a big step. Are you sure you're ready?"

"I've been 'ready' for this for a while now." A lie.

"I doubt that, love...Paris—Paris is a whole other world. The rules are different," Drake said, brushing his dark hair out of his face and leaning back again, trying to pull me across the fire with a stare that would halt anyone. What was this? A coded conversation? My imagination thought so.

Olivia glanced back and forth between Drake and me, knowing she was missing something.

Josh threw a football at Drake. "Come on, man, let's play."

Drake stood slowly, staring at me through the flames. A lump settled in my throat. I wanted to go home. As soon as Dane came, I was ditching this farewell party.

I went to take a drink of my water, only to find it empty.

"There's some water in the cooler I put in the trunk," Monica said.

I hadn't realized how warm the fire was until I stepped out into the darkness around it and found the night air cooler than usual. Trying to focus my eyes, I made my way to Monica's car. Once there, I had to open the car door to pop the trunk. When I rose up and closed the door, Drake was there. It was like he had appeared out of the darkness.

"Going somewhere?" he asked glancing down my body like I was puzzle piece he was sure was right, but felt wrong. At least that is what I gathered from the hints hidden in his placid expression.

"Just getting some water. Go play your game."

He laughed under his breath, reached his hand out, and ran his fingers under my eye. The warm sensation knocked the wind out of me. The feeling was beyond comprehension—stronger than any dream. It was a freaking weapon! Supernatural.

"I don't want games...I want you," he whispered.

I closed my eyes finding the vibration sliding through me. His arm moved around my waist, then he pulled me against him.

"Let me see your eyes...I went so long without them," he whispered.

I slowly opened my eyes, finding the will to face my fear once again.

"Our time has come. You belong to me," he said, staring somewhere deep inside of me. The absent, incredulous reflection in the dark of his eyes told me that he had expected a drastically different response from me, but I knew my response was on point. He had the wrong girl. I was not who he thought I was. Even though he had tormented my dreams, even though I knew I had a connection to him—this was wrong.

Dane! That's Dane's rage I sense. Those were his headlights that had just pulled in. He had seen Drake's pull me against him, my obvious resistance.

"What's going on here?" Dane shouted as he slammed his truck door closed. The others heard him and started making their way to Monica's car.

"Ahhh...does he think he's your boyfriend?" Drake asked sizing up Dane.

"Yeah, he does," Dane said fiercely.

Drake laughed. Dane charged forward and pushed Drake back, freeing me from the cage of Drake's arms. Drake caught his balance and stepped forward to charge Dane, but Dane was already stepping forward to charge Drake again. Josh and Chase jumped in the middle of them, Josh was holding Dane back while Chase stood in front of Drake.

"Look, man!" Josh screamed at Dane, trying to get him to look at him. "I know you're upset about Willow leaving, but that doesn't mean you need to take it out on strangers," he bellowed, using all his force to hold Dane back.

"Dane! Dane!" I yelled. "Take me home. Dane, do you hear me?"

Dane finally stopped pushing against Josh and held his hands up to show that he was done. Josh let go, and Dane reached for me. I ran to his side. He wrapped his arm around me and briskly walked me to his truck. He opened the driver side door and helped me in. Olivia ran and jumped in the passenger side.

When Dane turned his lights on and turned to leave, I locked eyes with Drake and gave him a murderous glare.

"Did he hurt you?" Dane yelled, still full of rage. I shook my head no, still stunned.

My soul was pulsing out of control like it was trying to get me to wake up. I could not shake the feeling that my nightmares were in some way a waste of time for Drake. He had me confused with someone else. Who? And why now? What triggered this? The Blue Moon? Was that it?

"I'm staying at your house tonight," Olivia announced, holding on as Dane peeled onto the highway.

"Was that the new guy that's staying at Chase's?" Dane demanded.

"Yeah, Drake," I said as I grasped my chest and remembered the pain of every single nightmare I'd endured.

"I'm glad I got there when I did," Dane said through his teeth.

"What did I miss?" Olivia asked, confused.

"Nothing...he just tried to make a move, no big deal," I said, dreading telling my father that Drake was there.

"I don't know where that guy is from, but he needs to learn his boundaries," Dane seethed, turning up the radio.

When we got to my house, Dane walked quickly inside. Once there, he climbed the front steps two at a time.

"Where are you going?" I called after him.

"To make sure your windows are locked," he threw over his shoulder.

My father stepped out of his study and looked up at Dane, then down at me.

"I'm going to go call my aunt," Olivia said, following Dane.

"What's going on?" my father asked.

"Is that kid's name Drake?"

The fear that spiked in my father told me that it was. He pulled me into his study and closed the door.

"Did you see him?"

"Yeah, he's been at the lake with me all day."

"Did he try anything?"

"He had just gotten me alone when Dane showed up...he's not what I imagined."

"Don't underestimate him, Willow," my father said sternly.

"What are we supposed to do now?"

"I'll move our flights up," he said, pulling his phone out of his pocket.

Dane knocked on the study door. "Did you tell him?" Dane whispered to me.

I nodded.

We listened as my father went back and forth with an operator, then he hung up the phone, questioning himself.

"Dane, can you stay here until tomorrow morning?" my father asked.

Dane muttered a 'sure,' a little taken back by the request.

"I've managed to move my flight to an hour from now, but I can't get theirs any earlier than 9 a.m. I just don't want to leave them alone if Willow is shaken up."

"That's fine. I'll call my mom," Dane said.

I motioned for my dad to come into the hallway. He moved swiftly thinking that maybe I had a better idea.

"Dad what's the deal? Why are we still flying all over the place? Let's just go."

"We have to leave a believable paper trail. We can't pass through the string now, anyway. When Ashten called, he said the others were separated from him in the storm."

"Are they hurt? Lost?"

"No, they know what they're doing. Ashten is sure they'll be here soon. He said Drake only uses the large passages. If he was trying to take you to one, he would've already."

"You fear him one minute, hide us in this life, and now its no biggy?" I was over this!

Dad clenched his jaw and fought with his own thoughts before he spoke. "Livingston has passionately argued this boy is not as dangerous as our fears led us to believe. He seems to think he can be reasoned with. I trust Livingston."

"But you asked Ashten and his family to take us home."

"I have my reasons," he said shortly. "I don't want you near Drake. I don't want you alone. When we get home we'll figure what needs to be done." He searched eyes. "I'm going off your instinct, Willow. You would've came home hours ago if Drake was an immediate threat."

"Not the one you should be counting on right now," I said quietly. Dane hung up the phone. I didn't need him to get the vibe there was more to Drake than an unwelcome advance.

"Okay," Dad said to himself. "I'm going to tell your mother. Make sure you're packed and ready."

I hugged him then climbed the stairs. In my room, Dane pushed my bed to the wall with the window on it. He stretched out on it with heavy eyelids. Olivia was pulling out the futon couch, which was big enough for the both of us. I went to my closet and pulled out the bags that I'd been packing to make sure I had everything.

"Do you need help?" Olivia whispered, trying not wake Dane, who had drifted to sleep.

"No, I think I have everything. I'm going to take a quick shower."

As I stood under the scalding water in the shower, I replayed the past few days. If I'd known what Drake had looked like, I don't think those nightmares would have been nearly as bad. I regretted not asking him what he wanted with me.

Then it hit me—if Drake were real, then the blue-eyed boy had to be, too. My eyes raced back and forth as I tried to think of a way to find him. I turned off the water, excited about going to sleep. I dressed like it was a marathon to do so, packing my stuff as I went. There was a soft tap on the door. I sensed my mother on the other side. I let her in.

"Are you all right?" she asked.

"Yeah."

"I have Libby all packed up," she said, leaning against the counter. It was like she'd been waiting for this day for far too long.

"I'm eager to go home," she said reading my expression.

"What was he like?" she asked when I didn't open a conversation up.

I didn't need to clarify who the 'he' was. "He's pretty hot," I said with a smirk.

"What did he feel like?" she finally asked, hunting for a reassurance that we had nothing to fear.

I froze for a second; no one had ever asked me a question like this before.

"I couldn't feel him..."

"I don't understand," she said, standing up.

"He was just a—void. He's the first person I've ever met like that." I grabbed my bag, clearly not wanting to talk about it.

"I'll see you in the morning," she said in a whisper when I opened the door.

Olivia had fallen asleep with her book open across her chest, and Dane was passed out cold. I tiptoed into my room, put all my things together, then set them in the hall. When I set my tote on the top of the pile, my sketchbook fell out. Laying on top and staring at me was the sketch that I had made of the blue-eyed boy.

Just the sight of him made me flushed. I just wanted to talk to him. I tore a page from the back of the book and pulled a pen out. With shaking hands, I wrote I need you, help me find you.

I lay down and stared at the note that I'd written. My plan was to focus on him and the words and hope that I could somehow take it with me. I didn't let any bad thoughts race through my mind, only him as my eyes felt heavier and heavier.

Feeling sunlight on my face, I opened my eyes and saw the house in front of me. I felt adrenaline rush through me as I realized I would see him. I looked down in my hand and saw that my note was there. I ran to the porch and circled it, but he wasn't there. I went through the house, searching every room. I found the place empty. My heart felt heavy as each moment passed. I didn't know how much longer I could stay asleep. I went back outside and searched the fields, trying to see if I could feel him, and in the distance, I was sure I did. I moved through the field toward a small hilltop. He was getting closer, so I started sprinting in his direction. All at once, I saw him coming over the hill.

He was astonished to see me. I crashed into his chest and hugged him, a tingling sensation filled with desire washed over me. The idea that he was real was almost too much to grasp. I felt his hands sway across my back, him lean down to catch my gaze. I would wake at any moment now. I leaned up wanting to feel the flesh of his lips once more, as I clenched the note I had in my hand against his chest.

I felt his hand clasp mine, the note, as those spellbinding eyes swam in my hungry gaze.

Right then I heard a loud crash and jumped to my feet. Wide awake.

Olivia had knocked over my bedside lamp while she was folding up some blankets.

"Sorry," she said in a loud whisper. "I didn't mean to scare you."

I glanced down to see my hand empty. The note wasn't there. Did it work? Was that real?

"Your mom came in here. You have to leave in an hour," Olivia said, pushing the bed into a couch.

I nudged Dane to wake him as I grabbed a change of clothes and went into the bathroom to dress. I convinced myself the blue-eyed boy had read my note and that the next time I slept he would tell me where he was. Then I would make my dad take me to him, and if he refused, I would find another traveler. They couldn't be that hard to convince, could they?

I heard the front door open and sensed Jessica, Hannah, and Monica climbing the stairs. I met them in the hall. They were so sad and full of dread. I led them into my room. I didn't have much time, and I wanted to make sure I wasn't leaving anything behind. When they saw Dane asleep on my bed, I felt embarrassment come from everyone but Monica. She found it hilarious.

"So I guess you were serious when you told Drake she was your girlfriend?" Monica said loudly, falling onto the bed next to him.

Dane sat up quickly and surveyed the room, replaying the last words he'd heard. He then rolled his eyes, slid by Monica off the bed, stretched, and grinned at me.

"I need a quick shower," he said to me as he left the room.

"So, are you guys serious?" Jessica asked, awestruck, not believing she'd missed something as big as Dane and me hooking up.

"I bet they are," Monica teased. "This whole time, Willow's been playing the innocent one, and then the day she leaves, the truth comes out."

As I listened to her, I shook my head and scanned the room for anything else I may want to take with me.

"Hey, Drake said to tell you he was sorry," Monica said in a more serious tone.

"For...?"

"He said he must have scared you, but he was only trying to carry the cooler to the fire for you," Monica said, believing every word she said. "He's not that bad of a guy. He invited us all to go to Florida with him. He has this huge boat, and he said we could go out on it."

"Tell me you aren't seriously considering going off with some guy you just met?"

Monica glanced down as the room grew awkwardly tense.

"We're all leaving for school in a few weeks. It would be nice to go to the beach first," Hannah said, defending Monica.

"Promise me you won't go anywhere with Drake," I begged, feeling a growing sense of dread.

"We got you something," Jessica said, breaking the tension. She handed me a black bag with burgundy tissue paper. I sat next to Olivia on my bed and pulled the ribbons on the bag. "We've all been working on it since graduation. We were going to give it to you last night, but you left so fast," Jessica said, proud of herself.

Inside was a large photo album, and on the front of it was an abstract painting of the five of us that Jessica had done. The photos started when we were all in diapers, and they went all the way through graduation night. The album was full of birthdays and summers. Everything we'd ever shared. I grinned as the flashbacks flew through my memory.

"I could not have asked for a better gift..." I said with a crack in my voice.

"Just don't forget us when you're famous, deal?" Jessica said.

I stood, pulled all of them together and hugged them.

When Dane was through in the shower, he loaded my mother's car with our luggage and drove us to the airport. He even went in with us, not leaving until we reached the security gates. My mother and Libby walked on, giving us a chance to say goodbye. I stared forward at the gate, then back at Dane.

I was so scared.

"You can't be afraid of the next step, Willow. We all have to grow."

"That's pretty deep," I teased.

"Maybe one day I will listen to my own advice," Dane said.

"You will," I promised.

Holding back my tears, I reached up and hugged him. I didn't understand why growing had to hurt so badly. After I let go of him, I kept my eyes down. I could feel his sorrow. It was ripping me apart. I never saw my life without Dane in it without any of my friends.

"Keep them safe," I said as I walked away. Trusting him to make sure Drake stayed far away from the ones who helped make me who I was.

Chapter 4

The flight was two hours long, so I decided to try and fall asleep. I needed to know if the blue-eyed boy had read my note. Dreams came fast, but I didn't find him...

All I saw was a Blue Moon filling the sky. I gazed at its detail and felt the energy that came from it. Slowly, it started to rise. In the gleam of blue light, I saw Drake to my right, and to my left I saw the boy I was searching for.

The landing gear hit the ground and I awoke with a start.

Libby had fallen asleep, too, so I carried her through the airport and cradled her as my mother rented us a car. My mother drove through the last hours of daylight. I took over at nightfall. As I drove, I searched the sky, looking for the moon and wondering what the dream could have meant.

My mother took over again at daybreak. She had been to Ashten's home before and knew the way. I gladly closed my eyes, needing the rest, the hope I wanted to find in sleep.

The weight that I always felt on my chest was immediate.

My sense of emotion was stripped from me. This time the people around me could see me. They gawked in my direction. The room I was in was more beautiful than any other room I had visited in these nightmares. It was regal. The floor was a red velvet carpet, and doors that stretched from the floor to the ceiling were centered on every wall. One of them led outside, into sunlight.

Women were lining the walls, dressed for a formal occasion; others made adjustments to what I was wearing. They'd dressed me in a gown, with lace and flowers woven into the design.

The wooden doors in front of me opened. I sensed someone. They were not afraid like the ones I always felt here. Instead, they were content. My heartbeat grew louder as I gasped for breath under the pressure on my chest. I wanted to wake, to help whoever needed me and leave. Through the doorway, I heard whispering.

A striking woman of age with spellbinding green eyes glided over to me. When she reached me, the ones around me scurried away. She took my hand, and as her smooth skin touched mine, the room vanished and I was surrounded by a white glow. In that moment, the weight on my chest was released. The woman smiled. I could feel her intensely now. She was compassionate, unconditional... at least when her emotions are aimed at me she was.

"You've been quite difficult to find," she said serenely.

"Who are you?".

"I am Perodine. You have known me from your first heartbeat."

"What do you want?" I asked, nervously.

She kept taking me in, like I was the supernatural element in this scene. "I've waited over four million years to see you this...strong."

"What?"

Perodine beamed. "You're powerful ..." she tilted her head. "Your heart is. The one who sees all must have it."

Sees what?

"I don't understand." I couldn't hide the tremble in my voice.

"When the Blue Moon rises, you will choose. Not for the first time or the last, but you will chose."

"Choose what?"

Perodine went to speak, and as she did, I saw pain absorb her body. With her eyes closed, she inhaled deeply and said in a hushed voice, "Our time now is over."

The room flashed back, and the others in the room gasped. The pain on my chest intensified. I panted for breath. Before I could focus on what was happening, men took Perodine away. She glanced over her shoulder at me, taking in one last disbelieving glance.

Someone's warm breath glided down my neck, as a hum swarmed through my body. I turned and saw Drake. He grinned and wrapped his arm around me. "They are waiting," he said.

The glass doors leading outside opened, the roar of a crowd erupted, and I walked unwittingly with Drake to the balcony. The sky was a beautiful blue, and the sunlight warmed my face. The crowd grew louder as they saw us standing side by side. Looking down, I saw a sea of color surrounding the people who cheered below. My nightmares had never had a happy ending even close to the vibration I felt then.

My eyes peered up at Drake. My willpower was losing a battle that any other girl would have lost the first time that she saw him. Then, above the crowd, I heard the sweetest voice.

"Willow..."

I turned to look back in the room and saw Libby standing there. I couldn't feel her, but I could see the fear in her eyes. I ran to where she was, but she vanished before my eyes.

The roar of the crowd grew silent.

The sky turned gray.

"You're mine," Drake said unsympathetically.

I turned back to where he was and raised my arms to block a light I was sure would come. As I moved my hand, I saw that my wrist was bare and that the Ankh was gone. I fell to my knees, gasping as I tried to understand why it was gone.

Chants echoed against the walls. I closed my eyes and found the image of the one who always made me feel safe: my blue eyes. The room shook, and the paintings crashed to the floor. The noise shocked my body, causing me to wake with a scream.

My mother was so frightened that she veered off the road.

"Willow? Are you okay?"

My eyes focused as I looked down at my wrist: the tattoo of the ankh and one lonely star was still there. I was safe, at least for now.

I had dreamed with Drake more times than I could count. Something was off about him in that last one...it was like I knew someone was playing his part, someone cold and deceitful. The question was how was any one of them getting into my head in the first place.

"Just a bad dream. I'm fine."

"We got you some breakfast, well, lunch. You were sleeping so soundly that I didn't want to wake you. I wish that I had now."

"How close are we?" I asked, looking at the secluded highway.

"Only an hour away. Are you sure you're okay?"

"Yeah, Mom, just a dream," I shuddered as it flashed into my memory.

I spent the rest of the trip watching Libby in the mirror. I had to keep her safe. Far from that place.

My mother turned off onto a small road where a picturesque mountain played the role of a breathtaking background. Then she turned off onto a less traveled path. Without warning, a beautiful, massive log home nestled next to a magnificent river came into view.

Excitement and relief overtook the emotions of the two people on the porch of the cabin. As we got closer, I could see my father standing next to an attractive man whom I assumed was Ashten. He was smiling and patting my father on the back. Strangely, he looked familiar to me.

I woke Libby up as we stopped. My mother was already in my father's arms. When we got to the porch, my father introduced Libby and me to his lifelong friend, Ashten Chambers.

"Jason, your girls are beautiful. You're a lucky man," Ashten said, looking curiously into my eyes, then to my father.

Overwhelming anxiety and anticipation started to build in the vibe around me. I should've questioned it, but I was so numb, so tired.

Dad told us the others should be there soon, then showed us into the cabin. The entire front room, from floor to ceiling, was made of a glossy wood. The ceiling was angled into an A-frame with wide beams that stretched across the room. All the furniture seemed to complement the mountain setting. The smell of pine lingered in the air. I unloaded my tote on the counter and picked up Libby's bag to carry it upstairs.

The cabin had six bedrooms, so Libby got her own room, which made her happy. I brushed her hair and listened to her tell me of all the fun she was going to have in her new home.

I decided to take a hot shower. All the traveling had given me jet lag, but the last thing I wanted to do was close my eyes again. When I got back to my room and started to dress, I couldn't find my brush anywhere. Libby walked in and handed it to me. I stood stunned, holding it. Libby didn't often go out of her way to help me out since she was used to us taking care of her.

"I couldn't find your sandals," she said sadly.

"Why were you looking for them?"

She furrowed her tiny brow. "Cause you told me you needed your brush and asked if I had your sandals."

"When did I say that...?"

"Just now. Mom wants you to come downstairs," she said, crossing her little arms.

My mother topped the stairs, looked in my direction, and said, "Willow, can you please come downstairs?"

Wide-eyed, I looked from my mother back to Libby, convinced I was now delusional.

"Mom, did you send Libby to tell me that?"

Slowly, she swayed her head no. I walked over to Libby, knelt down in front of her, and said, "Libby how did you know about the brush and Mom?"

"You told me to get your brush," she said flustered. "I heard Mom ask you to come downstairs."

Shock absorbed my mother, but it couldn't compare to mine. It was like watching Libby take her first steps all over again. She'd found her gift, but I knew she didn't understand it. She didn't even realize what she was doing.

"Hey, I'm sorry. I just forgot. I'm pretty tired from our trip," I said, straightening her shirt.

Libby hugged me tightly and said, "I guess it's okay that you're acting weird...just don't give me your cooties."

My mother turned on her heels and went downstairs. Reluctantly I followed her.

Ashten and my father were sitting on the couches in the center of the room. Their quiet conversation halted when my father saw the look on my mother's face. "I think Libby has a gift, Jason," Mom said when she got closer to him.

A surge of anxiety and denial came over Dad and Ashten.

"What is it?" Ashten asked dismayed.

Mom glanced to me. I guess she thought it would sound more believable coming from me.

Her reasoning made no sense, but I explained anyway. "She can see what's coming, short term, at least. Just now, she brought me my brush just as I began to look for it, and she told me Mom wanted me before Mom came upstairs. She doesn't know that she's doing it."

Dad glanced warily back at Ashten then forced a smile as he took in the concern in my mother's expression.

"If it's a true insight, it could grow stronger or leave her all together if we provoke her to use it. Leave her be, " he explained carefully.

"Willow," Mom said shifting the conversation. "I told your dad you had another nightmare. Could you please tell us what it was about?"

My stomach turned. "It was nothing," I muttered, looking away.

Libby. Let's talk about Libby, not Willow's slow fall into insanity.

"Was it the same as the other nightmares?" Dad asked.

"No," I admitted, swearing to myself that if I just told them what they wanted to hear I could get back to my own space. "I was in a huge home, like a palace. Libby was there, and so was Drake. There was a large crowd that cheered as we stood side by side. It was just a product of the last few days. Nothing to worry about."

Anxiety bloomed into the room.

"That'll never happen. You're going home to Chara, where you will always be safe," Dad said as he sat forward.

His words were soothing enough to chill Mom out, but I could still feel the unrest coming from Ashten. He kept his eyes low, avoiding mine.

Mom shook off the conversation, then went to the kitchen and started unloading bags of food. Dad glanced at Ashten then leaned back.

Gathering all my nerve, "Can we talk for a second," I asked.

"Ashten's hear to help, do you need him to leave?"

I didn't like the guilt trip I felt behind his words. As familiar as Ashten's vibe seemed I didn't know him, and I had a rather embarrassing enough topic on deck.

"Fine," I said under my breath. I stared at my dad. "On the way home, if I see a door that's bright or whatever, you gotta let me go in it. I'm looking for someone."

"Willow, you're only eighteen," Dad said. "I think you're just a little overwhelmed by what you've learned about Chara. You have your whole life ahead of you."

"Dad, it shouldn't matter how old I am. This isn't a freak teenage crush. I can't explain it. I just know I need him. His my best friend."

"Who?"

I didn't have a name. Only eighteen years of life with a soul that got me as we stood alone in our own world.

"You haven't even seen the string," Dad said as I blushed with embarrassment and anger. "It's not as easy as you think to see a beacon. It's a powerful moment. Most build up to this for months—years, before they even look."

I've been building up since my first breath! "He will tell me where to go. I dream of him—every night. Look, I can show you what he looks like," I said, walking to the counter to get the sketch out of my tote.

Ashten and my dad followed me over and watched as I turned the pages. I smiled when I flipped to the page he was on then turned it so they could see. Shock hit Ashten, and he ran his fingers through his hair, turned away, and started pacing. "Ashten, calm down," Dad said.

My mother circled the counter, took the sketch from me, and stared at it.

"Jason, I cannot do this," Ashten said through his teeth. He walked briskly back to the couch, sat down, and leaned forward stiffly. "Do you have any idea how furious he's going to be?"

My eyes raced back and forth between them, trying to understand what I'd triggered.

"This is just one part, Ashten," Dad said.

"Part of what?" I asked, protectively taking my sketch back.

Ashten stood and walked over to me.

"I want you to understand where I'm coming from," he said, trying to be polite.

Dad stepped defensively in front of me.

"Jason," Ashten said, raising his hand to let my father know he meant no harm. "I've made mistakes," he continued, looking at me. "I've overlooked a truth that lived before me, but my only intention was to protect my family."

"Protect your family," I repeated, then I realized why Ashten looked familiar to me—he had deep blue eyes, soft dimples, and was built just like the one in my dreams.

"He's...he's your son." My chest rose and fell rapidly. This was real. He was real. "What are you protecting him from? Me?" I asked as my cheeks filled with heat. I was so incensed that I felt sick to my stomach.

"Not from you," Ashten said.

Dad turned to face me. "Willow, I need you to calm down, you'll faint if you don't," he said, trying to catch my eyes.

"Tell me his name," I demanded, focusing on Ashten again.

"Landen...Landen Chambers," he answered, looking away.

"Willow, sit down. We need to talk about this," Dad said, reaching for my arm.

I stepped back, dodging his touch. I raised my hands and started to say something, but I was too angry—to confused. I took two steps back then walked to the door. I wanted to be alone. I opened and slammed it behind me as hard as I could.

No one dared follow me.

How? How was any of this real? How did I dream of my father's best friend's son for, like, my whole life? Why was all of this hidden from me only to explode in my face without warning?

The daylight was leaving, and the stars could be seen above the light blue sky. There was a river that ran behind the cabin. I walked down to it in a stunned trance.

Once there, I followed its path until I reached a mound of large rocks. I climbed up on them and listened to the aggressive river that rushed by. I'd come to the point in my life where everything I knew had changed. My nightmares had returned, I was told I was from another dimension, Drake had found me, and...Landen was real.

I replayed my last dreams, the one of the Blue Moon with Landen and Drake beneath it, and then the one where Perodine had told me I would have to choose. If that were all that I had to choose, then I'd made this bigger than it really was. I couldn't understand how that could be so important. Looking back at the cabin, I could see Libby sitting on a bed in the upstairs bedroom, coloring quietly. Her innocence touched my soul. She now had insight. I'd seen her vanish in my nightmare. I wanted to run from my life, but I had no choice now. Some way, somehow, I had to protect my little sister.

I felt a gentle pull in the air around me on me. An image was about to appear, a needed distraction. I stood slowly and stared into the darkness next to the river.

I vibe in the air lost its sting of anxiety. A blanket of peace wrapped around a sense of urgency shifted around me.

I knew this vibe...

The night air in front of me began to move; it looked like a wave gently swaying with a current. A thin light began to emerge then Landen stepped through the wave. Adrenaline rushed through my body as my heart violently hammered in my chest. I couldn't believe my eyes. I couldn't comprehend a wish that moved through my mind daily had come true.

"Landen..."

In the darkness, I could see his haunting blue eyes widen, we were both soaked in the emotion of disbelief, along with the fear that this wasn't real.

In that beat of my heart he'd reached my side. His hands were trembling ever so slightly as they cradled my face, and his thumbs grazed the flesh of my cheekbones. He was staring at me like I was a forbidden fruit, like I was every sin in the book, desire washed over that lasting look as he leaned in and let his lips frame mine.

When we fused our lips together, his hands fell from my face and slowly waved down my body, embracing me—proving to himself I was no longer a dream. I was doing the same to him. He was warm, he was on fire, I could hear his breaths, hear the sweet sound of our kiss.

He was real...

I was trembling with the need to be closer. I think he misunderstood my reaction; he slowed our kiss, as one arm went around me and the other cradled my face. His thumb reached to my lips just as his kiss ended.

"I found you," he said with the lips of an angel. His voice was deep and entrancing, those three simple words sounding like poetry as he spoke them.

His eyes danced over my image. "I've loved you...every day," he said as he leaned his forehead to mine.

I'd always felt this emotion coming from him, this deep claim, connection, and bond, but hearing the words...it was crazy fast and overdue at once.

"I've loved you," I said so faintly that I wasn't sure he heard me.

He pulled me to his chest, caging me in his arms like I was the most precious soul he'd ever laid eyes on.

I didn't care what hell was hunting me anymore. It didn't matter because I knew this boy would stand at my side and help me fight all my demons. He was strength. He was liberation. He was mine.

He slowly turn and look at the cabin, then down at me. He raised my chin so I would have to look at him.

"Willow?" he said with a disbelieving gaze.

I nodded shyly.

Anger came over him as he looked back at the cabin.

"What's wrong?"

"You were here the whole time, and he kept me from here," Landen raged under his breath. "How did you come to me before?" he asked as confusion came over him.

"What do you mean? I dreamt, just like I always do."

His haunting blue gaze filled with awe. "I wasn't asleep...I thought it was real."

"How is that possible?" I whispered breathlessly.

"I don't know. I've never known anyone who has dreamed of the same place and person so vividly, every night," he said, searching my eyes for answers I didn't have.

"Neither have I," I said, trying to catch my breath.

"You've always been real to me," he swore.

"It was all real, dream to dream, soul to soul," I said to myself.

Landen glanced at the cabin, then down at me. He tucked a loose lock of my hair behind my ear. "I've been following my beacon for the last few days, but it kept moving."

"We were traveling here to meet your father."

"What happened?" he asked as concern filled the stare I was lost in.

"There's this guy, Drake, who wants me to come to his dimension with him."

"Drake Blakeshire?" Landen asked, fury immediately overtaking him.

The astonished glint in my stare gave him his answer. How did he know him? Why did I feel an insane amount of emotions swelling within him? How much danger was I in? The sharp spikes of anger and grief in Landen's emotion gave me my answer: a lot.

He put his arm around me and started to walk in the direction of the wave from which he'd come. I looked over my shoulder to the cabin, where I could still see Libby. I wasn't going to leave her here.

"Wait, Libby, my sister. I can't leave her," I said, stopping in my tracks.

Landen followed my eyes to the window where she was sitting. His anger faded, compassion took its place.

"Let's get her, then we'll go." There was no room for compromise in the tone he used.

"Our parents won't let us take her without them," I warned.

He reached to caress my face once more, a shy smile emerged. "I finally found the missing part of me. My father is not going to make decisions for me anymore." The love he felt for me swelled inside him. "I should've listened to my soul," he said. "I'm sorry."

"For?"

"They held me back, and I let them."

I let out an uneasy breath. "They held you back and I stayed silent. I never told my parents about you. Maybe if I had I would've found you before now. I just...I just didn't want anyone to think I was going mad."

Those spellbinding eyes glanced over me. "You had the best intentions, Willow. Deep down I did, too. But that doesn't make me any less furious with my father at this point," he reached for my hand and began to lead me toward our parents.

I focused on the emotions coming from the cabin. They were of regret, sorrow, and anticipation.

"Being angry didn't get me very far," I said. "I can feel them. They're sorry for what they did. They had to have had their reasons. If we want to know why we were kept apart we need to listen to what they have to say." I said, staring up at him. "I don't want to fight with them. I want to understand why I'm the way I am. I need them safe."

He squeezed my hand. "I will never let you want for anything, Willow. I'll bring our family home."

My head was spinning. Too fast, too fast, the reasonable chick inside me said. The rest of me couldn't agree. The only thing different between right now and every single day Landen and I had spent together was words. Sound.

I for sure didn't know he was real, but I did know I'd give almost anything for him to be. He was bigger than life now. I was acutely aware of him. I didn't 'sense' his emotions. I knew them.

Too fast, too slow, either way, life was exploding around me. I had no choice but to make the most of every moment. Even if it sounded like a too good to be true fairy tale.

Chapter 5

When we stepped into the cabin hand and hand Ashten was pacing the living room floor. My parents were leaning against the bar that separated the kitchen and the living room. My mother gasped when her eyes met mine, then they moved to Landen's.

She rushed to us and embraced us both. Landen shyly hugged her back, refusing to lose his hold on me. Standing behind my mother, my father reached his hand out to shake Landen's hand. His relief to see Landen at my side was more than obvious in his eyes; it was as if his watch over me had ended.

"I'm proud to meet you, son. Your father is an honorable man, and I'm sure that you are as well."

Ashten had stopped pacing and was staring at Landen with a deep sense of pride and sorrow emanating from him. He looked in his son's eyes and mouthed the words, "I'm sorry."

Landen had no response. His respect for his father outweigh his anger, but under it all, Landen was hurt.

"I found her. That's all that matters," Landen said. "We need to leave now."

Ashten cautiously, stepped forward. "Son, we have to take them all. Libby may have been the only one in the dream, but you know just as well as I do that he'll stop at nothing to get what he wants."

"What is he talking about? What dream?" I heard Landen say.

"I had a nightmare. Drake was there...Libby disappeared."

As he pulled me closer, I felt Landen's sense of urgency grow; he realized why I wanted Libby to go with me. "I'll lead them both."

Ashten glanced at my father; both of their expressions matched the confusion coming from them.

"Landen," Dad said softly, "were you just speaking to Willow?"

Landen's jaw ticked up just so to answer.

"Did she answer you?"

"Dad, of course I did...what's wrong with you guys?"

"Are they always like this?" I heard Landen say.

My mother seemed to have figured out what was going on. Meanwhile, I was lost, embarrassed, and confused.

"Landen, Willow, you're not using words," Dad said almost like he was expecting this revelation.

My heart pounded in my ears. I couldn't comprehend what they were saying. Landen's emotions swarming out of control, too.

There was no way this was possible. I couldn't read minds! I didn't want anyone to be able to read mine. I turned crimson as I tried to remember if I had thought anything embarrassing around Landen tonight or even before.

I listened closely to see if I could hear Landen's thoughts, but I heard nothing. I closed my eyes. "Landen, can you hear me?"

"I can."

I looked up at him.

"Do you hear everything, or can you only hear me when I'm talking to you?"

"I guess when you're talking to me," he thought. His eyes raced over my face, the connection between us took the edge off the rightful shock I needed to have then.

"Do you think this is bad? I mean, is this common in Chara?"

His profound stare screamed no loud and clear.

"What is this, Dad? How are we doing it?" I asked, stumbling over my words.

"We all need to just have a seat and talk this through," Dad said.

We followed Dad to the kitchen table. Landen and I sat side by side. He held my hand under the table, his piercing blue eyes judging his father's every move.

Dad glanced at my mother, trying to size up her take on what she was seeing, then he nodded in Ashten's direction for him to begin. Ashten sighed as he gathered his words, first looking at Landen, then settling his eyes on me.

"The creators of our world, the woman Aliyanna and the man Guardian could speak without words, and they shared each other's dreams," Ashten said.

Landen swayed his head in denial. He knew this story. His disbelief told me so.

Ashten went on. "They were both born in Esterious. The priests in Esterious tried to gain control of the power between them. They needed to divide them. The priest pushed a force of energy at Aliyanna and Guardian. The force of vim used against them pushed them into the string, and once there they found their way to a different dimension: Chara. When their children grew up, Aliyanna and Guardian taught them the paths in the string so they could find the ones that they were meant to be with. Couple by couple, our world was born. Now everyone has to leave to find the one that they're meant to be with."

"What does that have to do with us?"

The tension in the room was so thick that I could barely breathe.

"There has never been another couple with the same insights, and you both are children of our dimension," Ashten answered quietly trying to get me to see the obvious.

"So...is this bad or good?" My voice cracked.

Ashten and my father exchanged weary glances. The strain between Landen and his father intensified within seconds.

Suddenly, Landen stood up. "Your silence gives me reason to leave now," he said, gently pulling me to his side.

Ashten stood and said, "Landen, it took you two days to get here, do you want to put that little girl upstairs through that? We need to wait for the storms to grow calm, or at least for Livingston and Marc to arrive."

"You know Livingston? Who is Marc?" I asked, using our new gift.

"Livingston is my uncle, and Marc is his son," Landen answered in the same manner.

Landen looked into my eyes, then to the stairs that led to where Libby was playing. Through his emotions, I felt him weigh each consequence. Calmly he sat back down. The room filled with relief.

Slowly I sat down next to Landen, trying to place all the names and faces with the story my father had told me.

The tightness in the room was broken when Libby appeared at the top of the stairs. "Is it time for dinner? I'm hungry," she asked as she walked down the stairs, smiling innocently at Landen. It was like she knew him and loved him already.

"Yeah, baby. We were just deciding what we're going to have," mom said "Let's have some dinner and get some rest. I'm sure everything will be clearer in the morning."

Dad and Ashten excused themselves to the back porch—I'm sure to discuss Landen and me in private. Libby walked over to Landen's side and slid her small body under his arm. They stared at each other, and the emotion between them seemed familiar to me, like I'd felt love between them, the love only a family could have. Libby reached her tiny hand to Landen's face, and when he smiled at her, she giggled. "I like the name Landen. Do you like the name 'Libby'?"

"I feel like I know her. How does she know my name?"

"It's her insight. She started using it today. She doesn't know that she has it yet."

His eyes filled with disbelief. "It has to be more than insight," he thought quietly.

"I do. It's one of my favorites," he said, humoring her.

"Is Willow your princess?" Libby asked, looking back and forth between us.

"Yes, she is," Landen agreed with a boyish grin.

"I told you princesses have green eyes," Libby said, crossing her arms, proud of her prediction. She then looked at Landen and said, "Daddy wants to talk to you." Landen looked down at his watch, and we waited as the seconds ticked by. Fifteen seconds later, my father opened the door.

"Landen, can you come out here please?"

Landen reluctantly stood, kissed the top of my head, and walked to the door, peering at me through the glass as he closed it. As their conversation began outside, I knew they weren't saying anything upsetting because calm came over the cabin.

When dinner was ready, Landen and our dads came back in; the calm emotions were still with them. For Libby's sake, the conversation had no stories of other dimensions. Instead, we listened to stories of my father and Ashten's childhood. I felt closer to my father. I'd never realized how little I knew of him before my mother came into his life.

Everyone was trying to act like this was ordinary, just two families hanging out. It worked until just after dinner when we ran out things to clean and small talk.

"It's been a long day, and a longer one awaits us," Ashten said. "I'm going to sleep in the living room in case anyone makes it through tonight. I don't want any false alarms."

Dad walked over to his medicine bag, pulled out a white tube, and handed it to me. "This is for the burn on his shoulder. It'll get infected if he doesn't treat it," he said, glancing to Landen.

"You're hurt?

"It's nothing," he thought.

I raised my brow, doubting his words, but he just gave me a playful grin.

"Good night," mom said over her shoulder as she carried Libby up the stairs.

I left Landen in the living room. I could tell that he wanted to talk to his father.

I changed into my pajamas—some simple cotton shorts and a white T-shirt. My sketchbook was lying across my bed with Landen's portrait facing up. Mom must have brought it up. I pulled out the photo album the girls had given to me, wanting so badly to tell them all about Landen, about the boy that had stolen my heart without uttering a single word.

I scooted to the center of the bed, turned to the sketch of flowers, and placed it next to a picture of the five of us. I realized that our lives were now like the flower: all original, beautiful, and living side by side, yet unaware of one another.

Sensing Landen coming up the stairs, I glanced to the hallway and saw him stop at Libby's room. As he gazed in and watched her sleep, I could feel his confusion and turmoil; I wondered what he was thinking. He looked down, wrestling with his thoughts before walking to my room.

"Are you okay?" I thought when he got closer.

He smiled at me, walked over to the bed, and slid by my side. "What happened? Why is Drake looking for you?" he thought.

I looked down at my wrist to the star that rested in the loop of the ankh. Landen followed my gaze, then looked back up at me.

"I didn't see his face when I dreamed, but I'm sure that Drake did this."

I felt relieved that I could finally talk to Landen about all of the odd things I'd endured.

His anger rose so high that I could see the heat behind his dimples. I knew then not to tell him that Drake had been in all my nightmares. He was the reason I was upset so many times in our dreams.

"How did he do it?"

"He just touched me."

"You told your dad, and he decided to run home," he guessed.

"He saw the star, then left. I never told him what happened."

"That was four nights ago, right?" Landen thought, sitting forward a little.

I nodded. "Why?" I asked, seeing that was important.

"Four days ago, Livingston came crashing into my father's house and pulled him away. They left, and only my father came back. He told us he'd found Jason and needed help bringing his daughters home."

"They found my dad a long time ago, when I was six. Dad said they knew Drake was searching for me and had decided to stay there until I was older."

"This doesn't make any sense," Landen thought, running his hands through his dark hair.

"Did you know about Drake? His parents, Adonia and Justus?" I asked.

Landen stiffened his jaw. "Marc and his brother, Chrispin, lost their mother that day. That's all we talk about...when we're alone."

His thoughts grew silent. I folded the album closed, set it on the side table, and reached for the sketchpad. When I picked it up, Landen slowly touched my arm and reached for the pad, pulling it closer and looking at the details of the flowers.

"How do you remember them so clearly?"

"It's easy to recall them," I tried to hide my blush.

I reached my finger to the pad and traced the outline of the blue and green flowers, each with different petals.

"I think they represent you and me," I thought, as the emerald of my eyes met the blue of his.

A slow sweet smile emerged as he eased his fingers through mine, gently squeezing my hand as if to tell me he agreed, that subtle move managed to rock my body, my pulse quickened, heat flushed in my chest.

"Where were we? Whose house was that?" I thought.

"Ours," he said softly.

A breathless smile escaped my lips. He leaned closer to kiss me, his lips feathered across mine ever so briefly, before his arm reached around me to pull me against him, when he drew me forward I felt him tense at the pain coming from his shoulder.

"Can I see?" I asked.

"Really, it's nothing," he thought, trying to smile.

I knew it was something. I could see the pain in his eyes. "I need to put the medicine on it anyway."

Landen gave me a wary look then began to unbutton his black shirt. I swallowed nervously. His body was flawless—his skin was tan and lush, his muscles were defined, he was built like a warrior, or an archangel. Pristine, too perfect to touch, yet it took all I had to hold myself back.

Underneath the black shirt was a white tank top. He pulled it over his head. At first I didn't see the damage, my eyes raked over every chiseled lean muscle in his chest. I had no idea how I was managing to look so calm.

I gasped at the sight of his shoulder.

"I told you it's nothing," he thought, trying to downplay it.

He was wrong. The burn started at the top of his shoulder and curved around his shoulder blade. "How did you do this?" I reached for the medicine my father had given me and gently rubbed the cool cream across his blazing skin.

"It's just the storm. I wasn't paying attention. I was being careless." His breath whooshed out in relief as I gently rubbed the cool cream over the wound, then he lay on his side, allowing the medicine to dry. His eyes drifted up to mine seeming to carry the same hungry desire that my soul was filling with.

The air around us was so warm, so numbingly calm, that I felt like I was locked in my own world with him.

"What did they want with you outside?" I asked.

Landen smiled up at me through his thick eyelashes. "Your father told me that he'd never shown you how to travel, that you didn't travel the way the rest of us do," he thought with a mischievous grin on his face.

He reached for my hand and let his fingertips glide across my skin. That simple sensation was mind-boggling.

"How do I do it differently?" I asked, shaking my head and bringing myself back to reality.

"The rest of us travel through the strings, like the one you saw me come from. Your dad said that you use people, that you see them through emotions." He tilted his head, finding it somewhat amusing.

I made a face. "How weird am I?" I asked, holding my eyes low.

I felt a fluttering kiss on my hand, then he leaned up and traced the side of my face, ever so sensually.

"It's not weird." He pulled my chin up, still smiling, so I'd have to look him in the eye. "It has to do with your insight. The insight of emotion is not a common one. It's unique that you, your father, and sister all have an insight."

"But, they're all different."

"You still all have one," he pointed out raising his brow to stress his point.

"Do you have one?" I asked.

"I do," he thought as he leaned down to the quilt at the end of the bed, pulling it over him, and settling in to sleep.

"Aren't you going to tell me?" I protested.

He let out a quiet, mischievous laugh. Clearly he was enjoying keeping me in suspense. He reached for me. I crawled into his arms as if it were the most natural thing in the world.

We had held each other like this for years, he knew how to make me feel safe. This time though, he reached for my chin and guided my lips to his. "I should've kissed you forever ago," he murmured.

"What is it?" I thought as loud as I could, knowing he was distracting me on purpose.

He reluctantly stopped kissing me, doing his best to suppress a sensual laugh, and stared into my eyes as his fingertip traced my bottom lip, then gently eased down my neck and settled just beside my collarbone.

"It's not as interesting as all of yours." His tone was deep, and entrancing. When he spoke aloud I felt the words caress my skin, when he spoke in his thoughts I felt them hum within my soul.

"I can determine truth or intent, but it's flawed. People can change their intent in an instant." The sinful smirk on the corner of his lips stopped my breath.

What was he saying? He could feel my intent? This internal war I had going on right now.

"How does it work?" I asked as I told myself to stop blushing.

Landen lay back down, still staring at me. "I feel it. I can feel if they believe what they're saying. The intent is harder to explain. I don't see it or hear it, but I know what they intend to do."

"Does Ashten have insight?"

"No. That's why your family is rare. There is usually one insight every other generation."

I realized that I didn't know anything about his mother or whether or not he had any brothers or sisters. We were backward. Every one

I knew built a relationship with words, the emotions drifted in with time. A bond was formed. I knew his soul inside and out, but not his life.

"Where is the rest of your family? Are they in Chara?" I asked, watching him grin as he tucked a piece of my hair behind my ear so he could see my face more clearly.

"Mom, Aubrey, and my sister, Clarissa, took a cab from an airport in New York to a hotel and have been shopping, using your mother's credit cards. My brother, Brady, is in Washington, using your father's credit cards."

"Why?"

"They're just trying to leave a paper trail for your world. Because you lived there so long they needed to fade you away."

I wasn't sure how I felt about fading away from all the people I loved here.

"It was just a precaution," Landen thought, seeing the effect that his words had on me.

I nodded shyly, forcing myself to focus on the wins of my life, not the losses. "What did you talk to your father about?" I asked needing to change the subject.

"It wasn't really a talk. I asked if he knew you were the one I dreamed of when he asked me to come here."

"What did he say?"

"He was silent." Landen paused then glanced up at me. "He understands my insight. He knows if he doesn't answer, I won't be able to tell if he's telling the truth."

"What is his intent?"

"All I can see is that he wants us safe at home," Landen thought.

"None of this makes any sense to me."

Landen pulled himself up on one arm and gazed over me. "Everything has its reason. It may not be clear to us tonight, but one day it will be. You and I have proved beyond any doubt that our beliefs are not false. We are meant to be with someone, the one. I found you. No one can keep us apart now. Our love will now be the story told to define how sacred love is."

Nervously I leaned up and framed his lips with mine. "I do love you," I thought softly, knowing that before he very well could've not heard my words. Mindlessly I settled against feeling a new kind of calm.

"What are you thinking...what do you want to know?" he thought.

"Everything. Tell me about your family. Are you sure your family is okay with running around this dimension for us?"

He grinned. "My sister loves Infante. She says her beacon is here, that she can feel it."

"Infante...is that what this dimension is called?"

Landen nodded "It means 'young.'"

"How is it young?"

He smirked. "Travelers consider it young because the cultures are still divided and war still occurs here."

"What does Chara mean?"

"'Joy,' 'happiness.'"

"Chara has no war or different cultures?"

His fingertips traced my eyes tenderly. "There has never been a war in Chara, and because everyone leaves to find someone, our culture is blended. Everyone has characteristics from several dimensions."

I smiled, thinking of how beautiful the people in Chara must be. "Has your brother, Brady, found his soul mate?"

A proud grin consumed his image. "Her name is Felicity. She's at home. Their first child will be here soon. Trust me, she's going to be thrilled to meet you."

Just the thought of meeting new people put me on edge, but it was hard to worry about that in this moment. "How old are they, Brady, and your sister Clarissa?"

"Clarissa is twenty and Brady is twenty-five. That's why my father didn't believe me when I told him about you. He thought I was too young."

"Thought," I pointed out.

I was struggling to keep my eyes open. "How come we need so many travelers to get us home?"

"I think my father and I can do it. You and your dad can travel, and Libby is close enough she wouldn't need a lot of help, so that only leaves your mother. We're really just waiting on the storms to settle."

"What causes the storms?"

He grinned as I set the intent to fight sleep just so I could hear his voice in my thoughts. "It's a disruption in the energy near the strings. They say the storms have only happened in the last two generations. One theory is that all the technology is disrupting the natural energy around us."

"Are they dangerous?" I asked. I was having second thoughts about taking Libby through something like that.

"They're more confusing than dangerous. It's like being out in open water—then all of a sudden a mass of waves turns you, and you lose your direction."

"How did you get hurt?"

"I thought there was a passage where there wasn't one, and I pushed through with my shoulder. I was just in a hurry to get here."

We lay in absolute silence, studying each other, lost in our own thoughts. I felt my eyes close against my will, and without hesitation, Landen was there beside me as we stood at the doorway to our home.

He smiled down at me, then wistfully picked me up and carried me across the threshold, kissing me gently as he sat me down inside. I walked through the house with him at my side.

We walked up the wide staircase into a large room, our room. A gentle breeze flowed through the long white curtains, framing the wide double doors; the sun glided over them, making them seem as if they were satin. We then passed through the open doors and stared into a field of beautiful flowers, the sun dancing across them. I truly did feel like I was home. Home was at his side.

Chapter 6

The sunlight peeked through the open window, warming my face. I smiled before I opened my eyes. When I reached for Landen, though, I didn't find him. Libby's small frame was under my hand. I opened my eyes to see her tiny sleeping head on my pillow. I hesitated, searching my memory. Then I franticly rose quickly, thinking it was all a dream.

I reached my senses out, finally finding Landen. Relief swept through me. He was downstairs with the others, maybe someone new?

Their emotions giving me no alarm, I lay back down and traced Libby's small features as she slept at my side. I couldn't recall when she'd come in there. Hoping that she hadn't had a nightmare, I shuddered as I remembered mine once again. Whatever the case, Libby seemed calm enough now, so I decided to get ready for whatever the day held for me.

When I returned to my room, Libby was sitting up in my bed. A smile filled my face; her hair was nothing less than a savage nest, though she did look well rested.

"Morning."

She smiled a sleepy smile at me.

"When did you come in here?"

She looked around the room, seeming shocked to find herself there.

"I don't remember."

"Are you hungry?"

She nodded.

"Then let's get you dressed. I think we have company downstairs."

I was brushing out her hair, a difficult task, when she looked at me. "I like Livingston. He's nice just like the others."

She was doing it again. I'd assumed we had company, but she already knew him. I didn't push her to tell me more. I was pretty positive my childhood ended the second I figured out I was different. I didn't want that to happen to Libby. I didn't want any of my darkness to touch her.

We heard laughter coming from the kitchen as we walked downstairs. Joy owned the vibe in the cabin.

"Ah, there they are," Dad said proudly.

Everyone was at the table—Ashten, Landen, and a man I assumed was Livingston, all dressed in black.

"Good morning," Landen thought, smiling at me as he got up from his chair and walked toward me with my favorite playful grin. Kissing me softly, he sent a tingle through my soul. I blushed. He was still real...everything was still real.

"You left me," I thought teasingly.

He shook his head, showing a playful pout. "Never."

I could feel everyone watching our wordless communication; it was embarrassing, spotlights were not my gig under the best of circumstances.

Livingston raised his brow as a grin spread across his face when Landen and I approached the table. He was slightly older than my Dad and Ashten, and he had dark brown hair with a hint of silver tracing through it. He also shared their same trait of dimples and deep blue eyes.

"Willow, Libby, this is Livingston," Dad said.

"Have a seat, girls. Breakfast is ready," Mom said.

Libby asked if she could have her breakfast in front of the TV. Normally, that would have gotten an instant no, but sensing the direction of the conversation, mom gave in.

"Willow," Livingston began when Libby was successfully distracted. "They tell me you can sense emotions, stronger the most empaths. Is it difficult to understand who is feeling what in a crowded room?"

I shrugged. "Sometimes its easier to just say a room has a vibe. If I focus on someone I know where they are at on the inside."

"How would you describe me?" Livingston asked with a mystified grin.

His tone was complacent, and he didn't hold any real expression in his face. One might say he was calm.

"Nervous."

Livingston shifted uneasily in his seat and looked cautiously at my father and Ashten. Landen noticed the exchange and stared at Livingston with his piercing blue eyes, judging his every move.

"Fascinating," Livingston finally said. "It does seem like you are advanced with your insight. More so, it complements Landen's insight."

I smiled at Landen, losing myself in his gaze. For a moment, I forgot I was in the middle of a serious conversation.

"Can you explain how you travel," Livingston asked.

"I see people who look like they need help, I feel a tug—this hidden force. I touch them, and then I'm there. But after seeing what Landen did yesterday with the string, I don't think I'm all the way there. They don't see me, and when I let go, I'm home again."

Dad sat forward. "I've followed Willow before. She makes a path where one doesn't exist. I was able to see the way back. If she were taught how we travel, she'd be able to see it, too."

"How far does she go?" asked Livingston.

"Mostly she stays here, but she's gone as far as Olecence before. More recently, she's gone further than I'd care for."

"Wait, what do you mean I 'stay here'? You can jump around in one dimension?" I asked.

The room erupted into laughter. It must've been a funny question to those in the room who could travel, the normal way, but my mother and I seemed to think it was a valid question.

"I'm going to show you the strings today. You'll see that Livingston is just in awe of you...they're only laughing because you have no idea the kind of the power you hold."

I turned crimson.

"Willow, I don't mean to upset you, but your mother told me something that I find just as fascinating. She said you couldn't feel anything coming from Drake. You told her he was a void," Livingston said, leaning forward in his seat.

Landen gave me a curious glance.

"Nothing there. That's what made me uncomfortable. Otherwise he was just guy."

I kept staring at Livingston. His emotions didn't match the room or the circumstance. He was broken, lost, weary.

"Are you ready?" Landen thought.

"Is it safe?"

"We're going to stay close. I'm going to show you my way, and then you're going to show me yours."

"I bet my way is cooler," I said slyly.

"I want to go, too, Willow," Libby said as she walked into the kitchen. Everyone looked at her with bemusement.

"Well, Jason, Ashten," Livingston said, sighing and staring at Libby. "I would have to say that you two have a very talented bunch on your hands."

Like my father and Ashten, Livingston was holding something back from Landen and me. He was holding something back from all of us.

Landen saw it, too. He gave his father a daring look as we left the cabin. As we walked along the river's path, he tried to prepare me for what I would see in the string.

"Have you ever swum in open water?"

I'd lived in a landlocked state my whole life. The few times that we had vacationed at the beach, I never went in any further than my knees. "Not exactly...do I need to be a good swimmer or something?"

He laughed as he searched for a different analogy. When he couldn't find one, he began again. "When you're in the string, it's like swimming in natural water. You're going to feel something like a current. It's easy to walk through, but I don't want it to scare you."

He glanced down at me. "Everything but the passages are going to be white."

When we reached the place where I'd found him, I breathed in deeply, feeling my unease and his excitement.

"Can you see the string?" he asked.

I could, but I still couldn't figure out why they called it a string. It looked like a ripple in the air, and you could see everything behind it. It reminded me of a glare coming off a scalding hot road in the summer's sun. I nodded, he took my hand, and we stepped into the ripple, the string.

It was so beautiful.

Everything was a glowing light, and there was no depth or height. I could feel solid ground beneath me, though the ground shared the same white glow. I felt the gentle current. It didn't scare me; it was very relaxing. The air wasn't cold or warm—it was perfect. I could hear a mesmerizing humming sound. A childlike smile ease across my face.

Landen reached to trace my bottom lip, grinning at the delight he saw in me.

"You're so beautiful."

" I'm just happy."

He leaned down and gave me the most innocent kiss, but the string, the energy behind the current, enhanced everything. I felt his lips hum against mine and gasped. When his hands moved down my sides I forgot to breathe for a second.

"That's not my touch, that's your soul reaching for mine." His eyes glinted "I can't wait to show you the universe." He took my hand and we began to walk. As we moved, the scenery never changed.

"How do you know where you're going? Do you visualize it, like my dad?"

Landen stopped, looked down at me, and grinned. The string had highlighted his eyes. It was like a light was shining through from behind. I'd never seen anything so absorbing.

"I follow intent. I can feel it through the string. When it changes, I know I'm either entering another part of the dimension that I'm near or approaching a different one. Can you feel emotions from here?" he asked as his eyes searched over my face.

I was so distracted by the beauty of the string that I hadn't noticed. I could feel Landen's powerful emotion around me, but in the background I could feel others. They were common emotions: worry, happiness, and sadness. I nodded.

"I think that when you learn the cultures of the dimensions, you'll be able to use your insight of emotion to help you navigate."

"How do Clarissa and Brady navigate?"

"Brady has a lot of Aquarius in his birth chart. He can hear music through the string. He says that every dimension has its own rhythm. Clarissa is dominant in Taurus, and she's known for her voice. She says that she listens to the tones of the voices through the string."

My eyes widened. I was beginning to see that they relied heavily on the Zodiac in the dimension of Chara.

"What's a birth chart?"

"A map of the heavens at the exact moment that you were born. When the planets align a certain way, they can highlight a dominant trait. They set the vibe. Our reaction and intent creates reality. The stars are a guide. A forecast that can help you navigate through your life, a valuable, timeless, tool. "

"Does Esterious study the Zodiac like Chara does?"

Disdain shimmered across his stare before he nodded once to answer me. He was clearly not a fan of Esterious.

"Chara looks to the heavens to find a positive way to impact the world around us. Esterious looks to the heavens to find a way to control others."

"Drake knows I'm a Scorpio," I thought, remembering that my father had said the people in Esterious had predicted my birth.

"I have a feeling that Drake knows more about what's going on with this Blue Moon than you and I do," Landen thought. He wrapped his arm around me, and we began to stroll through the string.

All at once, I could see a purple haze on the right side of the string. "It's turning purple!" I shouted.

He jumped at the sound of my voice. Laughing at my excitement, Landen pulled me closer. "Okay, purple is good. This is a natural path."

"Do you know where it leads?"

"I do," he thought as an amused smirk emerged on his lips. We walked for at least fifteen more minutes before we reached the purple haze. The color resembled a summer sunset; it was so breathtaking. I felt like I was standing on a rainbow.

"When you come to a passage, always step through it with cau-tion—you don't ever know for certain what you'll step into."

A wary look came across my face, and my curiosity was piqued. As he took the first step into the haze, Landen pulled me close, and a tingle teased my skin as the haze surrounded me. I then felt a burst of humidity in the air and heard a loud roaring noise. Fearing that we had somehow found our way into some horrible danger, I focused my eyes as the haze fell behind us. I couldn't believe what I was seeing: a vast waterfall. It was the most amazing thing I had ever seen.

"Where are we? Niagara Falls?" I asked completely humbled by this display of nature.

He grinned. "This is Victoria Falls."

"Where is Victoria Falls?"

"Zimbabwe," he thought, ducking his head slightly to catch my gaze, clearly wondering if I realized how those few steps we had taken in the string had moved me across the globe.

I couldn't fathom how we'd gotten there. "It's beautiful...so big..."

"It's over a mile wide and very old."

"How old?"

"One hundred and fifty million years. It's a powerful natural source of energy, and that's why it was so easy for you to see. We passed several other passages before we reached this one."

I didn't ever want to be alone in the strings. I was sure to be lost.

"Are they all this beautiful?"

"Everything that you see will amaze you, even if you've been there before. Each place has its own story to tell. If you listen, you can hear it and feel it."

True. I could feel this place. I could feel that all those who knew it, loved it, and respected it. The waterfall itself knew it was power ful...it was a life force all its own.

"Can you see your way back?"

I looked behind us, but there wasn't a purple haze or a wave in the air.

"No," I thought in a worried tone.

He didn't seem surprised by my answer. He stood behind me, wrapped his arms around me, and held me tightly.

"Close your eyes and remember the way you came...remember the feeling you had as you passed through... find the energy." He thought as his hands moved up my sides.

"I wish I knew you were real before yesterday."

"You doubted that I was?" He asked as he turned me in his arms. Concern was masking his playful image.

"Deep down I believed you were, I really did. There was always a lingering doubt that I had fabricated you to get me through each day. It was so exhausting to feel so much, to see what I saw for no reason, and not understand it. Closing my eyes at night and seeing you made it worth it."

"They never talked to you about your insights?"

"No, but I never asked either. They were worried enough about my sleeping patterns."

His hands squeezed my waist. " I struggled, too. I've always been treated differently. They look at me like they know something I don't, but at the same time like they think I know some cosmic secret. I ran away, a lot. I searching for a way to find you, looking for answers to questions I feel in my soul but cannot understand enough to clearly ask them. I fought every rule they put before me."

I don't know what would have been worse, not knowing we were more than just dreams, or knowing and not being able to do anything about it.

"How worried do I need to be about us right now? What secrets are they hiding? Do you really think they kept me hidden because of that dark dimension? I mean, are they expecting something out of us?"

His jaw clenched, he glanced away. "Chara can be just as superstitious as any dimension. I'm more worried about how our dimension is connected to Esterious, what Drake wants with you."

"Is it really wicked there?"

"Wicked doesn't begin to describe it."

A shiver ran down my spine.

"I'm not going to let him hurt you, or our home. I swear that to you."

"I trust you..." I thought as I glanced longingly at the massive waterfall before I turned in his arms. "Okay, I'm remembering how we came here, what the passage felt like," I said as I closed my eyes.

"Focus on that for a second or two." He swayed his hands against my arms. "Now open your eyes."

When I did, the wave was there again.

"I can see it!"

"Lead the way," he thought as he laughed aloud.

I walked slowly through the wave. The roar of the waterfall was gone, and the air was perfectly still again. Only the haze remained behind us.

"How come it wasn't there at first?" I asked, looking back at the haze daring to reach out and feel the color of the air.

"It was there—you just were never taught to see it. The strings are all over every dimension. You've walked by more than you could ever know. Our eyes can see them. You just have to learn to call on what you were born with."

I glanced around the string, and to my right I could see an array of colors that seemed to stretch out for miles in every direction. They looked like they were blocking our path.

"Is this a wall?"

"This is where the string divides. Focus on the hazes, and you'll see that the more dominant hazes are framing different paths."

I studied what I thought was a wall in front of me, and as I stared, I could see that the darker hazes outlined three passages. The colors of the three passages were so bright; they spilled out of their paths and joined the others. It looked like every color that existed was blended perfectly together. They flowed on the gentle current I was feeling. The glow of the white passages reflected on the hazes, looking like diamonds. I was humbled by the beauty before me.

"Three paths," I thought softly.

Landen grinned."The storms create these paths. More passages are created with each aggressive flow of energy. When our parents were young, storms were rare. They only really occurred once a year. Around the time we were born, they were so fierce that only the most experienced travelers were able to navigate through them."

"My father said his passage to my mother closed. Is that normal?"

His eyes told me no. "In our entire history it's only happened to your father. My grandfather, August, told me that everyone searched endlessly for the gifted healer."

"That's a little scary," I thought.

"I just wish they would have brought you home when they did find you," he thought with disdain.

We began to walk. I wasn't sure, but I thought we were going back the way we had just come. I searched the glow all around us, looking at all the hazes that had been absent to me before.

There were little speckles along the sides of the walls of the string. They were all different colors. Some small as dust, others as large as a doorway. We stopped before one of the large yellow doorways.

"I told you that purple was a natural path. Why do you think the color to this one is different?" Landen asked.

"Could be natural, just not as strong maybe?"

Landen held his arm out, indicating that he wanted me to lead the way. My steps were cautious. He may have known where it led, but I didn't. For all I knew, I could have been in Australia, and a big scary snake would be at my feet when the yellow haze left me.

When the haze passed, the same tingle as the last was there. The feeling was growing more familiar. As the haze faded, we stood on a rocky cliff overlooking a beautiful, deserted, white beach, the water was so clear. Suddenly, I heard a loud noise, and I turned to see water crashing through a hole in the rocks. As I stood in absolute astonishment, I could feel the energy leaving as the water fell.

"Do you want to stay here for a while?" he asked, laughing at my reaction.

I did, but I was hungry for more. Feeling proud of myself, I pulled Landen back into the string.

"You're quick. It took me almost ten times before I could find the string alone."

"I'm sure you were only a little boy. It's not the same for me."

All of a sudden my smile faded. I could feel someone in the string with us. I was certain of it. They had an eager but defensive vibe.

"Landen, someone else is here...I can feel them."

He was already looking past me his eyes grew brighter.

"Landen, is that you?" a deep voice said.

Out of the bright light, an image came forth. Dressed in all black was, a young, eye-catching boy. He was tall like Landen with wavy brown hair, and his eyes were so dark, but they had the same glow behind them as Landen's did.

"It's Marc."

"Where have you been?" Landen asked.

Marc stared at me as if he couldn't believe his eyes.

"You found her!" Marc's voice rang with astonishment. "Do you want me to help you get home before I go and help Jason's family?" he asked.

"This is Willow, Jason's daughter," Landen said.

Marc's was completely bewildered. "That isn't possible...that would mean you're both from Chara," he said, looking back and forth between us.

"Willow and I must be the exception in the history of Chara. Listen, Dad found Jason a long time ago. He only wanted to come home now because Drake Blakeshire is looking for Willow."

"Willow is the Scorpio? Why would he be looking for her?" It wasn't hard to tell he was not a fan of Esterious either.

"Everyone is silent when I ask. They're hiding something from us," Landen said in a tone that reflected the livid emotion his father always seemed to manifest within him.

"That must be why Ashten and Dad asked us to find a path that avoided Esterious," Marc said, looking back and forth in the string.

"Did you find one?" Landen asked.

"Yeah, the one you told me to check. A storm is beginning to stir that way. We need to wait at least a day before we pass through it. Where are the others?"

"Back in the cabin. I was showing Willow how we travel."

"Well, I guess I don't have to come up with an excuse for showing up without you. Are you sure you don't want to just go home? We can make it if we're really careful," Marc said.

"We're going to wait. We want to make sure Libby, Willow's baby sister, gets to Chara safely," Landen said.

Marc nodded. "I'm going to let you finish up your lessons. I'm beat," he said as he began to move past us. "Stay clear of the gray paths," he warned as he disappeared in the glow.

"Is gray bad?" I thought.

Landen gave me an impish grin. "No, they're just man made, so it's hard to judge what you're stepping into. Infante is known for having the most."

"Were you not going to come and help my family? Is that what Marc meant when he said at least he wouldn't have to come up with an excuse for showing up without you?"

He swayed his head. "We were leaving the day I saw you and you gave me that note. I told Marc and Brady I was going to find you, and I didn't care if my father wanted me to or not. They both agreed with me. Marc said he would find an excuse for me not showing up at the cabin."

My heart started to beat rapidly. He made me feel so safe, yet so empowered at the same time. I had no doubt that he would have moved mountains to find me after I gave him that note. I should have thought of doing something like that sooner.

Landen and I made our way through the string, stopping at every color that caught my eye. In one morning I had traveled from Montana to Zimbabwe, then to the beaches of Key West. We gazed at the northern lights and stood at the peak of Mt. Everest. As I looked at the Grand Canyon, in every single one of those places he took my breath away.

"Okay, so maybe your way is cooler," I teased.

"Not too bad for a first date," he thought.

I had asked him a million questions throughout the day. About places he went to, who taught him what he knew, and about his family. Everything I could think of. He answered each of them and asked me something about my past. I told him about my friends, how it was the hardest to leave Olivia and Dane behind, that we were the old souls of our group, and that we only seemed to get each other.

I heard all about his brother, and his cousins, the places they had gone, people they had helped, funny stories and scary stories. The ironic part was every story we told each other, in some way we already knew it, because of our dreams, we could remember each other's moods, or actions on that night.

"How do you know so much about my world, but have only found me now?"

"I was not allowed this far from my home, specifically to Infante. Marc and Brady would bring me there from time to time. I felt pulled here, but I could never see my beacon. My time was short here, someone or something always pulled me away."

"Did Ashten tell you why?"

"He was always silent when I asked...it doesn't matter anymore." He smiled and looked down at me, and I felt his enthusiasm rise. "It's your turn. Where do we need to go to help you get started?"

I didn't think I'd ever traveled outside of Franklin. It was easy to see someone out of place in your own hometown.

"I just need people."

"Jason said that I wouldn't be able to see the people you could see."

"Really?"

"That's what he said, you scared him a few times."

I laughed. "He looked extremely relieved to see you at my side last night."

He tried to hide a grin. "I have a reputation when it comes to the string. I'm sure he thought I could follow you no matter how twisted you got in here."

"What kind of reputation?" I asked, raising one brow.

He laughed, stealing a kiss before he answered. "I seem to see more paths." He winked. "That made running away easier than it should have been."

"They always found you, though."

"I let them. I was just proving a point." His gaze was all too serious right then. "We could run away now and never come back, but I know you feel pulled home just like I do."

"I do. I want it all. I want you and I want my family side by side, in Chara."

He brushed his nose across mine. "Then that is what you are going to get."

Chapter 7

W e found our way to a quaint little town that was a lot like Franklin. The buildings all dated back to the 1800s. Shops and restaurants lined the streets. We settled in at a little café, which was set in front of a square park that centered the town. People were pushing strollers, walking their dogs, and lounging on the benches. On the other side of the park was a beautiful church. Flowers and white lace decorated the step. I could only assume that a wedding was in progress.

"Are there places like that in Chara?"

"The building? Or what they do there?"

Knowing there was a wedding in process, I squirmed in my seat. I didn't want him to think I was insinuating anything.

"Either."

"Well, in some way, yes to both." He gazed at the historic church with the utmost respect. "That place is powerful, I feel the same kind of energy when I go to the places I took you today."

"I can see that." I let the tension slide out of my body. He misread my question.

He tilted his head and glanced at me curiously. "Were you talking about the wedding part? Or the higher power part?"

I started laughing, that's all I could do to hide the embarrassment.

"Do you want a wedding?" he asked sincerely.

I couldn't say or think a single thought. The boy had the insight of truth so I couldn't lie, and I refused to admit I was curious about how couples symbolized a bond.

Landen moved his chair closer to mine, wrapped his arm around me, and we watched the couples make their way out.

"They seem happy," Landen thought, glancing at the groom, then back to me.

I could sense the bride and groom from where I sat. There was a love between them, but, for some reason our love felt older. Bonded at the core of our being.

"In Chara, we celebrate when couples find one another. Friends and family welcome home the ones who were searching and their soul mates." Landen paused and looked deep into my eyes before continuing. "We believe that we are each other's gift from the heavens. We thank the heavens every moment for the love we feel. In Chara, 'I love you,' is more than just three words. They are never spoken unless that emotion is felt at our core. Right now we are just as, if not more so, committed as that couple. This is forever. This life and the next. I made you that promise the second I knew you could hear me."

He drew my face closer to his and said, "I love you, Willow. I always have, and I always will."

His voice, his words, they were so deep.

"I love you." I whispered.

He ticked his head toward the church. "Is there an image over there I need to be aware of? I can't stand waiting to see the way you do this any longer."

"All right. All right. I'm focusing."

I closed my eyes and let out a deep breath, only to open them and see him looking at me in a humorous way.

"Breathe deep? That's your trick."

I playfully glared. "Everyone seems to be in place. Images stick out."

One nod, a teasingly, disbelieving nod.

"I'm serious." I glanced around us. "Come on, let's walk."

We had only taken a few steps before I felt that familiar pull on me. I hesitated and searched the emotions around us. Somebody was painfully nervous. I spotted a young man pacing back and forth. He looked as if he were rehearsing a speech, playing the words across his lips. I watched him as he stopped his pacing and took a step forward, then halt and start pacing again. I was almost sure he was an image. He was stepping forward to a tree, but a tree would definitely not need a rehearsed speech.

"Do you see that guy over by the Dogwood tree?"

Landen followed my gaze. "What do you see?" he asked.

"A man preparing to give a speech to a tree."

He erupted into laughter.

"What? Trees can be intimidating. That or he's out of place just like I said he would be," I thought as I raised my chin to drive home my point.

"Is the tree making him nervous?"

"Something is," I thought.

"Your sure he's an image?" Landen asked as he continued searching the people on the streets.

"If I get closer to him then I'll know for sure. The pull will be stronger," I thought pulling him toward the man.

"What do you mean, 'pull?'"

"The images pull me to them, then after I help them, they push me back to where I began."

We began to walk closer to the young man. As we did, he stopped his pacing again, then stood in place and pulled a little box out of his pocket. I knew then what he was nervous about. I started to walk faster. I could tell he was losing his nerve.

"Okay, you hold onto me. I'll let go of him when it's over," I told him.

Landen held my hand tightly. The memory that I was going to use would be so powerful that this young man would have enough courage to last him for a lifetime. As I reached for his arm, the day shifted to evening, and the air had a gentle breeze. He was standing outside a quaint apartment building. I let the memory of seeing Landen outside my dreams for the first time come to me. The tension then left, and the young man took a deep breath and ran forward. I lost my touch.

Landen and I were back. I don't think I've ever felt as happy for one of my images before.

I smiled up at Landen. "Well, how was that?" I thought, proud of myself.

Landen looked around to see if anyone had seen us come or go. Finding no one paying attention to us, he thought, "I think you have me beat."

"What? There's no way—there was no wave or beautiful light."

"Yes, there was. You just didn't see it," he thought, smiling.

What did he mean by that?

"You just crossed the string and made your own light. The pull you feel is the energy of the string," he continued. "Look at where he was, remember the way you felt...do you see it?"

I could see. It was a wave, where one did not exist before. I took Landen's hand and stepped through, not knowing if we'd be with the young man or back in the string. When I heard the hum and felt the current, though, I knew we were in the string.

"Look, do you see the green in the wall?" Landen asked. I looked to the right and could see a light green haze, the same size as me. Landen walked to the left side of the string and pointed out the twin image on the other side of the string. As I realized what he was saying, a grin came across my face.

Without warning, the hum of the string grew louder. The current was moving faster. Landen pulled me down to the ground and wrapped his arms and body around me. The energy filling the string was so powerful, it vibrated every part of me. Just when I thought I couldn't stand another moment, everything was still again. I rose in a daze, and a numbing feeling came over me. The walls of the string had changed, and my green haze was no longer there. We had moved.

"Did I do that?" I asked, afraid of what his answer might be.

"It was just a storm. They're unpredictable."

"Do you know where we are?" I asked with a trembling voice.

Landen looked at the walls of the string. Once he found his place, a smile came across his face. "Well, we're back, a little faster than I would've preferred," he said reaching to help me up.

There was a light blue haze, and as we stepped through it the river that ran along the cabin was in front of us.

As we walked toward the cabin, I felt all the vibe that I loved, the ones that only a family could give you.

Libby was running down the river path as fast as she could, excitement pouring from her. When she reached us, she leaped into Landen's arms and reached across to pull me to them.

"You guys left me all day," she said in her fake pout voice. "Did you take Willow to your castle?" she asked Landen. He lifted her above his head making her scream with laughter.

"Did you?" she said through her giggles.

"No, not yet but I will very soon. When I do, you get to come, too. How does that sound?"

"I get to live with you?"

Landen was starting to learn that nothing got past Libby.

"Well, you get to live very close with your mom and dad."

"How close?" she pressured.

"Close enough that you can run there in less than a minute," Landen said, setting her down. Libby seemed to be satisfied with his answer, and I was, too. I needed Libby close to me.

At the cabin, dinner was on the table. Marc had made it there safely, and the cabin was filled with a sense of joy. The stories of all the places travelers had seen sent my imagination running wild. My eyes always found their way to Libby. She'd insisted on sitting in Landen's lap for dinner; he didn't seem to mind. I wondered what she'd filled her day with or if she'd picked up on her insight.

When Libby finished her dinner she slid off Landen's lap and went into the living room. Once there, she stretched out on the floor and began to color across one of my sketchpads. Landen and I stared at her as the others continued to reminisce.

"I wonder if she has a gift of art, too," Landen thought.

"If she does, she'll humble my talent."

"Landen, do you agree that we should wait another day before we travel home?" Livingston asked pulling us from our private conversation.

Landen's stare was still on Libby, "I don't want to take any risks. We should wait for the storm that's turning to pass."

I could feel eagerness inside Livingston. If it were up to him, we'd already be on our way.

"I'm going to get Libby ready for bed," I said, standing.

I wanted to spend some time alone with her, see if I could pick up on how well this insight of hers was developing, or at the very least let her know she could ask me about anything she thought was weird.

After she was ready for bed, I read her a story. I noticed that she was losing the excitement that I loved about her; it was as if she'd aged over the past few days.

"Libby, is there anything you want to talk about or ask me?" I whispered to her.

Her eyes found mine, and she searched my face. I could feel her running through different emotions: anxiety, a little fear, and then returning to the common thread of excitement. "I think I'm different," she said in a quiet voice.

"You are different. Everyone is, and that's what makes us all so special."

"Willow, I think that I am—I have—I can..." She was struggling to find the words. I felt her emotions rush, and I squeezed her tight.

"I know. Don't worry about it. It'll all make more sense as you get older. Don't rush it. You'll find your way," I said, playing with her long brown hair. I felt a calm come over her.

After she drifted off to sleep, I left her room. As I passed through the hallway to my room, I heard the discussion downstairs in full debate. I could still feel Livingston's eagerness. I could also feel Landen's frustration. It was obvious we weren't going to get any answers that night. I climbed on my bed with my sketchpad in my hand, then turned to a blank page and stared, trying to decide what to draw first. It was hard because my day had been so amazing. I sensed my mother. When I looked up she was leaning in the doorway. She smiled warmly at me. She had her energy and excitement with her again.

"Can I come in?" she asked. I scooted over on the bed, making room for her to sit beside me.

"I can only imagine what sketches will come out of the day that you've had," she said.

I smiled as it rushed through my mind. Mom saw the photo album on the table and grabbed it.

"Do you miss them?" she asked.

I nodded.

"What did you think of the string?"

"It was amazing, indescribable. It would change, the feelings, the colors, it all changed," I answered in a rush.

"I wish I could see it," she said, feeling envious.

I suddenly realized how scary only feeling it would be.

"So, Landen and you..." she said, shifting her emotion.

I felt myself blush. "Is everyone still shocked about us?" I asked, sitting up a little straighter.

"Not shocked. It's just amazing. I still cannot believe that you don't have to use any words to communicate. Did it scare you?"

"We didn't even realize it."

"Is it everything? I mean, can you hear his thoughts now?" she asked glancing to the doorway.

"We only hear each other when we speak to one another."

"What about the dreams, are they the same place?"

"I think so. The last few have been at this beautiful home."

"I bet it's the one he built," she said, smiling wider. "They all help. The family starts the house when the children are around the age of ten. It's not something that happens overnight. Your father said his was nearly finished when he left. He had spent ten years on it." She rand her fingers over the pictured in the album in her lap, "The houses are powered by natural energy. The whole dimension is. The power of sun, wind, and water is all they need."

This world was becoming a utopia to me. It was as if the world that I'd lived in had the same choices, but failed to take the right path.

"Ashten went to see Aubrey today. There must be something in the air...she said Clarissa found her soul mate."

I sly smirk rested on the edge of my lips. Landen was confident it wouldn't be long before she did.

Mom started to tell me about all the people I would meet when we finally got Chara. I drifted off to sleep somewhere in the middle of that conversation.

At first, I slept without any dreams. Slowly, though, my home came into view. I walked into the house, stopping to smell the flowers on the front steps. Once inside the house, I made my way through the rooms I'd seen the night before. I made plans to create paintings and place them, highlighting my first time in the string and the wonders of the world where my childhood was spent. I traced my fingers through the designs in the framework that bordered the center of the walls.

I was in a large room. The couches and chairs all had beautiful patterns on them, and I ran my fingers across each one. I could feel the handmade stitching.

In the center of the wall was a vast fireplace framed by a stunning mantel, and along it were pieces of what looked to be crystal. The shapes were all amazing, but one caught my eye: a willow tree. It was six inches high, and the branches and leaves each broke out into their own crystals. The sunlight peering through brought out an array of colors. Stepping closer, I could see a little knob on the base of the tree. I gently picked up the delicate tree and twisted the knob. I felt it wind up like a music box, and I could only imagine what song would come from it.

I felt Landen's hands on my shoulders; he moved them slowly down my back birthing a throbbing sensation from my soul. One hand reached for my waist, and the other reached for my arm, he gently lifted it, so that I was stretching back and threading my hand through his dark hair. As I gazed into his eyes, his fingertips feathered down my arm, it took all I had not to laugh, that tender caress fell further, tracing my chest, my ribs, all the way down to my waist. I held his stare as I leaned up to let my lips brush against his.

Every touch that night was innocent, yet provocatively sensual, holding the promise that we were eternal.

I didn't want to wake from the dream, but daylight brought us both back to reality.

"How did the convo go downstairs last night?" I asked.

He stared intently into my eyes and carefully thought his words through before he spoke. "All we came up with were more questions. It doesn't make sense why the string doesn't burn you when you pass through. Your dad said that was always his biggest fear. He could always see the green haze around you, but it didn't ever hurt you, inside or out. We can't figure out why you can't change the emotions of the ones that are in your presence, or why the emotions that call you are so simple. It's amazing that you can see them through an entire string."

"Do you know why they can't see me or feel me?"

"You never completely leave the string. You stay in the haze just on the edge. That might be why."

It bothered me that I'd never seen the haze before.

"Livingston thinks that if you focused your energy, you'd be able to affect the ones in your presence. If you could, you'd be able to give courage or a sense of empowerment to those who need it. He knows that there are good people in all the worlds, even in Esterious," Landen said, looking away. I could feel that he was uneasy with his thoughts.

"You don't like his ideas, do you?"

"He believes what he's saying, but they're guarding their intentions, not thinking about anything but the moment they're in."

"What do you think it is?"

"I don't know, but I don't think it's anything we should look forward to hearing," Landen said, tightening his jaw.

"The way we feel is a choice. I hope Livingston doesn't think I'll be able to change those who aren't willing."

"That's exactly what our fathers and I said."

"So when do we leave? What's the plan?"

"That storm we were in was just a little one. Marc looked in the string last night, and it got worse after we left. It should completely pass by late tonight. We're going to leave early tomorrow so Libby won't have to travel through the night. Today, we're going to go to one of the towns here and practice what you do so we can start to define it. You can't help anyone until you can control it."

It wasn't anyone's intention, but I felt like a science experiment. It made me uneasy. Showing Landen was one thing, but I already felt embarrassed, thinking of the others watching me and critiquing what I was doing. I rolled on my back and stared at the arched wood above us, wishing I could just tell them to save myself from embarrassment.

Libby ran into the room and dove onto the bed, making a place for herself between us. She was already dressed in a bright yellow swimsuit and sundress.

"I wish you guys would go swimming with me instead of a silly hiking trip," she said with a big pout on her face.

Questioning her words, I looked at Landen, but he was just as lost. I assumed it was another story my mother had told her to keep the peace.

"I promise to come back soon...we'll think of something we can do then."

Libby laughed out loud when I started to tickle her then all at once she went rigid and her eyes were somewhere else, looking past the room. I sat up quickly, feeling the fear coming from her. I shook her lightly and called her name. Landen stood up and lifted her to a sitting position. Her fear impacted us both, and we were reaching the point of panic. Then all at once it was gone, and she resumed her normal excitement. Landen and I sighed deeply, and Libby looked at us as if we'd lost our minds.

"Did her emotion change, too?" Landen thought.

"She had fear, but only for an instant, now she's fine. What do you think she saw?"

"I don't know. I just hope whatever it was passes just as quickly."

A sickening feeling came over me, accompanied by an intense sense of dread.

Landen and I got ready for our day. When we went downstairs, I was surprised to see that only my mom and dad were there.

"Where is everyone?"

"Marc and Livingston went to check the progress of the storm. Dad went to see my mother."

Relief came over me. I wouldn't have to be anyone's science experiment after all. When I glanced at Landen he was grinning.

"You didn't think I'd let them make you uncomfortable, now did you?"

"You might just be too perfect, Landen Chambers."

"Doubt that, you just bring out the best in me."

I could feel his disdain but I didn't understand it. When my eyes questioned him he responded. "I'm a bit adventurous and stubborn, even reckless, but...I was that way because I wanted to find you. Figure out why I'm different. You've calmed me down."

"Is that why your dad and the others are looking at you like you are a ticking time bomb?"

He laugh. "Not a time bomb, they just know they crossed a line by keeping secrets from me. If there is one thing you do not mess with in Chara it's a persons soul mate. They're still hiding something and they know I won't take it well."

"Whatever it is...we'll get through it."

"I promise we will."

We'd forgotten we were standing in the den, with my parents a few feet away. Until we heard my dad say, "I hope you guys are hungry. There's more than enough."

Mom, was sketching the mountain view. "Are you going with me and Landen today, Dad?"

He was surprised and flattered by my question. "I think I'm going to stay here with your mom and Libby," he said, sitting down. "I heard you had a good day traveling yesterday, that it came quickly to you."

I glanced at Landen, "I promise I didn't tell them everything. They don't even know where we went," Landen thought.

"So where did you two go anyway?" my father asked.

Landen raised his brow and tilted his head as he took a big bite of his omelet.

"Well, a lot of places. We started at Victoria Falls."

We had my mother's attention now. She'd put her sketch down and was looking at me, a surge of energy coming from her. "Zimbabwe?"

There was no holding back the laughter from my father, Landen, and me. My mother sat back in her chair and tried to imagine how.

Right after breakfast, Landen and I took the rental car and drove to the closest town. It was a tourist town, and we hoped it would be easy to find someone who was unhappy when they were vacationing.

"Landen, do you think I could really help people close to me, like Livingston does?" I thought as we strolled across the sidewalk that lined the town.

"I think there's a reason for your gift. I don't want you to rush it. It'll happen when it's supposed to."

"Do you really think I can, though?"

"I know you're special," he said, giving me my favorite playful grin. "Did you like your tree last night?"

It had been dancing through my thoughts all morning. I wanted to ask him if everything was really that perfect in our home.

"Is it really there?" His eyes told me it was. "Where did you get it from?"

"Your grandmother, Rose, gave it to me almost two years ago. She told me when she saw it, all she could think about was me. I thought it was strange then. Looking back, I think she was trying to give me an advantage."

Out of the corner of my eye, I saw someone. It was Monica's mother, Sharon, and she was hysterical. I felt a panic rush through me. Something was wrong. Why would she be in Montana? Then I felt a pull come across me, and a sinking feeling fell through my stomach as my eyes raced over her. Sharon was an image.

"What's wrong, Willow? Willow?" Landen said, trying to follow my gaze.

"Sharon is an image," I thought with a shaking voice.

"Who is Sharon?" he asked.

"Sharon lives in Franklin. I'm friends with her daughter, Monica. Remember I told you about her yesterday? She's the outspoken friend of mine."

"Are you sure she's an image? What does she look like?" He'd followed my stare and was searching for her.

"She has on a black dress. Long blonde hair. She's crying, scream-ing." I knew he couldn't see her. There was no way not to feel sympathy for her.

"I have to help her, Landen."

Landen's gift of intent was working. He knew that's what I was planning to do, and he was ready to argue his point of view. "It could be a trap. She's in Franklin. If Drake is anywhere near her, he'll see you."

"Landen, I have to help her! Something has to be really wrong—what if he's hurting them?" I felt a sick feeling rise and settle in my throat.

It would be my fault, and I wouldn't be able to live with myself.

"What if you just call and see?" He knew he was fighting a battle that I wasn't going to let him win.

"Landen, I have to help her," I thought in a pleading tone. "You'll be there, and you can pull me back into the string if he's there. I'll even let you take me all the way home if he tries anything."

Landen clenched his jaw. I could feel the turmoil stirring inside him. I felt his pain. He knew I was going to go, and I knew he was trying to think of ways to stop me. He knew if he tried by force, I'd just find another way.

"Okay, let's just compromise. You can't stay, no matter what you see. If it's bad, we'll get the others and we'll all help," he thought.

I could handle that compromise. I didn't want to put myself in danger. I just wanted to help her. I had to help her. No choice in the matter.

We walked to where Sharon was. She wasn't screaming anymore, and she looked like she was calming down. Landen held my hand as we passed through the crowd.

"Willow, don't say anything to her. You have to keep your concentration. You can't do anything differently than you normally do. I don't know what could happen if you do."

I was having doubts. What if I put Landen in danger? I argued with myself. I had to help, though.

When we reached Sharon, Landen stood behind me and wrapped his arms tightly around my waist. His anxiety was growing stronger by the second. Putting him through this was torture. Taking in a deep breath, we reached for Sharon, and the string pulled us through with a rush of energy.

We were in the police station. Sharon was not alone. Other parents were there, in fact, all the parents of my friends were in the room with her. Using all my strength, bringing her a feeling of safety was all I could do. Her tears stopped, but she didn't smile. I knew I was only giving her temporary peace. Deciding that was the most that we could do, we let go.

Stopping in the string, I could still feel Landen's arms around me. His anxiety was replaced by sorrow. When I turned to face him, his face held the same emotion. He pulled me closer to him. He saw more than I did. He knew what was wrong, why they were so upset.

"What happened?" I asked.

I knew my thoughts were as pleading as my face. Landen hesitated, just like he always did when he didn't want to tell me something.

"Landen."

He breathed in. "There are six missing." I heard his words, but I couldn't process them at first.

"He took her," I thought, remembering how Monica had wanted to go with Drake to the beach to go out on his boat.

"I don't know how. He'd have had to take them one by one. Esterious is dimensions away."

He was rocking me back and forth, trying to calm me down. The humming and gentle current of the string was helping him. All at once, Landen stopped. His whole body became ridged. Rage coursed through him. Then I heard who was making him angry.

"Well, well...what do we have here?" It was Drake's deep, charismatic voice.

Landen moved, shielding me with his body.

"Have you hand delivered my queen to me?" Drake asked.

My adrenaline rushed to my defense. I was infuriated with Drake. He had now crossed the line.

"You know, I'd expected to have to deal with her father, or maybe her little boyfriend, Dane. But you, my friend," Drake paused while looking Landen up and down, "are a worthy opponent." He began to circle us. "Mmm...yes...a degree of chivalry always makes for a good story." Drake tilted his head, smiling arrogantly and winking at me. "It will be a good one to tell our sons, when I tell him how I won you and every dimension." He stopped in front of us, his eyes moved from me to Landen. They were locked in a dead stare.

"She's not leaving with you," Landen growled through his teeth.

"You would think that a man of Chara would want the color to return to Esterious," Drake said, folding his arms across his chest. "Would respect soul mates."

"You don't need Willow to release those people. It's you and your beloved Donalt that holds them captive," Landen said in a harsh tone full of disgust for Drake.

"Willow's destiny is threaded through mine," Drake said, glancing at the tattoo of the dragon on his arm, then to my ankh.

I lunged at him, pushing him into the wall of the string. I could hear the singe of his clothes as he quickly stepped forward. The wrath in the string intensified. Every muscle in my body hardened, trying to block out the sheer force of the emotions coursing through the string.

Drake didn't scream in pain. Instead, a proud grin filled his face, and he chuckled under his breath.

"Where are they?" I screamed at him as Landen pulled me behind him and blocked Drake, who was stepping toward us.

Drake looked at Landen with an arrogant sneer. "She's always belonged to me...I've been with her more nights than you could ever imagine," Drake said, clearly enticed by my outburst. "Willow, are you going to make this easy or hard on yourself?" he said, glaring at Landen.

Before I could answer or manage to pull a thought forward, a rush of energy with an unbearable force plowed through my back, knocking me into Landen. The flow intensified, and Landen pushed into Drake, then turned and pulled me close to him. We were both watching the sides of the string. The hazes were rushing by so fast, there was no way to be sure where the passages were. The hum suddenly rose to a roar. I felt every part of my body vibrate violently.

"Let me go first. It won't burn me," I thought, feeling my confidence build. I pulled Landen's arm and stepped through the moving wall into an open field.

"Do you know where we are?" I asked, shaking.

I looked back at him. The string had burned his arm—there was a large hole in sleeve of his shirt, blood oozing out. "You're hurt again!" I gasped.

Landen looked down at his arm, then around to find our place. My body was so weak from the storm it started to tremble.

"It's all right. It'll be all right. I promise," Landen said as he picked me up and held me as tight as he could. Over his shoulder, I saw Libby. I blinked a few times, thinking the stress had caused me to hallucinate. She seemed frantic. I felt a pull reach for me.

"Libby!" I gasped. "It's Libby—she's scared!" I screamed.

We ran the twenty-yard distance between her and us.

"Landen, hold on to me!" I yelled, reaching for his hand as I reached for Libby.

When my hand touched her, I screamed her name. When she looked at me, all the fear vanished from her face. I'd brought us back to the cabin. Everyone was there with her.

Landen shouted toward Ashten. "Drake is in the string! Willow's friends are in danger!"

Without hesitation, Ashten, Marc, Livingston, and my father stepped through the passage I'd made. Landen was still holding my hand.

"Stay here. I love you. Stay here." He let go, and my passage was gone.

"LANDEN!" I screamed.

He had vanished.

Chapter 8

<hr>

Mom was kneeling in front of me, saying something, but I couldn't hear her. A pain was creeping through my body. Everything hurt. I felt like I was being torn apart. I desperately tried to see my passage so I could follow Landen, but it was gone. I was still holding tight to Libby, and she was holding just as tight to me.

"Willow, what happened?" My mother's words finally reached me. When I didn't respond, she fumbled with her phone, finally dialing a number. When the other person answered, she said, "They're in the string—all of them. Willow made a passage in the center of the cabin, but she won't tell me what happened...is that safe...are you sure?"

There was a pause.

"Okay, okay, okay." She hung up. "Willow, I need you to calm down. You're scaring me. They know what they're doing. He can't hurt them. I promise."

I knew I was scaring her, but I couldn't calm down. As the seconds passed by, the pain intensified.

When I could think all my friends flashed before my eyes, and a different kind of pain settled in my soul.

The cabin door opened, and there stood a beautiful woman, the same age as my mother. Sympathy filled her face, and she ran to where my mother was holding me in the center on the cabin floor.

"Did you see them on your way here?" mom asked. The woman shook her head no.

"Is it safe for Clarissa to be in there?" mom asked.

She had to be Landen's mom.

"She's fine. Her soul mate can see in the string. It's like he was born to travel through them. She went back for him. Brady will be here any minute."

"I'm sorry," I whispered. I don't know if I was talking to her or everyone who was up in arms or hurt because of me.

I laid my head on my knees and rocked myself, trying to focus. Aubrey brushed my hair out of my eyes. "You're so beautiful," she said, smiling as if nothing was wrong.

My mother took her phone outside, leaving Aubrey to watch me. Libby was still sitting next to me. I tried to focus on her. Wondering what had her so upset, why I could see her before.

My emotion was still overpowering everyone else's, but my eyes found a solution to my agony: someone was on the porch. A rush of excitement came through me.

"Landen!" I said breathlessly.

Aubrey followed my eyes and pulled me close to her. "No, sweetie, that's Brady."

He opened the door, and when the sunlight hit his face, I could see that she was right. Brady's resemblance was remarkable. He had the same build and wavy dark brown hair, but his eyes couldn't begin to compare to Landen's. He smiled at me, and I saw his dimples come to life. He narrowed his stare disbelief as he walked closer.

"Now there are those eyes my baby brother told me about," he said, looking down at me.

"Did you see them?" Aubrey asked.

"I didn't expect to. The storm is blowing the other way," Brady answered, still staring at me.

"Will you tell me what happened so I can help Landen and the others if they need me?" he asked.

I nodded quickly. "I made a passage from a town down the street to Franklin. Drake has taken people from there. When we were in the string, Drake showed up, then the string roared and the current erupted. Landen and I pushed through. He's hurt. His arm is burned really bad." I said it so fast that my words collided together.

"It's going to be fine," Brady said confidently.

My words and reason were slowly coming back to me. "What is taking so long? You two traveled in just moments?"

"They'd have had to find Drake first. The storm could've taken Drake anywhere."

Brady moved me to the couch. My mind was replaying what had happened in the string, as well as how confident Drake was. What did he mean, 'our destiny was threaded together'?

The cabin door opened. I didn't bothering turning; it wasn't Landen. Brady was talking to someone. I heard a beautiful girl's voice. It had to be Clarissa and her soul mate.

"Willow," I heard my name from a familiar voice, one that didn't belong there.

My mind had to be playing tricks on me, and my eyes joined in. Before me stood an old friend, the one I'd always shared a kinship with: Dane. Behind him stood a girl our age with olive skin, short dark brown hair, and pale green eyes like Aubrey's. She was dressed in a black dress. A red belt gave shape to her petite figure, and long gold necklaces tangled around her. Why was she there with Dane? He was in Franklin, not New York.

"Willow, are you okay?" Dane asked me in an alarming tone.

I just stared back and forth between Dane and Clarissa. "How... how did you...you went to New York?" was all I managed.

Dane glanced up at Clarissa. That one glance told me everything I needed to know, the emotion between them was remarkable. Soul mates. I was too freaked out with all that was going on to realize how ironic that was.

Too fast...my Infante raised morals screamed in my thoughts.

"I told you I knew if I stayed close to you, I'd find what I was looking for. After you left, all I could think about was New York. I flew there the next morning and found your hotel. I knocked on your door, Clarissa answered, and..."

"Do you know where Drake took Willow's friends?" Brady asked.

"I know they were all talking about going to Florida to sail on his boat," Dane said, looking at me. "Monica was trying to convince everyone to go."

"Who is 'everyone'?" I asked, realizing I didn't know who was missing.

"Chase, Josh, Jessica, Hannah...and Olivia," Dane said, feeling guilty. "I'm sorry, Willow, I didn't think she'd go."

"I'm the one that left...I'm the one he really wants," I said through my teeth, trying to block out the pain I was feeling.

"This is not your fault," Aubrey said, squeezing her arm around me.

Mom came back in and sat down next to me.

"Did you find anything out?" Aubrey asked.

"Sharon said she panicked when Monica didn't call. No one will help her. They keep telling her it's summer love and that she'll come home in a few days."

"I bet they're still here, at least some of them," Brady said. "There's no way he could have carried that many people through the string within a seventy-two hour window, not with as bad as the storms have been across the last few hours."

Clarissa nodded in agreement. I stood quickly, thinking that if I moved, the pain would go away. I could deal with this, think clearly, if I didn't have to deal with ripping pain.

"Do you know where he would have taken them?" I asked.

Brady and Dane shadowed me, thinking I was going to fall. I started to pace the floor—or run, either way they didn't trust me.

"If they're right about him, he'd need to use a large passage, and the only one down there would be the Great Barrier Reef," Clarissa said eyeing me.

A chill rippled through me. I knew we were all over the string yesterday, and we could have crossed him at any moment. How did we not see him?

"Are you going to look?" mom asked Brady.

"I'm not going anywhere until Landen is back. He'd kill me if I left her unprotected."

"Could he still come here?" Dane asked, looking across me at Brady.

"He could if he lost them. It's a long shot, but I'm not going to risk it. I'd want Landen to do the same if the situation were reversed," Brady said.

I remembered that Brady had someone at home, not to mention a baby on the way.

Their voices faded into the background, and I went somewhere inside myself, looking for answers, wondering what I ever could have done to deserve this pain. I began to regain my balance. Brady stepped back, trusting me more. Dane stayed close. I turned my eyes slowly to the last place I'd seen Landen. The air was clear, and there was no evidence that it had ever happened. The absence of the string began to fill me with hopelessness, but then I remembered the first lesson Landen had taught me—I had to 'remember what is natural to me.'

I let what I thought the passage should be like run through my mind. I imagined the way it would feel as I passed through; the hum I would hear inside the string. Essentially, I let myself feel as if I'd already seen it.

The room faded, and all I heard was utter silence. Before me, the air was divided by a thin glow of light. Suddenly, a pull of energy came over me. I'd found my passage. I knew Landen was in the string, and I wanted to find him, to find my friends. I couldn't stand there any longer and play the part of the damsel in distress. Feeling someone grasp my elbow, I stepped forward with confidence.

The white light passed through me with a soothing vibration of energy. I sighed, feeling a tinge of relief from the agonizing pain that I'd felt everywhere; I felt closer to Landen. The grip on my elbow tightened, and I looked back to see Dane in the string with me.

"Willow, take us back," he said calmly.

I shook my head in defiance. "I have to find him. I have to find all of them," I said, choking on my words.

"Don't cry."

"Cry? Are you kidding me?"

"Most people would've lost their minds by now. Hell, I'm still having a hard time—I keep thinking I'm gonna to wake up and this is some wild dream. That Clarissa's not real."

He glanced nervously down the string. "You need to calm down. Get us back."

I squinted as pain licked through my body; it was milder in the sting, but still hurt. "It hurts. I don't get what hurts or why but its better in here. If I find Landen it'll stop. I'll be able to think and find our friends."

"It's not safe," he said, struggling to keep his cool.

"Not safe?" Was he serious? "I have a darkness hunting me. I'm not going to sit there in pain and just wait."

He lifted his chin in stubborn defiance. "You and me, we're break-ing all the rules again."

His one phrase brought me right back 'round. For a split second I was who I was a week a go, a southern girl doing her thing, hiding her weirdness. Dane and me were not troublemakers, by any means. But we didn't follow the obvious path. If we had, we would've hooked up years ago. He'd be plotting to take over his families business and I'd be determined to honor my mothers name by becoming a creative legend. We had it all in front of us, and left it on the table. We waited for what felt right. Turns out, our right—was out of this freaking world.

"I shouldn't be able to see in this string," Dane said. "I should've never been able to follow you through impossible paths you made.

That's just me—to hear 'em talk you and Landen are starring in an ancient prophecy. This is the wrong kinda magic to taunt. You gotta play it smart. It's a came of wits, not strength."

He was making sense, too much freaking sense.

"Your Dad—hell, Landen thinks you're safe here. If they come back and you're gone...nothing good is gonna come of it. They'll be looking for you while our town is torn upside down. Families are going to be devastated."

I blankly stared forward, not knowing what to do. "I have to help," I said knowing myself, knowing this urge I felt swelling inside me. It was like sensing a thousand images calling out to me and ignoring them. It wasn't in me to sit on the sidelines.

"If Landen is half as good as they've told me he is—he's got this. Game of wits, Willow. Game of wits."

I closed my eyes trying to regain my composure.

"Take us back," he whispered.

Fine, I'd give this a few hours, nothing more.

I ticked my head telling him to step aside. My green haze was behind him. I reached my hand back and held his. One step later, we were in the center of the cabin. The pain roared through my body, so violently I nearly fainted.

"Told you so," Libby said. She was sitting on the couch. Mom and Aubrey were standing in front of her. They followed Libby's eyes and found Dane and me standing in the cabin. Aubrey ran to the door and swung it open. "Clarissa, Brady, they're back!" she called toward the river.

I glanced out the window; in the distance Clarissa and Brady were at the opening of the string. When they heard Aubrey the vibe of relief booming form them and the cabin itself was my own personal pain reliever.

Too bad it didn't last long.

Grimacing I moved tensely to the couch to sit with Libby. Dane stayed inches behind me, sitting on the coffee table and guarding me from the string.

Aubrey sat next to me while Mom fidgeted in place. Seconds later, Clarissa and Brady breathlessly rushed through the door.

I pulled my legs as close as I could to my body, pushing the thought of the pain away. Brady prowled closer, having a hard time hiding his suspicion and admiration. I took him as a guy who didn't really like things that didn't fit inside clean lines.

"Did you know she could do that?" Brady asked Dane.

Dane nodded.

"How?" Brady asked mystified.

Dane shrugged his shoulders. "All I know is she gets a look in her eyes, then she's gone before she ever really leaves. I started holding on when I was eight."

"Has Landen seen you do that?" Brady asked me.

I waited for the wave of pain I was breathing quietly through to leave before I answered. "He taught me to control it...started to, anyway."

Brady arched a brow as he crossed his arms. His curiosity, disbelief, and hope entangled around dread pretty much made me feel like I was mystical being who'd just stepped out of the pages of ancient lore. These people needed to get over thinking I was some kind of remake. I was an original soul, this much I knew.

Everyone fell silently into the background as I drifted into dark thoughts.

I never thought I was hurting anyone when I dealt with my issues on my own, and if I was, it was only me. Now I know my entire family, maybe even Landen's, had felt my burdens. Even worse, if I had asked, if I had learned anything about who they thought I was, or where I was from, my friends would be safe. I would've recognized Drake as a threat and left before he had a chance to see who mattered to me. For all I knew, I could've been in Chara, been there for years, if I had just asked for help—just asked someone to help me understand what was going on inside of me.

The day aged. The sun had set long ago. Libby never left me, even when Mom begged her to eat. She was sleeping on my lap now. Even though she was warm, I trembled.

Why didn't I tell Landen about the other nightmares? Did he even know that's what Drake meant?

"What was Libby upset about earlier when I saw her?" I asked Mom who was at my side. Aubrey was at the other.

Mom glanced at Libby and ran her hand across her forehead. "We'd just gotten back, and I was about to fix lunch for everyone. She was dancing around and playing with Ashten and Marc, then...fear filled her eyes. Like she was watching a horrible accident. We tried to talk to her to bring her out of whatever trance she was in, then after three or four minutes she started screaming your name. She told your dad he had to go get you, that you were lost in a field. Then you appeared out of nowhere."

A chill slithered down my spine. God please don't let Libby see my hells, please...let her be a kid.

"Willow," Clarissa said "I bet your friends don't even know they're in danger."

Offense flooded my expression. I liked her vibe. I did. But to be real, she was hooking up with my best friend. I got soul mates. I believed in them. Insta-love was another gig all together. It was different from how Landen and me were. We had years—every night of our lives—they had days. Until I could think again, she was going to be at arms length. Dane was family. Dane had been my sanity for years. Only the best would do for him.

Her telling me my friends were just chilling somewhere was not a good start. Clarissa read my expression and went on to explain. "It just seems that if they were scared, you would've seen them."

Okay. Smart and logical, she was back to winning my trust again.

Mom's phone rang. Brady and Dane came back in from the porch while

"Hello? Hey, is there good news?" Mom said cheerfully.

Hope speared the vibe in the cabin, but as Mom listened, I could feel her heart breaking.

"I—I need to talk to Jason...I'll call you back...I'm fine...I promise," she said, fighting back tears. She hung up and stared at her phone.

"Are they okay, Mom?"

Nothing.

"MOM!" I yelled.

"I don't know...she didn't say."

"What do you mean? She said something."

"There was...well, there's some kind of a fire at our house...they're working on it."

Mom was shattered. That house was all she had left of my grandparents. Inside of it was every relic her family had, stretching back to before America was home, to when the mystic land of Romania sprouted our roots.

I think Brady said something to her, pulled her to another room. I wasn't really locked on to reality. When I focused again only Brady and Dane were downstairs with me, the others were shuffling around upstairs.

Landen wouldn't have been gone this long unless something had happened. Perodine's words circled in my mind. I wondered what price my choice would cost, and who would pay it.

I wanted answers.

"Do you know who Perodine is?"

My question astounded Brady. "Do you?" he asked bleakly.

She was real...just as real as Drake and Landen. Aubrey was standing on the balcony that overlooked the living room when I'd asked.

Brady glanced up, then walked to the window and stared out at the passageway to the string.

After a moment of thought Aubrey came back down the stairs. Mom and Clarissa were not far behind her.

"Where are they?" I asked.

When no one answered me, I stood and started to pace.

"Willow, I think you should sit back down; you don't look so good," Mom said.

Considering I was in so much pain I couldn't even feel it anymore, I didn't doubt her. Moving felt better. Moving made me feel like I was still capable.

Mom went on. "You need some food. You really look pale."

"How are you so calm? All of you," I said glancing to Brady and Aubrey. "You're all separated from them...does it not hurt? You don't feel it? "

Confusion dancing in the unstable vibe of emotions clearly told me I'd just publicly highlighted a weird trait. The embarrassed feeling I had—the one I felt wash down my crimson cheeks reminded me why I'd kept my oddities to myself.

"We have to go in the string and find them. Something could've happened," I said before they could analyze how weird I really was.

I swayed. Brady moved to my side, waiting to catch me if I fell or tried to leave—whichever came first.

Out of nowhere, a rush of vigorous vim came through the room. I glanced to all of them then finally settled my stare on Libby.

A second later, Libby shot up from the couch and ran up the stairs.

Mom walked over to the stairs and yelled Libby's name. When she didn't answer, my mom started to go up the stairs at the same time Libby was coming down them. She had taken off her bathing suit and put on her favorite little pink sundress and sandals, and she was holding the rabbit that she'd slept with her whole life. A smile was brightly lit across her face. When she got to the bottom of the stairs, she screamed, "Come on, Willow, it's time to go to Landen's castle!"

"Libby, do you see them?" I said, feeling life seeping into me.

"Come on, Willow," she said, holding me by the hand and pulling me to the door.

I wasn't going to ask any more questions. I followed her out the door and down the steps. I could feel the confusion coming from everyone behind me. I didn't care, though; Libby had to have seen something.

My eyes were weak, my whole body was. I wanted to run faster, but I didn't have the strength.

I felt him.

"Landen? Landen, are you here?"

He didn't answer.

I closed my eyes and fell to my knees but before I could fall any further, I felt his hands on my face. When I opened my eyes and saw him, a lazy smile came to my face. The pain was going away. Sweet relief was humming through the shredded paths inside my body

"I know... I know it hurt, but it's over now.

My body fell limp. I was drifting away.

Landen yelled behind him, "Jason, something's wrong with Willow!"

"Willow, speak to me." I wanted to, but I couldn't.

"She's fine," Dad said. "Get her home, you're the medicine."

"Can you carry her?" I heard Ashten say.

"Brady, get Libby," Landen said.

"Willow, baby, hold on. I'll carry you home."

I fell into a deep sleep, dreamless at first.

When I opened my eyes I saw a canopy above me.

I'd made it to my home again.

When I reached next to me, Landen wasn't there, but I could feel him just outside the doorway that led to the porch. I felt his turmoil. I was sure he was still lost in the worst day we'd lived through so far.

Rising from the bed, I noticed that I was wearing a white night gown that barely reached my thighs. The straps were a beautiful lace. It looked like nothing that I'd ever owned. I loved the way it felt against my skin.

Where had I fallen asleep? Where did this come from? The thoughts were dangerous; at least they were if I wanted to stay asleep. I'd learned to never question a dream, to float on its current and work out all the whys later.

I walked slowly toward where Landen was, feeling the pain in my sore muscles with each step. I had to be in serious agony in my waking life for it to follow me to the dream state.

No, there was no way I wanted to wake up yet. I needed to heal.

Landen was gazing out at the crescent moon. His arms were spread wide across the banister. The gleam from the night sky highlighted every lean muscle in his back.

The site of him rushed my heart. It pumped good adrenaline through me—the kind that makes the bad in life bearable, the kind that was created to highlight unforgettable moments. Moments that write a story on our soul.

My dad had treated his wound; a wide white bandage was wrapped around his arm, and another was on his shoulder. When I reached him I wrapped my arms around him.

Relief filled him.

He felt so real, more real than he had in any dream I'd ever had before. He kissed my hands softly before slowly turning around. When I saw his eyes, I could see how troubled and tired they were. I reached up and ran my fingers over them. He drew my chin up and kissed me tenderly as his hands moved down my sides, and mine eased up his chest.

Each temperate movement of his hands across my gown left me breathless.

His kiss gained power. His long arms reached down and grasped my legs, lifting me so that I fell perfectly around him.

The closer I was to him the less I hurt, the less I felt like I had a care in the world. I was weightless, eternal, part of everything.

A heartbeat later he carried me through the doors to our bed. His hunting blue eyes slowly traveled over every inch of me as he carefully laid me down.

I reached for his face wanting to feel his lips against mine.

An insane tingling sensation encased my soul as when he leaned forward and stared at me just before our lips touched. Kiss by kiss, touch by touch I realized we were not new lovers. We were old lovers welcoming the other home after a long absence.

A euphoric high came over me. I found myself losing my breath—the sound my heart thrashing in my chest deafening. I couldn't believe how real it all seemed to be.

He whispered, "I love you," just beneath my ear.

No, this wasn't a dream.

It was real.

We were home.

We were together, both embracing this sacred, breathless first.

Chapter 9

Sunlight filling the room brought me out of a deep sleep. I glanced to my side and saw Landen sleeping soundly. I watched his chest rise and fall, assuring myself that he was real. Smiling, I let my memory flow over the night that we'd shared, but then the day that we'd lived before came crashing through my thoughts.

I had so many questions.

Is everyone safe now?

Is Drake only a bad memory?

What now?

He looked too serene to wake. I decided to get up and explore. There was a long dresser on the opposite wall of our bed. I saw the bag that I'd packed in Franklin sitting on top of it.

My photo album was open to the picture of graduation night. Monica was the valedictorian, and Olivia and I were kissing her cheeks as she smiled widely. An uneasy breath escaped me. I wanted them all to be safe and wished only for a moment that they'd never known my darkness or me.

With my purple top, white shorts, and all my toiletries, I found my way to the master bath.

When I was ready for the day, I tiptoed past Landen's sleeping body and went down the stairs. The house was even more perfect in reality, not a single stich of uniformity could be found, it did seem like it was manufacture made to capture the almighty dollar. Like the home I grew up in, it felt like it was made with love, made to protect a family, to hold all the laughter and memories tightly inside its vibration.

I searched for the willow tree first. Rainbows danced across the walls as the sun touched the crystals. While I was standing star struck, I heard something. It sounded like a car door closing.

Odd...cars.

I peeked out the front window and saw a little white car, just like the ones we had at home. The only difference was that the top of the car had a gray panel. Someone was pulling things out of the back seat. She was young, her hair was long and blonde—almost white—and her skin was the color of honey. I walked to the front door and opened it a bit shyly. She turned as I stepped on the front porch, a smile filling her beautiful face. I assumed she was Felicity, Brady's soul mate. The massive baby bump gave it away.

"Did I wake you?" she said.

"I was exploring..."

She had reached the porch wither her large basket, and I could smell the baked goods coming from it. My stomach adamantly reminded me that my last meal had been breakfast yesterday.

"I'm Felicity."

"Willow," I said under my breath.

I felt like a fool. She knew who I was. "Here, let me take that," I said.

"Is Landen still asleep?" she asked.

I nodded and watched her walk into the house. A bit confused, I followed her through the entry hall to the kitchen.

"This is my favorite room. It was the only one I got to help with," she said over her shoulder.

The kitchen was one of the rooms I hadn't been in yet, but I found it perfect, just like the others. The counters were made of a beautiful gray stone, the cabinets were a dark wood that matched the table and chairs, and there were beautiful bouquets of flowers set in the center of the table and counter. The room was extremely large. It had a long window across one wall and a wide doorway on the back wall that led to the porch. She walked over to the cupboard and pulled out two glasses and plates. I sat down at the large kitchen table and just watched her. She had a beautiful glow about her.

"I don't remember anything. Is my family okay? Do you know where they are?" I asked.

"Their house is just over that hill," she said, looking out the back door. "Libby is the best. I played with her for hours after you all came home. I love her vibe. I'm sure they're still asleep. It was well into the night before they went home. Brady was sleeping like a baby when I left."

"Do you live close, too?"

"We all live within a mile of each other. It's still very private, though. The hills give each home solitude."

She felt so safe, comfortable. It was reassuring. I knew she had come from another dimension, left her family behind and started a new life. The lack of fear and stress inside her promised me I had a shot at finding the same.

"Is it as amazing as I think it is here? I mean, how does it all work—its ah, its not so...happy, at least all the time, where I come from."

Felicity laughed. "What I love about here is that each person does what they're meant to do. Everyone has a purpose threaded into their soul. In this world, its a priority to discover what yours is. I think that helps with the 'happy.'"

"What do you mean? Everyone has insight?"

She swayed her head. "I mean we all have a purpose, something inside us meant to bring not only personal joy, but also those who surround us. We are here to make it better than we found it. You can see it in everyone if you really look, it's almost as beautiful as love."

"I can't imagine that's easy. Figuring out what you're meant for." I was sure if it was my world would have the same philosophy. It didn't make sense for us or anyone to want to live a life without purpose—without a fire burning inside driving us to see what others can't.

"Its not hard, not really. Well, okay, Libby is six," Felicity said. What they'll do is look at her birth chart and find her characteristics, teach her math, science, everything in the way she learns best. Brady's sun sign was Aquarius, but he has several other planets there too. Aquarius's hear differently—they hear the sound, not the words. With Brady, every subject was related back to music. He's not a musician, but being confident enough to learn and explore helped him find that traveling wasn't just in his blood it was in his soul. Loving to learn and explore is the first step to looking inside yourself. It can be scary in there, even for kids." She pursed her lips. "It is the last place most explore."

The most I'd ever done as far as the Zodiac was concerned was looked at my horoscope, which was always wrong. To think that an education system was balanced on the stars in the sky seemed insane to me. Then again, I still didn't understand what a birth chart was or how it could hold any answers.

"What?" She asked when she read the debated in my stare. "How do they do it in your dimension?"

"We all just go to school and learn the same subjects." I lifted a shoulder. "Some of us are pushed by our parents down a path they know."

"What dimension did you come from again?" Felicity asked, raising one brow.

"Um...Infante," I said, hoping I'd remembered the name correctly.

She nodded as if my thought process matched my home dimension. "I still find it intriguing to meet the people they bring home. You would not believe how differently we come to conclusions on the way life should be lived."

When I glanced to her stomach, to the innocent vibe there, Felicity landed her hand right where I felt it the strongest. "Traveling is a dominant purpose in our family. They are vital to Chara, they guide us. If they see something in another dimension that has brought harm to the people, they guide us away from that tragedy. If they see something that has brought peace and bliss to a dimension, they teach us so we can grow more peaceful. Traveling is one of the most respected gifts. Without travel, our children would never find the love that we have."

"Everyone in this family travels?"

Felicity nodded. "So far. We're well known throughout Chara," she said. "Landen is the youngest and most admired traveler of all."

I raised my brows to question her.

"Landen's insight of truth is not what he is known for. Instead, he is known across Chara as 'the one who can see all'," she explained.

Mystified I slanted my head in thought. Perodine told me in my dream that 'the one who sees...,'. Did she mean the string?

One problem at a time, Willow...

"Do you know what happened before we got here? Did Landen find them?"

Her smile lessened. "I think Landen wants to talk to you about it." She sighed, "I felt so bad for him. He was worried about you. Jason must have told him a hundred times that you just needed to rest."

She reached for my hand. "I'm so happy for you two. I knew he would find you. When Brady told me the names of your family, all I could think about was that music box on the mantel." Letting go of me she said. "Everyone is coming to your celebration."

"Mine? What about Dane? Isn't this fast? We got some things to take care of, and stuff."

Was I fumbling my words? Yep. I didn't like parties. I loathed them. The ones I feared had a spotlight aimed to find me.

"The news has spread across Chara. Jason Haywood home at last, Clarissa's soul mate being able to see the string, and, of course, the youngest couple—the ones who need no words!"

Nope I needed to run from this topic before I had an all out panic attack.

"Which dimension did you come from?" I asked.

"Neime. Just next door, so to speak."

"Is Neime a good one?"

"Yeah. We live a lot like they do here. I think Neime is the smallest. The biggest difference is time. I didn't know what it was until I came here."

She shrugged when she saw how baffled I was. "We do not mark hours or days or even years. It's a good place for Gemini signs." She glanced to her basket then to me. "I need to go. I want to help Aubrey get ready for tonight."

"Tonight?"

"It's just going to be family and close friends," she promised. "This whole week will be filled with celebrations. People are coming from everywhere," she said, walking softly toward the front room, beckoning me to follow her.

When we reached the porch, she said, "I have some clothes for you. I wanted you to have something nice to wear. I remember how I felt when I got here, not having more than a satchel of things from my world."

I followed her to the car, and she handed me a handful of clothes. They were all dresses; some long, others short, and the colors were vibrant and balanced all at the same time. They felt so smooth, like the gown I found myself in last night...I wondered who had put that on me.

"I made these, so if they are too big, I can take them in for you."

"You made these?"

Her grin was proud. "Its my thing. I'll stop back by before the party and make sure they fit you well. See ya when the sun goes down."

I found the way she kept time very comforting I gave her a shallow nod then watched her leave.

When I walked back in the house, I found Landen standing at the bottom of the stairs. I could tell he had been up for awhile; his hair was wet from where he had showered, and he was dressed for the day, all in black again.

I shyly smiled at him. I couldn't believe this was real. I was home.

Then the distance between us seemed too far, so I let the dresses fall and ran into his arms. He laughed out loud at my unconventional enthusiasm.

"Why didn't you wake me?" he asked against my neck before he kissed the tender skin there.

"No way, you looked to happy."

I glanced at his arm to make sure he'd dressed his wound again. My eyes widened as I stared at his unbroken skin.

"How?" I thought.

"I don't know. It was healed when I woke up. My shoulder is healed too," Landen said, pulling his shirt up to show me.

It was like it had never happened, but both of his burns had been severe enough to cause scarring. I kissed his shoulder softly before I lowered his shirt. He turned and stared at me with utter devotion.

I felt like a mystical lore character all over again.

"You healed me," he whispered as he put his hands around my waist.

"I'm weird, but not that weird."

"Do you hurt," he asked leaning his forehead to mine.

I didn't. Not one single sore muscle.

"We're both weird," I said only halfway teasing. I was scared. Scared that I was changing too fast. I was becoming someone new. I didn't' even know who the old me was.

"Don't let it scare you. Don't let anyone scare you," he said holding me a little tighter. "We're in this together."

I pulled him closer and laid my head on his chest, hearing his heart racing, too.

When his heart had settled into a rhythmic beat and we a second to take in the latest revelation he said. "I see you met Felicity. She wanted you to wake up just as badly as I did last night. I was surprised that Brady got her to go home," he said in an amused tone as his hands slowly glided down my back.

I let my arms fall from around him, then picked up the dresses I'd let fall to the floor and draped them across the banister.

"She brought some food. Are you hungry?"

Landen eyes brightened up. I smiled and pulled him to the kitchen. After a bit of hunting with only a nudge here and there from Landen I found all I needed to plate breakfast.

"What?" I asked, glancing up at him as he helped.

"Nothing."

"Tell me."

"You just look...you look like you belong here. I just can't believe it—that you're here," he answered shyly.

We fell into an odd silence. I had questions; he had things he needed to tell me, but neither one of us were ready. It was like we knew any breath we could take we needed to savor it.

After breakfast we moved out to the back porch.

Large white windmills were scattered across the fields. I could see the wind turning them. Long benches, padded chairs, planters, all made up a cozy clean setting. We settled on the biggest bench against the house.

"Landen, are you going to tell me?"

He lowered his eyes.

I reached for his hand. "Landen, tell me...is it really that bad? What did he do?"

Landen adjusted himself in his seat then looked out past the fields and back at me, replaying the day in his mind.

"When we got into the string, we split up. Your father and Marc went back to Franklin so they'd know who he'd taken. Livingston and my father went with me to find Drake."

Landen stood and started to walk back and forth in front of me, rage was threatening to flood his emotion.

"When we finally found him, he'd almost made it back to Esterious. I was so livid. I wanted to throw him off the nearest cliff. He kept taunting me, wanting me to follow him into his world."

He was so furious you'd have thought Drake was standing there at that very moment. I stood and moved in front of him to silently remind him we were here, not trapped in yesterday.

"Livingston told me that if I followed Drake." He glanced down at me, then reached to trace of eye. A few seconds later he said. "I just wanted to talk to him. Get some things straight. I was determined to do so, but then Drake hit Livingston. He wailed on him. I pulled them apart and threw Drake through his passage."

He lifted his chin. "I would've gone after Drake but...I wasn't thinking right." He glanced down at me. "It was getting harder for me to fight the pain. A place like Esterious, it sucks the life out of you on a good day."

I was glad didn't go but I wasn't going to strike his ego and tell him if he felt anything like I did yesterday, he would've lost a fight with Drake.

"Did you find the others?" I asked.

As Landen's remorse grew, my stomach turned. It was bad. I could feel it through him.

"Marc and your dad had gone to a passage that Livingston told them to search...they ...they...found what was left of a boat."

"What do you mean, 'left?'" I asked. I could barely hear him over my heartbeat.

"It was wrecked. There were survivors...two."

"Two? Where are the rest? Does Drake have them?" I said, covering my mouth in disbelief. The pain in Landen's eyes was ripping me apart.

"The two guys, Josh and Chase, saw Drake take three girls, Hannah, Jessica and...Olivia," Landen said as his eyes judged every inch of my body, looking for an emotional break.

My eyes raced back and forth, trying to process and count the names that he'd said, and I suddenly realized he didn't say Monica's name. She was there—it was her idea—why didn't he say her name?

"Monica?"

Tears were pooling in my eyes. Landen looked down at the ground, then back up at me through his dark lashes. His remorse told me she was gone.

"Josh and Chase said they couldn't reach her before she...drowned," he said slowly.

Feeling like I was going to be physically sick, I walked to the side of the porch, trying to hide my failing composure from Landen. I couldn't breathe. Monica's face was rolling through my memory. Landen came to my side and caressed my back. "Where are the others?" I said in an angry whisper.

"With Drake."

"How...how are we going to get them back?" I needed action. I needed revenge.

Landen didn't answer me; his stare begged me to give him time to work it out. "I gotta to protect you, first. The priest in Esterious are known for their dark magic."

"How can you stop something like that?"

"Erasing you from your world was step one."

I grimaced. Someone had done half the work for him. "Was Dad in Franklin when our house was burning? Did he see it happen?"

"We burned the house...your room, at least. I don't know how far it spread."

"What? Why?" I raged.

"I told you. For all I know it didn't help. Drake had days to take what he wanted. He could've taken something from when you met him. Our dads said it was better to be safe than sorry."

"That house meant the world to my mother."

Landen moved closer to me, trying to make me understand. "And she'd give anything to make sure you were safe."

I wrestled with blame and grief before I spoke again. "Can we bring my friends home before Drake decides to hurt them?" He nodded as he pulled. "How?" I asked.

"They'll call you. You're connected to them."

"What if they're under some spell or something? Can we not just go get them? They may not even know they're in danger? You sister said that."

"She's not wrong," Landen agreed. "What I'm saying is taking them will do Drake no good unless they lure you in. At some point he will do so, and we'll be ready."

I wasn't good with this wait and see plan.

"I sent travelers out last night to find my grandfather, August. If there is another way, he'll know what to do."

"What if they call me, like now? What then?"

"Then we go together. I don't think we can survive long without one another."

"I told your mom, your family it hurt when we were apart. They thought I was crazy. I should not have said anything. I wasn't digging the look in their eye. Like they separated themselves from us."

Landen clenched his jaw, "You're dad would've told them anyway. He said we were hurt on the inside. Inflamed from so much pain." Landen glanced to the fields then back. "Don't let them scare you with the way they look at us. It superstation. They want to see something, so they do."

"You're worried," I said quietly.

"No, not yet. Not til' I have a reason to believe. Even then...we can't help what we were born to do. Being terrified of it makes it real—it means glory is hiding and we only have to earn it."

I wasn't signing up to run through any hell. Not until I survived this Blue Moon. Before then, I had a mess to clean up. Friends to save. I kept them in a loop in my mind. Dad told me when I was a kid that what I thought about was a magnet. To think about what I wanted to come to me. I was still working on it. It was easier to think about what I wanted to stay away.

I'd give anything a shot right about now.

My head was spinning. I walked back to the bench on the porch. He came to my side and wrapped his arm around me. I laid my head on his shoulder and let yesterday play through my mind.

Landen's emotions were shifting from moment to moment. I felt them finally settle on jealousy. I knew what he was about to ask me, and I braced myself for the emotion that he would feel.

"Are you going to tell me what he meant about the nights together?" His voice was low and calm.

I stayed very still and quietly answered him. "He meant the nightmares."

Landen shifted his shoulder to face me with anxious eyes. "He was in more than that one?" he asked. I let my eyes tell him yes. "Is he the reason you'd be so upset all those nights?"

He knew the answer to that question, too. He stood quickly and paced the porch. The anger inside him reached the point of wrath. All at once, he stopped and knelt before me. "Tell me what happens, when they happen," Landen said in a desperate tone.

"There's a heavy, painful weight on my chest. I can only feel one person, a person who's afraid. In my nightmares, I can change emotion, and help that person feel at peace. Then they disappear, and Drake shows up and reaches for me, a bright light takes me away."

Landen placed his hand in the center of my chest, as if he wanted to take away all the times that I'd suffered under the overpowering weight.

"I've had a nightmare every new moon of my life until last November, and the last two nightmares don't fit any pattern. I don't understand why they're different."

Landen lowered his hand and looked down. "Do they see you, or are they like the images?" he asked quietly. I could feel his fear laced with rage. He was aiming to destroy Drake.

"Like the images," I said.

He turned from me and leaned up against my legs.

"Does that mean something?" I asked.

"If we met in the same place every night...I'd think that you met Drake in Esterious in your nightmares. The thought of you there alone there..."

"Did we always meet in Chara?" I asked.

Landen turned and looked into my eyes, then swayed his head. "I have no idea where we're meeting. I've never seen anything like it."

"Was Drake ever in your nightmares?" I asked.

"I've only dreamed of you."

"Who's Perodine?" I blurted out faster than I intended.

Landen's confusion was twice as thick as Brady' when I asked him.

"Who told you about her?"

"No one. I dreamed of her."

"You dreamed of Perodine?" He was angry and alarmed all at once.

"Is that bad?"

"It can't be good," he said moving the bench beside me. "She's older than time itself. She's portrayed as Donalt's wife—the queen. If you look at paintings from hundreds of years ago—millions of years, you'd see her portrait. They say she lives on and on, never dying, and that she's the source of all the good and bad magic that the dimension uses."

I closed my eyes, exhausted from the constant twists that life kept throwing at me.

"What did she say to you?"

"Nothing that made any sense," I said, frustrated with the added conflict of Perodine.

"Listen," he said. "Keep this to us. When August gets here, we'll tell him. He'll be honest with us."

"Are the others not being honest?"

"Your Dad is walking this way," he said leaving my question hanging there.

I glanced the field, but I didn't see him. Landen ticked his head toward the front door. "He's coming to see how we're feeling after yesterday."

Chapter 10

When I followed Landen inside I did sense my dad approaching. Landen reached for the door just as my father knocked. Landen then pulled the door wide open, and my father was standing there with a bright smile on his face.

"Morning, Jason," Landen said, extending his arm as an invitation.

"I was just coming to see how the two of you were fee-" my father stopped in mid-sentence. He was staring at Landen's arm, then his eyes quickly looked over Landen's entire body, then over mine.

"Come in, Jason," Landen said again.

Landen led my father into the living room, which was beside the front door. My father quickly looked us over again while reaching for Landen's arm and inspecting it closer.

"How did you heal so fast?" Dad asked.

"I don't know. It was gone this morning," Landen took a seat on the large tan couch in the center of the room.

My father walked over to one of the matching chairs that faced the couch and sat down, still completely astonished. "Both of you are healed. Last night I could see damage, painful—slow healing damage. I've been up all night trying to figure out how it was possible."

"Have you seen my dad and Livingston today?" Landen asked, trying to change the subject.

"Livingston went to Esterious to see if he could find a way to the girls, and Ashten is helping Aubrey get ready for tonight."

"Is Mom okay?" I asked.

"She's fine. Trying to stay busy and positive. She's worried about your friends." Dad gave me the same gravity filled stare he aways did when he need me to pull my shoulders back and weather through something. "It was an accident. Josh and Chase said that a storm came quick. Olivia and Monica were knocked out of the boat. They said that Olivia would've drowned if Drake hadn't pulled her out of the water."

"What are you going to tell Sharon?" I asked.

"Sharon knows there was an accident. The Coast Guard told her that Monica was on a boat with Chase and Josh and that they couldn't find her. Right now, she wants to believe that Monica is just missing. She'll say goodbye when she's ready."

"Where do they think Olivia, Hannah, and Jessica are?"

"They don't know. I altered a manifest for a cruise ship that showed the three of them docking in the Florida Keys. It was all I could think to do at that moment. That'll buy us some time to get them home safely, though"

"I thought you said Chase and Josh saw Drake take the girls. Wouldn't they have told everyone? Did they see the string?"

"There is an herb that grows in Chara. It erases recent memory. I gave them the herb to help them with their misery. Both of them blamed themselves for not reaching Monica." I could feel grief from my dad. "Now, the last memory they have is of arriving in Florida. The doctors will assume that their memory loss is due to shock."

"We have to go and get them," I said, standing.

"Willow," Landen said. "They aren't in danger now."

"Landen's right," Dad said. "Drake wants you, and he knows that if he hurts them you'll never come to him."

"Why does he want me?" I demanded.

The color left my dad's face. He glanced to Landen, then to me. He stood. "I'm hoping that one of the girls will appear as an image to you," he said deciding he didn't have an answer he wanted to give me about Drake.

"Now he's being silent," I thought.

"Will you show Brady and Marc how you travel? If they appear as an image, it would be good to have them at our side," Landen thought.

"I'll show whoever you want me to. I just want them back," I thought, still staring at my father as feelings of betrayal welled inside me.

"We're going to teach Brady and the others how Willow travels so that when the time comes, we'll be able to get them all back safely," Landen said to my father.

My father turned quickly. "That's a good idea, but do you think it's safe for the two of you to leave Chara?"

"We'll stay close," Landen promised.

"Just make sure the two of you stay close to each other...I still don't understand what happened to your bodies yesterday."

Landen nodded. My father then looked at me, leaned down and kissed my cheek. "Be safe. I'll see you tonight," he said quietly as he turned to leave.

I sat patiently on the couch as Landen called his brother and Marc to come over, but my stomach was tied in knots. I needed a pause button. Something to slow my life down, there was too much right and wrong side by side. Too much supernatural.

While we waited on the front porch for everyone to arrive, I stared out into the field, taking in the pure beauty of Chara.

Brady was the first one to make it to the house. He stepped out of a large white Jeep that had gray glass panels running across the hood and doors. I noticed he was dressed almost completely in black. As he walked toward us, I couldn't help but ask.

"What is it with all the black? Do I need to change?" I asked, looking down at my white shorts and purple top.

Landen smiled at my new observation. "No, I'll keep you close. It's just easier to see each other in the string if your wear black. If you get more than ten feet apart, you seem to fade."

Brady and Landen were now standing side by side, and their resemblance to one another was more than apparent. It wouldn't be difficult for a stranger to mistake one for the other.

"How's your—" Brady started to say as he looked at Landen's arm.

"I don't know," Landen answered before Brady could ask.

Brady dropped the subject. The respect in the vibe between them told me these two had a tight bond. No explanation was needed. They'd been through too much, seen too much to not know how to ride the wave of unknown.

Another Jeep pulled up. It was dark gray. I could see the same panels that were on Brady's Jeep. I studied the panels on both vehicles, trying to understand how they were powering the Jeeps. Landen grinned as he watched my eyes take in all the details.

"I keep forgetting that this is all new to you. It's like you've always been here with me."

I grinned. "I have been. I just never paid much attention to the scenery around us."

"You two are talking, aren't you?" asked Brady. "Now that's weird. I don't know if I'd want Felicity in my head...I mean she is the one, but this is just—just something else."

Landen smirked. "Its awesome."

There were two people in the Jeep. I recognized Marc; he was the one driving. The other guy was tall and had a lean build like the others, but with a baby face. His hair was a dirty blond and very curly, and he had a playful emotion wrapped in anticipation. "That's Chrispin. He's Marc's baby brother," Landen answered my question before I could even ask it.

"I have to say, you two look a lot better today. You had me worried, little one," Marc said to me as he reached the porch and hugged me.

"Can I see your arm?" Chrispin asked as he got closer.

Landen looked at Marc, then down to his arm. I felt the shock come from Marc, but Landen just shrugged his shoulders. Marc then looked back at Chrispin and shook his head, letting him know to drop the subject. I felt the confusion coming from Chrispin as he looked nervously back and forth between Landen and me.

I followed Landen's lead, and we walked off the porch to the fields that surrounded the house. Along the way, we passed a large windmill about a mile away from our house. "We're going to take a shortcut to another dimension, Olence. It has towns like yours."

"I'm worried my insight won't work outside of Infante," I thought.

"I know it will. When we were in the string yesterday, I could see your paths everywhere. You've gone farther than your father thought."

"Did that upset him?"

"I don't think he saw them. It seems that they're only really clear to you and me." I looked at him with an astonished expression on my face. "I know, weird."

Just before we reached the windmill, I could see the string come into view. Brady stepped in first, but Landen held me back; he was waiting for something. Brady then reached his arm out and waved us in. The string was calm. The hum was a low murmur, and you could barely feel the current.

"Are there any storms close?" I thought nervously, remembering how painful the last one had been.

"Storms never occur close to Chara," Landen promised. "We don't encounter them until we pass Esterious."

I smiled faintly and took his hand for my own personal comfort. I began to take in the beauty of the string.

"So what do you think about Dane being able to see in here?" Brady asked Landen.

Landen raised his brow, and pressed his lips together. I could feel a tinge of jealousy coming from him. "I knew there was something else I wanted to ask you about."

"Dane is the brother I never had," I explained.

I watched as a grin came across Landen's face. He then wrapped his arm around my shoulder and kissed the top of my head. "I know. He told me about that night at the lake. I've already thanked him for keeping you safe when I couldn't."

We came to the passage that they'd chosen. It was a light blue haze. I was the last to step through. I didn't know what to expect, having no idea what this world would be like. The passage was behind a large building, next to a generator.

We walked around the front to the streets, and much to my surprise, it looked the same as my world did. We were in a small town, the buildings were all made of brick, and the roads were made of what looked liked pea gravel. The people seemed ordinary enough, and the clothes even seemed to be the same as they were in my hometown. I reached out with my sense of emotion to see if this place were truly as safe as I thought it was, and I could feel that the mood was ordinary—the common stress, pride, and energy that I would have felt at home.

I did find it odd, though, that I didn't see any children anywhere. There wasn't a stroller in sight. I didn't even see a dog on a leash. I noticed a few admiring feelings aimed at my escorts, and it was easy to see that they all went unnoticed by them.

"Where are the children?" I asked.

"Here, the children are the most precious assets. They keep them safely at home until they're young adults, for fear that if they mingle with any adult beyond their family, their ambition will be altered."

Chrispin began to grill Marc and Brady about the dimensions he'd recently traveled. He was so ambitious and young at heart. The guys were telling Chrispin tall tales about giants and flying dragons, and at one point they had him convinced that trolls taught in the schools in my world.

As we passed a street crossing, something caught my eye. I hesitated, and Landen stopped with me, but the others didn't notice and kept their stroll.

"What is it? Do you see something?"

"You said no children, right?"

"Right."

"Do you see that woman with the crying baby?"

"No."

Landen called out to the others. They were confused. Maybe they were waiting for something more dramatic, or perhaps they thought they'd be able to see my images.

We turned down the alleyway and followed the woman. I was grateful that I'd found someone off the beaten path. I could imagine that someone might notice five people disappearing into thin air. This was a young girl. I could see that this was her first child. The inexperience was in her eyes. She was dancing and singing above the crying. I could see that she needed strength and that the baby needed to be calmed down. I was starting to doubt that I'd be strong enough to help them both and carry us all through the string.

"Okay, we're here. What's your plan?"

"Look, I'm going to hold Willow, and you guys hold onto me," Landen instructed.

"Wait. Are you sure about this? I don't want them to get burned," I thought in a nervous tone.

"I was only burned because Drake pulled me back through. I shifted out of the path you made. They'll be fine. I promise."

I tightened my jaw. I was even angrier with Drake now, and all I could think about was how I was going to make him pay for hurting the ones I loved.

Brady stepped forward quickly. I was sure that after my display yesterday, he was eager to see how I did this. As their anticipation rose, I could feel the excitement running through the guys. I felt the gentle pull of the string, and as I reached out, I could see a white light reach back toward me.

I reached forward and placed one hand on the baby's back and one hand on its mother. I felt the hum pass through my body. They were so beautiful. I'd have to find the time to sketch these two. I let my mother's energy and my father's peace flow through my memory. I hesitated longer than I normally would. I watched as the baby succumbed to a peaceful sleep. His mother's eyes sparkled. She looked refreshed and happy. I lingered, taking one last look at all the details, then I took in a deep breath, gathered my strength, and let go. I felt my body being pulled back, so I focused on the energy and stopped myself in the string.

Suddenly, a roar of laughter erupted from Landen, Brady, and Marc. Brady was laughing so hard tears were coming out of his eyes.

"Get him, Marc," Landen said as he tried to calm himself. Marc stepped through the other side of the string and returned with a humiliated Chrispin. I felt so bad for him.

"Don't let go until she stops," Landen said as he tried to stop laughing.

"Sorry," I said, apologizing for the others' laughter.

His face was so red. "You guys can tease me all you want, but that was epic," Chrispin said, grinning. The others nodded their heads in agreement.

"I'm glad I got you back when I did. The passage is already gone," Marc said, slapping Chrispin on the back. I looked in front of and behind myself, and I could still see it just as clearly as I had before.

"I told you so, they can't see it anymore," Landen thought.

"Can they still pass through it?"

"I don't know. We should try."

"Hey, we're going to try something. Line up behind Willow," Landen instructed. The irony was unbelievable. They were nervous, but they were so macho on the outside. I walked back through my passage, and one by one we were all back in the alley.

"That has to give us an advantage," Brady said.

They followed me back into the string again, and Landen led the way back to Chara. I noticed that Brady's emotion had changed. He was nervous. The others must have sensed his mood change as well because Marc grinned at Brady and said, "Don't worry, Brady. I'm sure Willow will learn to affect the emotions around her soon enough to help you if you really need it."

I glanced up at Landen, questioning what I'd just heard.

"He's nervous about being a dad. Can you blame him after seeing your image?"

"It's not always like that." I could remember what a happy baby Libby was.

"It's not the crying. The two biggest challenges we face in our lives are finding the right person and being good parents. He was just as nervous when he went to find Felicity. I remember telling him it should be easy, that he already knew what she looked like. That was when I realized that by my seeing you I was different from the others. They only have a feeling to follow."

I halted as my mind raced through my memory, touching on every image I'd ever helped.

"What is it, Willow?"

I smiled up at Landen. "I attract them." Landen questioned me with his eyes, but I continued. "Listen, if I'm lonely, I find someone who's lonely. If I feel lost, that's who I find. The other day, we were talking about marriage, and I found someone who was about to propose. This morning, I was with Felicity and I could feel the baby's emotion."

"But, Sharon—Libby."

"I think that was personal. Like you said, they're connected to me, so I have to be sensitive to their pain."

Landen grinned, agreeing with me. "Well, we can take that off our list of unanswered questions," he thought.

When we reached our dimension, it was almost sunset. Landen had told the others about the nightmares and our dreams, how they were more like out-of-body experiences. They seemed to take what we were saying well, but I could tell it bothered them the same way it bothered Landen that I'd been in Esterious so many times alone. That place must be wretched.

When our house came into view, I could see Felicity's car. She was standing on the porch with her arms crossed, which reminded me that I hadn't even tried on the dresses that she'd brought me.

"Looks like somebody's in trouble," Chrispin taunted.

When we got to the house, I could sense her. She wasn't angry; she was excited. She wrapped her arms around Brady and said, "I heard that you've been playing with babies all afternoon."

Shock came from everyone but Landen and me. We both knew Libby must have told her. I couldn't wait to see her.

Felicity smiled at Brady, knowing that she'd bewildered them. "My new best friend, Libby, told me."

"I wonder how she fits into all of this?" I asked Landen.

"She's zoned into you, at least what happens to you."

Felicity had Brady unload her car. She must have been expecting us to be late coming home because she'd brought clothes for the guys to change into. It was refreshing to see them in colors other than black; like changing out of a uniform, the seriousness left them for a moment as they prepared for the night.

Chapter 11

Felicity helped me choose a dress for the night. It was a beautiful combination of royal green and blue, fitting for the warm weather. The straps were thin, and it flowed from beneath the chest to just above my thighs. I blushed as Felicity complimented the way it brought out my eyes. I was trying to absorb all the positive energy she was exuding. My nerves were on edge. I was looking forward to seeing Libby and my mom, but I had no idea what to expect from my long lost grandparents or whoever else.

Landen was waiting for me at the bottom of the stairs, dressed in a royal blue shirt and brown khaki pants. He politely told Felicity and the others that we wanted to walk and would be there soon. Their understanding was undeniable. We had been alone for less than an hour that day, and it was easy to see that, though we were an admired couple, no one would desire to bear our burden.

We walked in silence for a while, lost in the last few days. With each step we took, I could feel the dread building inside me. When my breathing became measured, Landen hesitated, and then stopped walking. I could feel his concern as he tried to understand why I was so upset.

"I'm fine, just not so good with crowds," I thought, looking around for an escape.

Relief came over him as he heard my simple explanation. "It's not going to be like it was at home. They know what your insight is, and they're going to do whatever it takes to make you comfortable. If it gets to be too much, just tell me. They'll understand," he said as his eyes tried to catch my gaze.

"Landen, I just don't think I can go and smile and have a party. I just lost one of my friends, and I don't know if the rest of them are safe or not. I can't block that out and the emotions of the crowd at the same time," I said, stumbling over my words while trying to hold back tears of grief. I turned away from him so he wouldn't see me struggle. He quickly circled me, not allowing me to hide anything from him.

"Look, there's nothing I can say to take all of that away. No one is asking you to forget them. This 'celebration' is just a way for you to meet your family, a family that you should already know," Landen said, cradling my face.

As I looked in his eyes, I felt a peace come over me, and my body relaxed as the calm took over.

Landen smiled as he felt the tension leave me. "I don't want to go either. I want you all to myself. It feels like we're never alone, awake, anyway," he said as he looked across the field in the direction we were walking. He looked like he was listening to a distant conversation. "I can feel Rose's intent from here. She wants to guide us. Right now we need to be guided if we're going to be strong enough to bring your friends home safely."

I glanced across the field at the distant hill, then back at Landen and nodded. As we began to walk, he wrapped his arm around my shoulder and pulled me closer to him. When we reached the top of the hill on the south side of our house, Landen pointed to where my parents' house was. You could only see the rooftop behind the hills around it. Their home was to the left, and his parents' was to the right.

Landen explained that not only had our fathers been close friends, our grandfathers had been as well. For generations, the Haywood and Chambers families had lived side by side, the only two families with generation after generation of travelers. Even the women were fierce explorers. Others came to learn from them—some only trusting them to carry them home to visit the ones that were left in other dimensions.

We walked in the direction of his parents' house. I assumed the party was going to be there, but I wanted desperately to see my mother's home. The next hilltop revealed the home in which Landen had been raised. It became clear to me that porches were a way of life in Chara. The house was large, two stories, and white, outlined with wide porches and long columns. White lights outlined the bottom porch as well as the pathway to the front door. Music was playing, and laughter surrounded the house. There were several cars parked along the road just before the house. This "small group" of friends and family was larger than I'd expected.

A tiny figure ran toward us. It was Libby. My fear dissipated as soon as she fell into my arms. We couldn't even say hello before she began to rush over her day, telling us about everyone she now had as friends, her room, and how much she loved it all here.

"So you didn't miss me at all today? I see how it is," I teased.

"Willow, I was with you, too, you can't see me sometimes, though," she said as she slid down and ran toward the house to announce our arrival.

Glancing up at Landen, I could sense his despair. He wanted nothing more than for me and Libby to be safe, and at that moment he saw that as an impossibility. He grinned at me, then guided me toward the house. I took a deep breath and squeezed his hand as we climbed the front steps.

"Don't be scared," he whispered into my ear, kissing my neck softly. He was putting off a blissful emotion, giving me a blanket to hide behind.

We walked through the front door, and I noticed that his house was so much different from ours. Everything was white and very bright, the walls accented the rooms with a light teal blue, and even the floors were a light wood color. Flowers decorated the banister and the doorways. No one was in the house. They'd all gathered in the back. Landen led me through the living room to the double doorway that opened to the back of the house. As we opened the doors, an eruption of applause began.

The group of family and friends was close to two hundred people. Heat filled my cheeks and my ears. The spotlight couldn't be more uncomfortable. My mother and father stood in the front of the crowd, smiling up at us. My mother was glowing in a silver dress, her long hair was curled and her happiness unmistakable. Ashten, Aubrey, my father and mother proudly walked up to the porch where we were standing, which had been transformed into a stage.

Ashten began a heartwarming speech. "Aubrey and I, along with Jason and Grace, are pleased to introduce each of you to Landen and Willow, the newest and youngest couple of Chara."

Applause erupted again, then Ashten continued, "We have faced many trials and triumphs over the years. The time that Jason was lost will haunt me for a lifetime, just as the time that I found him will be celebrated for all of time." Ashten raised his glass to my father while tears streamed down Aubrey's face. It was easy to see that she'd helped Ashten carry the burden when my father was missing.

"Today, we celebrate Jason and Grace. They have been returned to us at last. We also celebrate that my only daughter, Clarissa, has found her soul mate, Dane."

I noticed Clarissa and Dane standing beside Landen and me. I didn't know if they'd been there the whole time. They were locked in each other's gaze, not appearing to notice the world around them.

"We also celebrate that life is not predictable. We are not all the same. Uniformity doesn't apply to any dimension, not even ours. Landen has proven this to us all as he stands here joined at last with Willow."

The applause erupted again, and I felt an overwhelming joy beaming from the crowd. An older woman handed Landen and me a glass of champagne. Ashten then raised his glass, and the crowd toasted. Landen turned into me and kissed me softly. I could hear the applause begin again as my head spun with his touch.

My father put his hand around the older woman who had handed me the glass and said, "Willow, this is Rose, your grandmother."

My eyes widened—she was not what I expected. Rose looked so young. The only sign of age she had was her solid white hair, which fell just to her shoulders. Her eyes were a beautiful green, and beside her was an older man whose hair was short and dark with silver running through it. He looked like my father, only much older.

"And this is your grandfather, Karsten," my father said, tilting his head in the direction of Karsten.

Rose hugged me tightly. "Oh, I've been on edge all day, wanting to meet you. Your father said you needed your rest. Do you feel better now?" Rose asked, looking at me then smiling over my shoulder to Landen.

I nodded, not knowing what to say. Karsten stepped forward and hugged me. "You are just as beautiful as your mother," he said, grinning at me, then at my father.

The band began to play, and we were flooded with welcomes from the crowd. Everywhere we looked, there were smiling faces, handshakes, and hugs from everyone that was introduced to me, but the names escaped me as soon as they were said. You could see the resemblance in some of them, and it was clear that they were from Landen's family. Others, I wasn't so sure.

Rose stepped in front of Landen and me. "All right then, give her some room. I'm sure crowds are difficult for her," she said. Everyone stepped back a little.

"No, no, I'm fine. These emotions are the ones that I like," I said, a little embarrassed. Out of all of them, I couldn't help noticing that Rose seemed to have an even greater understanding of my gift than my father did.

"You may want to hide her on the dance floor," Rose said, grinning at Landen. He nodded his head and winked at her. It was easy to see the favor he had with her.

The dance floor was full. All the couples seemed so immersed in each other; it was hard to imagine that Landen and I were the only ones who didn't need to use words. They all seemed locked in a world of their own. Even my parents seemed lost in themselves.

The grief and danger that had been hovering over me took a back seat as I took my place in Landen's arms on the dance floor. With each new song, I was passed on to an eager partner: first my father, then Ashten, Brady, Livingston, my grandfather, and finally Dane.

"You look so happy," I said to Dane as he took my hand.

"Just as happy as you," he answered, glancing at Landen and Clarissa dancing.

I sighed, feeling the guilt come over me. It didn't seem right to be this happy, knowing that our friends were in danger. Dane felt my body tense up and looked down at me. "It's going to be fine, Willow. We'll find them and make it all right," he said, sounding sure of himself.

"We can't make what happened to Monica right," I said under my breath, holding back tears. I felt grief inside Dane. He may have teased her growing up, but he still cared about her.

"No, but her memory will always be with us, and we can learn to never take anyone or anything for granted. You know if she were here, she'd be furious with you for not enjoying yourself. Monica lived in the moment, and that's where we need to live. We can't change the past, and the details of the future have yet to be seen."

I'd never heard him speak so deeply. I guess love changes every-one.

After my dance with Dane, he returned me to Landen and took possession of Clarissa. I made a conscious effort to be friendly to her. "I'm sorry for the way I acted yesterday. Dane can tell you that I'm saner than that."

Clarissa put her hand on my shoulder. "You held yourself together more than I would have been able to," she said, smiling back at Dane.

Libby demanded that Landen dance with her. I stood back and watched as he picked her up and swayed her to the lullaby of a song that was playing, smiling at me over her tiny shoulder. I made my way to one of the tables, so lost in my thoughts that I didn't notice that my grandmother, Rose, had taken the seat next to me.

"He's such a good man. We couldn't have dreamed of another so perfect for you," she said as she watched with me. Libby laid her head on Landen's shoulder, fighting heavy eyelids.

"I still have a hard time thinking that he's real. For so long, he was lost in my dreams."

Rose folded her hands under her chin and stared at me. Her green eyes were outlined in silver, reminding me of what the string did to the eyes of its passengers.

"I can remember the first time Ashten told me about Landen's dreams," she said. "He was so worried about him. I knew then that Landen was going to stand out from the rest."

"I didn't realize how close our families are until today," I confessed, remembering the story Landen had told me on the way to the celebration.

"It seems that we always have been, at least since before my great grandmother's time, anyway."

She began surveying the crowd around us. Her eyes settled on Livingston and Marc, who were lingering by the side of the dance floor. Marc was talking to Livingston, but it was clear that Livingston wasn't listening.

"Do you find it odd that, in the midst of this celebration, you feel a deep sorrow?" she asked. I looked at her quickly, then in the direction of Livingston and Marc. "Is your insight strong enough to tell me whom it is coming from?" she continued, glancing back at me.

"Livingston," I whispered. Rose nodded. "Do you have the same insight?" I asked.

Rose smiled to answer my question.

For the first time, I felt normal. Others having a gift was not the same as knowing someone who knew exactly how it worked. My peace started to fade when I realized that this was the first time I'd heard of anyone being like me, let alone my grandmother. Why did my father not tell me when he knew what mine was, even when he told me who we were?

"He doesn't know," Rose answered the unasked question. "Your feeling of betrayal isn't called for. You, August, and Karsten are the only ones alive that know."

"Why? Is it a bad thing? Is that why you keep it a secret?" I asked as the feeling of being a fluke came back over me.

"No...it's a beautiful gift," Rose said, reaching for my shoulder. "My father believed that for me to truly understand my gift, I should keep it to myself," Rose said, smiling.

"I don't understand," I said, leaning closer, hanging on her every word.

"If people guard themselves around me, I can't help them. The beauty of the gift of emotion is that you truly walk in another's footsteps for a moment."

I watched Livingston walk over to my father and Ashten. They glanced nervously in my direction, and I could feel a building anxiety coming from the three of them. I looked back at Rose. "What is my father not telling me?" I asked.

Rose caught my father's gaze, and I could feel his emotion through her. She sighed and looked in my direction. "That you are the one who will bring color to Esterious, its one of many things predicted about you," she said quietly, beaming with pride.

"What?" I asked, bewildered.

"You have a power inside you that will move both of our dimensions," Rose said.

My mother walked over to Rose and me and took a seat, ending our conversation.

"Are you two getting acquainted?" my mother asked, putting her arm around me and smiling at Rose.

I looked anxiously for Landen. I found him across the floor, handing Libby's sleeping body to my father. He caught my gaze, almost as if he could sense that I needed him.

"Are you okay?" he thought as he began to walk toward me.

"I just have no idea what she just told me, but it doesn't sound good."

"What did she say?"

"That I would bring color to Esterious."

I could feel confusion and fear come over Landen. Reaching me, he took a seat next to me and stared at Rose, who nodded in his direction.

"Well, it looks like it's time for me to go," my mother said, noticing that Libby had fallen asleep.

"You're going home?" I asked.

"I'm going to take Libby home and lay her down."

"Are you okay, Mom?" I asked, realizing this had to be a lot for her to take in as well. She nodded and tried to smile.

"I'm sorry about the house," I said, my voice echoing the guilt that I felt.

She heard it and tried to make me feel better. "Those are just things. You, Landen, and Libby are safe and sound," she said, smiling first at me, then at Landen. "That's all I could ask for."

Landen and I hugged her goodbye, then my father waved goodbye in our direction as my mother approached him. Landen looked slowly back at Rose, who smiled.

"Would the two of you care to follow me to the living room for a more private conversation?" she asked, sliding her chair back.

Landen and I followed her without hesitation. As we passed by Livingston and Ashten, I felt their anxiety rise. Once inside the house, Landen closed the door behind him. We were both nervous. We watched as Rose walked to the center of the room, then wavered before turning around Slowly, she reached her hand into her pocket and pulled out a silver chain.

"I wanted to wait until August came home to give you this," Rose said as she looked at the necklace in her hand, "but I think it may help you bring your friends home."

I walked slowly to her, feeling my heart rise in my chest. She reached for my hand and placed the chain in it, and I felt a warm tingle as it touched my skin. I looked down and noticed a medallion attached to the silver necklace. It was shaped like a sun with wavy, detailed rays, and in the center of the sun was what looked like black glass with a crescent moon carved into the surface. As I studied the details, I had a sudden, sickening sense of déjà vu. Landen leaned in to look closer as my hands began to shake.

"I think I've seen this before," Landen thought.

"Me, too," I thought, looking up at him.

"It should look familiar to you," Rose said.

She smiled and reached for the necklace in my hand. She then opened the clasp and reached for my neck. I leaned in slowly to help her. She leaned back and looked at my neck, then gazed into my eyes and smiled.

"Where did this come from?" I asked as I moved my hand to the charm, feeling all the details of its surface.

"From you," Rose said, tilting her head. Landen and I both looked at her with wide eyes.

"When I was a child, you and Landen approached me and August one day. You told me to give this to you the day you returned home to Chara."

"What are you talking about?" I asked, looking from her to Landen.

"Rose, you're scaring her," Landen said, putting his arm around me. "Now is not the time for myths."

"What myths?" I asked, looking back and forth from Rose to Landen.

"Some people in Chara believe that travelers have led past lives. They think that's why we can see more passages than them. Myth, our lore," Landen said.

"Myth or not, there's not a doubt in my mind that this is not the first time you've walked this earth," Rose said, looking at me, then up at Landen. "You need to know that you're missing a part of the medallion." Rose reached for the medallion and turned it for me to see. On the back of it was a ridge, and there were five holes spread around the inside edge.

"The star was lost," Rose said quietly.

I heard the back door open, and I could feel the anxiety of Livingston and Ashten pouring into the room. I also felt the curiosity of Brady and Marc. Ashten and Livingston walked cautiously to Rose's side. Landen looked back and forth between them. Marc walked to Livingston's side, and Brady came to my side. I felt his confusion as he saw the medallion I was tracing with my fingertips.

"Where was it lost? Does it matter that it is?" Landen asked.

"It was lost in Esterious," Rose said.

"Where?" Landen asked quickly.

"In the Blakeshire Palace," Rose answered. "You knew it would be lost," she continued, looking in my eyes. "You told me, 'Do not fear when the supremacy was taken, it is but one of many battles.'"

"Are you saying this medallion has power?" Landen asked in disbelief.

"I am," Rose said.

From the shock that ran through Landen, I could tell Rose was telling the truth.

"Was Drake able to hurt her because he has that star?" Landen asked in a low tone as anger began to come over him.

"He hasn't hurt her," Livingston said defensively.

Everyone in the room looked at Livingston. I felt heat rise in my cheeks as anger coursed through me. I stepped forward and peered up at Livingston with a dominant stare.

"He hasn't, has he?" I said sarcastically. "So what would you call a suffocating weight on your chest that makes breathing painful? How about being stripped of your senses and forced to feel a trembling fear of innocent people—not to mention that he's taken someone I love deeply away from me?" I said, poking my finger in Livingston's chest as angry tears came to the corners of my eyes. As

Marc stepped between his dad and me I felt Landen's hands on my shoulders pulling me back..

"Why are you defending him?" Brady asked Livingston.

"I just...I just...I didn't realize she suffered when she met Drake," Livingston said quietly. The deep sorrow I sensed coming from him told me he truly believed that.

"I want to know what you're hiding from me." Land said in a harsh tone.

"Where is the star? Does Donalt have it?" Brady asked, pulling his shoulders back. "If it belonged to Willow, they can use it in their magic. It might be why and how they got in her dreams in the first place."

"You're not going to get it," Landen said, looking at Brady.

"If it's hurting either of you, yes, I am," Brady said shortly.

"I'm going, too," Marc said, looking at Brady.

"I'm going alone," Landen said.

I stared up at him with panic in my eyes. He wasn't going without me.

Livingston's face turned red. "You're not going anywhere near Esterious. I told you they'll kill you," he said, stepping closer to Landen.

Landen pulled his shoulders back. "I know you believe what you say is true, now tell me how you know that," he said, staring into Livingston's eyes. "Tell me what you know. Tell me what you're shielding me from!" Landen demanded.

Livingston didn't answer him.

"Now is not the time to be silent," Brady said, pushing Livingston to answer Landen.

"Dad," Marc said, putting his hand on Livingston's shoulder. Livingston looked down, avoiding all of our eyes.

I looked at Rose for some kind of help, and even though she held no expression on her face, I could still feel her confidence and pride in me. Landen's eyes moved to Ashten, only to find him staring at the floor.

"Rose, will you please tell my mother that Willow and I said goodnight," Landen said as he let his hand fall into mine and led me to the door.

"I'll drive you," Brady said, following us. "I'm coming, too," Marc said as he followed us outside. Landen opened the back door of the Jeep for me to slide in. He then slid in beside me and wrapped his arm around me. Marc climbed in the front seat as Brady started to drive away.

"What's going on around here?" Brady asked.

"Marc, has your dad said anything to you?" Landen asked.

Marc turned in his seat. "He's been acting strange for the past week or so. I don't understand what's gotten into him," he said, first looking at me, then to Landen.

"Right now, I don't care. I'm going to bring Willow's friends home and put all of this behind us," Landen said, glancing at me.

Hearing his words, I exhaled, hoping it would be that simple. Brady pulled in front of our house, and Landen and I climbed out of the back seat. "Just get some rest tonight. We'll go back and talk to them, and maybe they'll tell us something," Marc said as he looked out the window at us.

Landen nodded and waved. We then turned to climb the steps, and as Landen reached for the doorknob, he hesitated and looked at me.

"Can you still feel their emotions?" he thought. I nodded, feeling the distant anguish and dread.

"Come on," he said, taking my hand and leading me off the porch.

"Where are we going?" I asked as we stepped off the porch and began to walk through the dark field.

"A different part of Chara. We won't be able to rest if we try to untangle their emotions or intent through the night," Landen said, looking down at me, he squeezed my hand. "I want to be alone with you."

I wrapped my arm around his waist as he led us into the string. Within the white light, we both felt a peace come over us, and the swarm of mixed emotions I felt was replaced by an overpowering love that I felt from him. We turned to the left and walked ten short feet, and there I could see a light yellow passage. I closed my eyes as we stepped through the haze, taking in the tingle. The sky was just as dark as it was at our home, and the half moon showed the way. I could hear waves breaking and smell the salt in the air. A small beach house was just a few feet away from us.

"Now we're alone," he said, smiling down at me.

I grinned and took off in a sprint to the dark beach house. Once I arrived, I climbed the short steps that led to the porch and pushed open the front door. Landen caught me in his arms, laughing, and I turned and looked up at him. He quelled that laugh with a deep kiss as he reached down and clasped my thighs before wrapping them around him and pressing us against the door.

"This dress has been the death of me all night," he thought as his body pinned me in place and his hands glided over me.

"You don't like it," I whispered as my eyes fluttered closed.

He rocked against me; at the same time his lips had eased down my throat and were passing my collarbone. "Love this dress..."

He gripped me in his arms and carried me to the table that was a few feet away. I fought with his clothes, searching for the smooth feel of his skin against mine.

We went wild in that embrace, the danger, the threat, and the dark emotions had built up throughout the day, we were both trying to heal the other, to wash those emotions away and replace them with unbridled passion. It took us forever to reach the bedroom, each step of the way we left a trail of clothes behind.

One second I was giggling, the next I was gasping for breath, then I would find a way to return every touch he gave me.

As we held each other that tingling sensation swarmed within me, his presence was embracing my soul. Filling in all the cracks of my heart, elevating me to a level of exaltation that I didn't know existed.

Chapter 12

As we lay staring into each other's eyes, sleep escaped us. I rolled onto my back, so I could look through the sky light, at the night sky. I could see the moon. It seemed to be growing fuller by the moment. I reached my hand to my chest and let my fingers dance across the details of my medallion. Landen rolled to his side and stared down at the sun and crescent moon. I sensed his confusion.

"Do you really think we lived before?" I asked him.

He looked from the medallion into my eyes. "I've never given credit to the myth of living past lives before," he whispered, "but I know I've seen you wear this before." He looked back to the sun and the moon.

"Are there any other myths about travelers?" I asked in a light-hearted tone, reaching for his face to trace his perfect profile.

Landen smiled and looked back into my eyes. "Some believe that the gifted travelers are the oldest souls bound by past lives," he answered, tilting his head and smiling at me as his eyes searched my face.

"I guess that means our families have always been with us," I whispered.

I heard him laugh under his breath. "Right now, I don't know if I'd see that as a positive," he said, trying to hold the sarcasm out of his tone.

I playfully glared at him.

"I didn't mean it," he said, wrapping his arm around my waist. "I just want to know what we're up against so I can protect you. It bothers me that my father doesn't think I'll be able to handle it."

"You're wrong. I can almost guarantee you that your father thinks you can handle anything. He has a strong pride that comes from him every time he looks at you." Seeing his doubt I went on. "Maybe he's the one that can't handle it. I don't think my father or Livingston can either."

"August will tell us," Landen murmured.

"Does your father realize that?"

"My grandfather has always played peacemaker between me and my father. He has a way of making my father let go and me slow down both at the same time."

"Maybe that's what our fathers are waiting on, the peacemaker."

"He should be home soon..."

"Do you think they lost the star when Justus and Livingston went to bring home Adonia?" I asked, rolling to my side so I could get closer to him.

Landen arched a brow "Livingston is the only one besides Justus that's ever been inside the Blakeshire Palace."

"Why did Beth go with them? Why didn't they take more travelers?"

"August told me that just before I was born, that the storms were so bad that travelers would be gone for months at a time. Justus and Livingston were the only ones close enough to go. Beth was from Esterious, so she went to help them find a new way in the palace."

"I think it's strange that no one knows where Beth and Adonia are," I muttered as I furrowed my brow.

"Marc and I do as well. Marc is convinced that Beth is locked in that palace and that he needs to bring her home." Unconsciously his arms flexed for an instant around my body.

"What do you think?" I whispered.

"I know that if I were Adonia and I lost my soul mate, I wouldn't want to live anymore, and if I were Beth, no palace would be able to hold me."

"Are they as strong as you?"

"I've never met them."

I felt my eyes growing heavy and smiled at Landen.

"Where shall we dream tonight?" I asked.

"Do you think we can choose?" Landen thought as he sat up with a rush of excitement.

"I think you choose. I've only ever gone to where you are," I thought, pulling him back down to my side.

Landen had beaten me to our dreams almost every time. The only time I'd ever been first was the night we danced to the willow tree music box. He was focusing in a straight stare. "What if we plan to go to a place to see if we can control it?" he thought.

"Where?"

"Here sounds safe enough," he thought as a grin spread across his face.

"If it works then what?"

"Let's just test it, see what we can do. We never even tried to communicate this way."

He rushed from the bed, I sat up completely confused, he came back a second later with our clothes.

I grinned and shook my head. It didn't cross my mind that we needed them, but if we managed to make this work, if we could control this and explore, clothes were needed.

I pulled my dress back on, and turned so he could help me with the zipper.

"This is a tragedy." He thought in a teasing manner, as his lips touched my shoulder and his hands waved over the dress he had fought so hard to remove.

After a moment I closed my eyes, keeping my focus both on the space around me and Landen, refusing any other thoughts or fears. I began to drift. It felt like only a moment had passed before I opened my eyes again. My body lay sleeping on the bed before me. Landen's body was still; only his chest rose and fell. The scene was so surreal. My first reaction was panic, and then I heard, "Can you hear me?"

He stood at my side, staring at our bodies as they lay sleeping. Not only could I hear him, I could also feel his discomfort.

"I can feel you, too."

Landen looked slowly at me, a sinful grin spread across his face. We were both feeling control of this heart-racing gift we shared.

He moved to the wall and knocked on it. Sound. We could clearly hear.

I furrowed my brow, he shrugged. "It might be because we are in Chara, it could be because we are controlling it." He came to my side. "Come on, I want to try something," he said, holding my hand and leading us from the beach house to the path that led to the string. Once there, we walked back through the passage close to our home. Landen hesitated as he used his gift to tell him where everyone was.

"My father is on his way to Jason's house," he thought.

"Where's Livingston?"

"I can't feel him anywhere close," Landen thought. "Can you?"

I focused on the emotions around me, feeling the same dread and anxiousness that I'd felt before, but unsure as to where it was coming from. I shook my head no. We passed through the field in the direction of my father's house, and in the distance I could see Ashten walking from the other direction. My father was standing on the front porch of a beautiful two-story brick home, the front of which was framed by bay windows.

"Do you think they'll be able to see us?" I asked.

"Brady was right behind me that day you gave me that note, and he didn't see you."

"I don't remember seeing him," I thought.

"You terrified him. All he saw were my arms going around thin air and a note appearing in my hand," Landen thought, grinning.

"I think I would have been bothered if I'd seen that happen."

We reached my father's house at the same time that Ashten did. You didn't need the insight of emotion to realize how concerned they both were.

Landen and I stepped cautiously closer, my father and Ashten never looked in our direction. It was an eerie feeling, almost ghostly.

"Are you sure they didn't go to Esterious?" Dad asked Ashten.

"More than sure. Landen is not one to make decisions without thinking them through. Rose believes they just went far enough not to feel us," Ashten answered.

"Did it upset Willow when she was told that the medallion belonged to her before?"

"I wasn't there when Rose told her, but I was there when Willow told Livingston how she felt about Drake," Ashten said, raising his brows.

Dad stared at Ashten in utter confusion.

"Livingston made the comment that Drake had never hurt her, and she told him exactly what she lived through."

"Maybe I should have brought her home sooner," Dad said to himself.

"You don't know if that would have stopped the nightmares," Ashten said, defending my father.

"I know that she's a new person now that she has Landen. She's more sure of herself now than she's ever been."

"Landen is, too," Ashten said, looking in the direction of our house. "He's calmer now, she gives him pause and he needs that." Ashten cleared his throat. "We need to get those girls home so the two of them can just live here in peace."

"It's not going to be that simple," my father said, looking at Ashten with pain in his eyes.

"Jason, I will not allow them to face Donalt or anyone in Esterious," Ashten said shortly. I felt his anger rise.

"We cannot make their choices for them anymore. All we're doing is pushing them away from us. I'd rather stand at their side."

Ashten crossed his arms over his chest and looked down. "I don't know what scares me more—what they're capable of now, or what they will be capable of," he said quietly.

My father nodded.

"Where's Livingston?" my father asked.

"He left right after Landen and Willow. I think he went to Esterious."

"Is he insane? It's well after curfew there," my father said with wide eyes.

"He always goes there at night. I think he wants to bring those girls home before Landen has a chance to."

"Did you figure out how he knew that Willow's nightmares had come back?" my father asked.

"He said he saw it in the stars," Ashten answered.

My father shook his head from side to side, clearly not believing what he'd just heard.

"I don't know, Jason. He's not the same person you knew twenty years ago. The only one he really talks to is August, and it kills me to see Marc and Chrispin reach out to him only to be ignored," Ashten said in an exhausted tone.

"They have you and Aubrey. You made them the men that they are. You should be proud of the family you raised."

"I am. I just feel like I'm going to lose them now," Ashten said, looking down. I felt his sorrow deepen.

"I'm going to try something," I thought.

I reached my hand carefully to Ashten's shoulder. He didn't seem to notice my touch. I thought of the emotions I felt from the celebration, the overwhelming love and peace. I remembered the smiling faces and the laughter.

His emotion began to change. As he surrendered to his peace, I felt the medallion on my neck tingle, then a warm rush flowed through my hand. It was a mesmerizing feeling. As it began to intensify, I looked back at Landen and felt the sensation flowing through him, too.

"You feel this?"

"It's amazing. Does it always feel like this?"

"No, never."

I reached my other hand out to my father's shoulder. Letting the same memories flow through my mind. The charm hummed, and the sensation pushed through my hand. A smile came across my father's face, and he looked at Ashten. "They're going to be fine," he said confidently.

Ashten nodded and stepped away from me, and I lost my touch. He glanced over his shoulder at my father as he walked away. I could still feel the peace that I gave him. My father sighed and turned to walk inside his house, causing me to lose my touch on him as well. The high that I felt began to fade.

"Let's follow him," I thought, stepping toward my dad.

We passed through the front door behind my father. My mother was sitting in the front room on a long white couch. She had a sketchpad in her lap and was outlining the house I was raised in.

"Is everything okay?" she asked my father as he took a seat next to her.

"It will be," he said.

"Do you want to check on Libby?" I thought knowing my parents had a way of taking care of each other. I also knew if anyone could bust me for playing with these insights of dream walking and emotions it would be the people who raised me.

Landen took my hand, and led me to the staircase that was in front of the door.

I could sense Libby sleeping peacefully. At the top of the stairs, we opened the first door to the left. It was a very large room with high ceilings. The far wall of her room had a large bay window, and baby dolls and books lined the windowsill. It was a room made for the princess that she was. When we both walked to her bed to sneak a peek at her sleeping face, her eyelids fluttered open softly, a smile spread across her baby face, and she whispered, "Willow, is it time to get up?"

Being seen by her sent a surge of shock through the two of us. Our eyes flew open, and we were back in the beach house. Catching our breath, we sat up with a start. When we realized what we'd done, laughter exploded from the two of us.

When the rush wore off we drifted back to sleep, and our souls walked along the beach through the sunrise.

The peaceful feeling of another person and the sound of the wood creaking on the front porch of the beach house brought us both back to our sleeping bodies. Landen jumped up and tiptoed toward the front of the house. He then looked back at me. "Rose," he thought. I nodded in agreement.

Landen pulled the front door open, expecting to see Rose, but instead he found a large basket sitting on the floor of the porch. He brought it into the house and set it on the coffee table in the front room. A note was attached to the top of the basket that said:

I thought you two would need a few things. Take your time. Love you.

In the basket under a blanket was a new sketchbook and food, along with a change of clothes.

"How did she know where we were?" I asked.

Landen smiled at himself as he read the note again. "This is her place. Sometimes trying to understand the intent around me can be difficult. Rose and August brought me here when I was fourteen and told me that whenever I needed peace, I could come here."

We settled on the floor, making a picnic out of the fruit and muffins that Rose had brought.

"I could feel Rose differently just now," he said, looking at me. "I felt her emotion of peace."

I looked at him with wide eyes.

"Did you feel her differently?" he asked.

"I don't know. I mean, I knew she didn't want to disturb us, but I just took that as my own insight."

"That's how my gift feels. You just know what they want to do," he said, smiling at me as his eyes drifted to my lips for an instant.

"How are they merging?"

"I don't know. I didn't feel any emotion until you touched my dad last night."

"Can we look for images today? For my friends?" I asked, rising to my knees.

"If we find them, we need to come back and get Brady and the others," Landen said, standing.

I stood and began to pull out the clothes in the basket. Rose had packed the traditional travel clothes for Landen—black pants and a black T- shirt. For me, a solid black dress with wide straps. I looked at Landen and shook my head. I wasn't sure how much I cared for always wearing black. He laughed at my expression. I then sighed and began to change into the dress. It felt soft against my skin, and it fell just above my knees. I pulled my necklace out and looked down at the sun and moon again, wondering for a moment about all it had witnessed.

The string was calm, even relaxing when we entered. When we passed by the passages to our world we saw several others were in the string. Smiling faces and pleasant greetings were given as we ushered by. Landen didn't even know most of them by name. Whatever reputation he had before I came with drama was bound to have intensified.

The string became empty as other passages came into view.

I stopped walking right as we reached cluster of doorways. I could feel something, a terror so powerful that it took my breath away. It was coming from Landen, too, but it didn't belong to him. Landen looked forward, then back. After a moment of indecision, we walked back to where we'd just been.

"You could feel that, couldn't you?" I asked.

"I want to get Brady and the others. I'm not sure if that's coming from in the string or around it."

"How far are we from Esterious?"

"Only a few passages," Landen said, guiding me back to Chara.

After reaching our dimension, we walked back to our house and Landen went to the kitchen to call Brady while I waited impatiently on the front porch for help to arrive.

Moments later, two Jeeps pulled up in front of the house. Brady was in one with Marc. Chrispin was driving the other one with Dane and Clarissa. I climbed into the back seat of Brady's Jeep with Landen, and then both Jeeps sped across the open field to the windmill.

Just before we entered, Landen told Brady that he would lead. He wanted Brady to bring up the tail and Marc and Chrispin to flank the sides, and he wanted Dane and me in the center with Clarissa. Brady argued with Landen, but he ultimately lost the argument. The others agreed that it didn't matter where we stood. Being in the string was risky, no matter where you were.

Our group weaved through the others making their way to the celebration. As we walked in silence, Landen would glance back at me, checking my expression. We'd already passed the point where we'd felt the fear earlier, but the tension was growing among the others. I had a feeling we were almost to Esterious. The hum of the current flowed more aggressively, then reached an annoying high pitch. Landen stopped, and everyone stared at him, waiting for him to lead.

"Do you feel that?" asked Landen.

"No," I answered, now concentrating on his emotion. I walked closer to him, and through him I felt the fear again. When I reached his side, I felt it firsthand. "I do now."

"Do you recognize them?" he asked.

"The vibe is all fear. I don't know. They never...," he stopped me with a tick of his head before I had to explain I'd never known any of my friend to have this kind of fear drowning them.

Landen motioned for the others to come closer as we crept forward.

"He's here," Landen thought.

He reached out to stop Brady from walking any further. In cat-like fashion, we took a few steps back then slid through a purple haze. Passing into this dimension, we were close to another waterfall. It wasn't nearly as powerful as Victoria Falls, but the beauty was still breathtaking.

Landen paced, then stopped and checked himself to make sure he was confident before he spoke. "Drake is just a few feet away from here. This is a trap. He has someone with him, more than one, several, actually, and they're expecting conflict."

Anger swelled in the energy around us.

"Charging in is not the answer," Clarissa said eyeing her brother, and cousins. "What if I passed through the string? He doesn't know me. I could get a better understanding of what's going on in there."

After an onslaught of arguments erupted, Brady convinced Clarissa that it didn't matter who went Drake would take us—Landen would come definitely come after one of our own.

One plan was put on the table, then another by all of them.

I ventured out, looking at the waterfall and the tall overhanging trees. There was thunder in the distance; the breeze announcing its approach moved my sweat drenched my dress against my body.

Horror slammed into energy around me.

I glanced to see if the others were in danger. I'd managed to walk almost fifty feet away from them. They were still discussing options. Their mood was tense, but no horror was with them.

I took a few more brave steps toward the worst emotion I'd ever felt. The trees covered the gray sky, giving the illusion of darkness. The branches swayed with the wind, causing a light whistle and drying the sweat on my face.

When I looked back at the others again, Landen was staring at me, no longer listening as everyone pleaded their case to him at once.

"What is it? Do you see something?"

"I feel something, this way."

Landen pushed through the others and made his way to me. As he got closer, I could feel it through him, too.

"I bet there's an image in there," I thought, looking into the dense darkness.

The others came to where we were. Landen glanced back and said. "She's hunting an emotion, kept yours in check."

We made our way into the forest. We could hear the sound of rain on the canopy of leaves that shielded the ground. When the darkness was all around us, three figures came into my view—Hannah, Olivia, and Jessica. They were all dressed in white gowns, and their hair was up and decorated with jewels. Lines of mascara streaked down each of their faces. They trembled as they gripped each other. Hannah was the only one not screaming. It was hard not to rush in to touch them, to help them.

"I found them," I said, swallowing hard and feeling the nauseating sensation of guilt overcome me.

The others stared into the darkness, trying to see what I saw.

"How's this going to work?" Chrispin asked. "I mean, if they're in the string, won't Willow pass by them?"

"I don't think they're in the string. I can feel the intent of several people," Landen said.

"Can you see around them?" Clarissa asked calmly.

"Not until I touch them," I said.

"Regardless, she has to touch them, at least one of them. Two of us can grab the others," Landen said. "We're not going to have time to lead them. They're going to have to be carried."

"To where?" Marc asked.

"We can't take them to their home, not in this condition. Jason is going to need to look them over," Landen said.

"So who wants to go with us? We need two of you." No indecision came from any of them. They all stepped forward, even Dane. Seeing their eagerness, Landen made the decision for them.

"Okay. Brady and Dane, flank me and Willow. When we're back here, Chrispin, you grab the girl Willow is holding. Clarissa, Marc, you lead us back to the string. Dane and Willow are the only ones that need to talk. If they struggle, we'll never make it back to Chara."

I circled around feeling the pull of energy draw me in, I stopped just behind my friend's. I wasn't brave enough to look them in the eye yet. Landen took his place behind me, and Brady and Dane held on to him. I felt a pull come over me. When I reached my trembling hands out, the charm on my chest hummed, and the sensation brought a calm over me.

Olivia was in the middle. I laid my head on her back, then wrapped my arms around Hannah and Jessica. When the green haze passed, taking the tingle with it, I moved my arms around Olivia's small frame. The room they were in was dark and damp, and the only light came from an open ceiling, with a gray sky as a canopy, adding a degree of eeriness. An altar was centered in the room, and un-lit candles lined the table. Black roses served as a centerpiece. Chants could be heard from all around the room.

Assuring myself that the other two were secure, I pushed back the haze of green, and a warm tingle rushed passed me.

The forest replaced the dark room again. Chrispin took possession of Olivia the moment we came into sight. In the blink of an eye, we'd passed through the forest and were in the string again. Jessica was screaming. I pleaded with her to calm down, but she screamed louder.

"Willow, is that you?" asked Olivia.

"Yeah, you're fine, I promise. Is Jessica hurt? Why is she screaming?"

Tears streamed down Olivia's face as she leaned into Crispin's chest, not caring that she didn't know him. "She can't hear you. They took it."

"What do you mean?"

"Jessica can't hear, Hannah can't talk, and I can't see."

I looked at Hannah. She was afraid. In here, she couldn't see or talk.

"Hannah you can still see. It's just dark in here. You'll see in just a few minutes."

I reached for Jessica. I had to help her, so I concentrated as hard as I could to take away her fear and give her peace. After a moment, her screaming stopped, and she laid her head on Brady's chest and fell asleep.

"You changed it," thought Landen.

"I don't know if I did or not. She may have just given up."

"I felt it," he assured me.

Others were beginning to come into view. We were close to Chara. People shot us concerned looks as we passed, and someone in the crowd called out to Landen as we got closer.

"You kids all right?" It was an older man with a long gray beard.

"We're fine. If you see Jason Haywood, will you tell him we need him at my house?"

The man nodded and pushed past the others, going into the passage. Our passage was just a few minutes past the large entrance. As we left the string, Hannah's eyes brightened as she realized she could see. Dane sat her down to let her walk. Jessica still lay sleeping in Brady's arms. Knowing that Olivia couldn't see, Chrispin carried her to the jeep. He was whispering to her. I couldn't hear him, but I knew that whatever he was saying was making her feel happy and at ease.

Chapter 13

W hen we reached our house, the girls were laid on the couches in the living room. When Chrispin tried to step away from Olivia, she pulled him back to her. He didn't falter and sat by her side.

"What was that? That place, what they were doing?" Brady asked.

"Evil," Landen said.

Clarissa had gotten a warm towel and was wiping away the streaks of Hannah's mascara, telling her she was fine.

"Do you know where you were?" I asked Olivia as I hovered over her.

Olivia stared blankly into the room, then said, "I remember being on the boat. I woke in a chamber. A massive bed was there, and chairs around a fireplace. The walls were made of stone. No windows. When the fire went out, darkness filled the room. Once a day, we'd find a large cart of food and water. After we ate, we'd fall into a deep sleep—so drugged. I convinced Hannah and Jessica not to eat."

Tears drizzled down her face, "We pretended to sleep, and after an hour or so the fireplace slid aside. The room was filled with people wearing long black robes, and shadows covered any signs of their faces. They lined the room. When I opened my eyes wider to focus, I lost my sight, Jessica screamed as the chants began, and Hannah started to pray out loud. That is when she lost her voice." She pressed her lips together and pulled her shoulders back. "We were carried into another room..."

She tried to speak a few times before she got the story to come out. "They...they stripped our clothes and washed our bodies. Dressed us. Then we walked. It was cold, and the ground was uneven, uphill. The air was damp. We stopped. The chants began again then you came like they said you would."

Everyone was hanging on Olivia's every word, and now the fear she felt was filling the room.

"Who said she would come?" Chrispin asked softly, being gentler than anyone else was capable of being.

"When they were dressing us, I focused on the people talking. I heard Drake talking to a man with a husky voice. Drake was angry with him, telling him 'Now you've done it. Willow is sure to feel this, and the moon is not full.' The husky voice just laughed, saying there were always more people to be taken if need be. I prayed you'd come, Willow. I didn't know what you could do to help, but it was easy to see that Drake was afraid of what you could do."

Hannah had been nodding along as Olivia spoke, she motioned to me; she wanted something to write on. Dane left the room swiftly and returned with one of my sketchbooks. I tore out a clean sheet and handed it to her.

Hannah began trying to sketch. She drew a necklace it had a star, and she shadowed it to make it look like it was glowing. She then drew arrows pointing to it. Then wrote: old man had it.

"Did that star do something?" Brady asked.

Hannah nodded and drew what looked like a small tornado on the back of the page.

"Okay, Okay. Just calm down. We'll figure it out," I promised her, halfway trying to convince myself.

I sensed my father and Ashten's panic. I glanced to the window and saw them pulling up in front of my house.

Brady glanced to Landen. "Are you ready for this?" he asked. Landen shrugged.

We met them on the front porch. My father's eyes danced over Landen and me.

"What happened?" Ashten shouted, trying to look behind us. My father quickly looked us both over again. "They're fine," he said to Ashten.

I spoke up first, telling them what had happened—how the girls were hurt.

Dad walked in the house. Ashten went to speak, but Landen raised his hand, stopping him. Right then everyone filed outside giving my dad room to work. Almost fifteen minutes passed before Landen and I went back in, hoping he'd figured out what was wrong.

My father was still looking over Jessica as she lay sleeping. Hannah's confusion was apparent. She couldn't understand why Dane, my father, and I were all there.

My father smiled warmly back at her. "Listen, we're going to make you all better, okay. You just need to calm down."

He then led us into the kitchen and paced before he spoke. "There's nothing wrong with them—they just think that they can't see, hear, or speak."

"What do you mean?" I asked quietly.

"I can see that they've been given narcotics or something close to that, but beyond that they're fine."

Brady had stepped in the kitchen as Dad was talking.

"I think they're under some kind of spell," Brady said. "You heard the chants, didn't you, Landen?"

My father promptly stood at attention. I seemed to have left that small detail out earlier.

"Chants?" he repeated, making sure he wasn't mistaken.

"They...umm...were in a room with an altar and chants, but they were sick before that," Brady said, looking guiltily in our direction.

Dad slid to the floor against the cabinets, bowing his head to his knees. We all rushed to his side. Landen and I could feel how distraught he was, almost to the point of grief. He looked up slowly, reaching for my face and leaning his head toward mine.

"Dad, it's okay. What's wrong?" I asked.

He stared forward for a moment before he spoke. "If I'd brought you home, the two of you would have had enough time to prepare yourself. We could have all helped, but now you're defenseless."

Landen and I glanced at one another. We knew that we weren't completely defenseless; our gifts were merging. Not to mention we could leave our bodies as they slept.

"We're going to be fine, all of us," Landen said.

My mother tapped lightly on the back door, causing us all to rise. She was genuinely concerned when she saw my father and his composure, but she listened as he gave us instructions. "You need to see if they want to go home now, or if they want to wait until they're better. If they want to stay, you need to find a way to tell their parents that they're okay."

Landen, Brady, and I left the room, giving my father time to explain everything in his own way to my mother. When Brady passed through the entry hall and went back outside, Landen stopped me before we walked into the living room.

"Listen, if we take them back, I want to give them the herb to help them forget. I don't want them to have to remember that place," Landen thought.

"If they forget the chants would it break the spell?"

"I don't know," Landen thought softly.

I nodded and walked into the living room. They all looked up as I walked into the room, staring at me for some kind of explanation.

"Listen, I don't know how to explain any of this to you. I can't tell you when you'll be better. If you want to go home to your parents, we'll take you there. If you want to stay here a while longer, you can."

Hannah turned the page in the sketchbook she was holding and wrote "HOME PLEASE."

Jessica glanced at her, then back at me for some kind of understanding. Landen walked over, gently took the pad from Hannah, and wrote what I said for Jessica to read.

Jessica wrote the words "Which way will make us better faster?"

I swayed my head, "We don't know. Dad says that there's nothing physically wrong that he can see. It's unexplainable."

Olivia leaned forward, reaching for my arm. "Do they want to go home?" she asked, I whispered yes, then she turned to where she knew they were sitting and said, "I'm going to stay here...it feels right here."

I felt like I had won a battle. I wanted to stuff Olivia in my suitcase days ago, but I'd never take her from a comfort she knew. I guess it felt to know as bad luck as I may be, I'd helped someone by just being me.

"Are you sure you want to stay here?" I asked softly.

Olivia grinned. "You get me. I get your crazy. The vibe is right here," she said glancing blinding around.

Landen then left the room to tell the others what the girls had decided, and I slid down in one of the big chairs in the room trying to plot my next move. I had my friends back, but the draw—need to confront Drake had me chains that I could not break free from.

Olivia asked, "Willow, where are we? Who are these people who are trying to help us?"

"My family."

Jessica tried to speak, but not being able to hear her voice, she was rather loud. "Drake knows that guy with you. He asked if we'd met him yet."

"Landen? He knows Landen?" My rush of fear caused Landen to look in the window at me.

I thought back to when Drake and Landen were face to face. I couldn't figure out if they acted like they knew each other or not.

Seeing my surprise, Jessica went on. "He just described him. He thought you two were together."

Landen came in, hearing the last part of what Jessica said.

"Did he say anything else about us?" I asked.

"He asked a lot about you, Willow. He wanted to know what you painted, why you have that tattoo, if you ever talked about your dreams. What made you scared or happy," Olivia said.

Landen and I were locked in a stare both questioning what Drake had to do with us.

Aubrey and Felicity arrived. My mom and Felicity gave the girls food and changed them out of the dresses they were in. Brady and Marc took the dresses and jewels the girls were wearing and burned them in one of the side fields. Chrispin hovered near Olivia every chance he could; he seemed to have a goal to make her laugh and succeeded with only a few whispered words.

"Are you getting the same vibe I am," I asked Landen when he leaned against the wall with me and could see what was in my line of sight.

Landen smirked. "Yeah...I was going to say something to you."

I glanced up.

"Chrispin saw his beacon right before I made him go into the one with the waterfall. When we came back out, he looked back and it was gone."

"He doesn't think that..."

Landen shrugged a shoulder. "I don't think he's had a chance to think anything. I just knew you're still having a hard time with Dane and Carissa. This might too weird, even for us."

"Not a hard time," I said grimacing. "I'm just not that lucky. When I do find luck, there's always a consequence."

His furrowed brow questioned me.

"If I could've only taken two friend's it would've been them. We run with a circle, but...I don't know, we were just different. Waiting or something." I tilted my head as I promised myself the worse was behind us. "I just don't want them hurt. Anyone hurt."

Our conversation was cut short as Rose arrived at the house. She motioned for us to come to her. We followed her through the kitchen, off the porch, and into the backfield, far away from earshot of the house full of people. Coming to a stop, she turned and crossed her arms, looking at us over her small square glasses.

"Libby mentioned that she saw the two of you in her room last night," Rose said. She had a proud smile on her face as she measured our response. We looked at each other with guilty smiles on our faces until the realization that our secret was no more suddenly set in.

"The others won't learn what you can do from me," she reassured us. "It's your gift. All I want to do is help you with it."

"Do you know how she could see us?" I asked.

"Libby is connected to the both of you. The only vision she has directly involves the two of you, or your surroundings. It makes sense that she can see you when others can't."

I stared at Landen. Both of us had deep concern coming from us. We felt protective over her. We didn't want her to see anything as dark as we'd seen that day.

"When your father told me of the way you dream, I was sure that you did meet soul-to-soul. Your bodies are only vessels," Rose said proudly. "That's why I agreed with the decision to keep Willow in Infante. I knew you two were never really apart." Her eyes looked over Landen and me carefully. "Have you learned to use each other's insight as one yet?"

"If you mean that I can feel emotions and she can see intent, then yes."

Rose gave off an emotion of surprise, meaning that wasn't what she meant.

"You now have both," she said, trying to hold down her excitement.

"We're just now learning our new ones. It can easily be overlooked because our own is so familiar to us."

"You both should try to intensify your primary gift."

"How do you mean?" Landen asked.

"Try seeing intent further away or changing emotions with a touch to those that are here. Don't push it, or you could hinder your progress. Let it come to you."

"Can you change emotions?" I asked.

Landen looked fleetingly at me, astonished, then back to Rose. "No wonder you always understood me," Landen muttered under his breath.

Rose grinned. "We all have the power to change the emotions of the ones around us. A kind word could make someone's day, just as a harsh one will bring pain. The secret is to know your own energy and use it to fill the room around you. By being connected the way the two of you are, I can only imagine the energy you could find as one."

It was just after noon in our dimension, and it had already been a long day. I explained to Olivia that she needed to tell her aunt and uncle that she was safe. She agreed, and we handed her a blank page. She told them that she'd met someone and was going to see the world before she went to school, explaining that the line was busy each time she'd tried to call. We enclosed a snap shot of Chrispin and Olivia using the sun as a backdrop, covering her eyes with sunglasses.

My father had given Jessica and Hannah the herb that would take their short-term memory away, and it would soon take effect. The girls hugged Olivia goodbye.

Chrispin stayed behind with Olivia. Ashten and my father joined us as we walked back to the string. Landen led us. We were going to use the new paths he'd discovered, avoiding Esterious all together. Jessica and Hannah held their eyes down as we led them. As we walked, their eyes grew heavy, and eventually Marc and Brady carried them as they drifted off to sleep.

Landen found a passage that was on the roof of the only hospital in Franklin. The street lights started to blink yellow, meaning it was past midnight. My father had worked in the hospital for close to twenty years, and he knew everything there was to know about it. He went in to put the girls names in the computer and assigned them a room. When he returned, he had two beds with him. Brady and Marc laid the girls down, and Ashten went with my father to take them to their rooms.

Taking advantage of the time that they were gone, I walked to the edge of the roof and gazed toward the town. The streets were empty, but my memory took me back to so many happy days that I'd spent growing up within a four-block radius. Landen came to my side, smiling as if they were his memories as well.

The walk home was quiet, the mood complacent. No one wanted to comment on what had happened to the girls, or where we'd found them. Talking seemed to confuse the issue more. We made two stops on the way back, one in the Florida Keys to mail Olivia's letter, and one in New York to mail letters my mother had prepared for her friends that she'd left behind. Sharon's letter was on top.

Landen and I had agreed to return to Franklin that night while our bodies slept. It would be daylight soon, and the girls would be awake, and we could see if forgetting had healed their hearing and voice. Once home, everyone departed to dress for the celebration.

My father and Ashten lingered behind the others. Worried glances came from Aubrey as she helped Olivia into the car.

Ashten chose not to resume his lecture, a promise I felt him make Aubrey.

"Now that Willow's friends are safe, will you stay here?" Ashten asked.

Landen glanced down at me, then to his father. "I won't make you a promise I can't keep," he said respectfully.

"Landen, this is the only dimension that will protect the both of you," Ashten said, stepping forward and trying to hide his frustration.

"What do you mean?" I asked, looking from Ashten to Landen.

"Chara can only be found by those who were born here," Ashten said, looking at me, hoping I'd be able to convince Landen to stay.

"Then why didn't you just bring me here when you found me? Drake never would have found me."

"We didn't know that until Drake started looking for you. He passed by the passages to Chara blindly," Ashten said defensively.

I believed him. Landen's gift of truth was making itself known inside me. Yet, I also knew that wasn't the entire story.

Ashten sighed and walked down the front steps. "Just promise me you won't ever go to Esterious alone," he said, looking back at Landen. "We'll get the star one way or another."

Landen stared back at him.

My father hugged me. "I'll see you in a little bit," he said as he let me go.

Landen and I walked inside our house to get ready for the celebration in town. "Why do you think they're so worried about that star?" I asked, "Do you really think it's that important?"

"I don't know. I do know I don't want Drake to have anything that belongs to you," Landen said.

"Do you think if we got the star we'd be able to heal my friends?" I asked.

"I do," he said quietly.

"Then that's what we'll do," I said confident as ever it was the right choice.

Chapter 14

Dinner was at sunset. We drove Landen's black Jeep into town; this was the first time I'd left the area around our home. My eyes widened as I gazed at the lush fields, homes sprinkling the horizon. None of them looked the same, a unique personality accompanying each of them. The outline of the town was coming into view on the horizon; from where we were, it looked broader than Franklin.

Landen parked on one of the side streets. The roads were made of stones set perfectly together. The buildings were crafted uniquely, with light colors and wood framework. Each stoop had beautiful flowers sitting on it. The town was full of people, each of them beautifully original; their skin was as dark as night, yet their eyes were a crystal blue. Others would be as light as snow and every shade in between; the one common factor was the peace you could feel emanating from them.

Along the streets, banners were stretched across with our names written in a beautiful script. My parents, Dane and Clarissa, had banners as well. Lights reached out from building to building, giving the street a picturesque canopy. Music could be heard throughout the town. Children ran through the streets dressed in beautiful bright colors. Their laughter energized us as we walked by.

The atmosphere was electric. It reminded me of how a crowded concert would be at home—energized, joyful, and carefree. Some were braver than others, stopping and shaking hands with Landen and me, others would only bow their heads, with a sweet smile. Landen introduced me to several couples he'd carried home. I met well over thirty of them in a one-block radius; the pride of having known him was overwhelming around them.

As we neared the center of town, large tables with white cloths lined the streets, and beautiful candles surrounded by roses set the centerpieces. The center of town was transformed into a dance floor, and the band played a beautiful melody.

A path was made for us as we crossed the dance floor, and as Landen swirled me into the center of everyone, applause erupted. He caught me in my spin and pulled me to him, kissing me softly for the world to see. The crowd grew louder, their energy rushing through us. We lost ourselves inside each other's eyes, dancing to song after song.

The impatience of our favorite little girl, Libby, caught our attention. We went to the other side where we could see our family sitting along a large U-shaped table; others that I hadn't met sat amongst them.

We took our place near the center, next to my parents, Dane and Clarissa. Landen, with Libby in his lap, sat next to my father. Rose was to my right, Karsten to her side. I watched as they stood and greeted another older couple. A small crowd lingered around them, causing me to lose my stare. Desperate to regain it, I adjusted my seat. The man's skin was dark, his hair was short and white, and his eyes were as pale as clear water. The woman was small with long black curly hair, her eyes were as black as coal, and I could feel their admiration. Feeling my stare, the man turned to me and smiled as he bowed his head.

"Landen, who is that next to Karsten?"

Landen looked up from his quiet conversation with my father to follow my gaze. It was clear he hadn't noticed them before. I could feel respect, joy, and love coming from Landen. He stood, putting Libby in my father's lap, and pulled me up with him.

"That is my grandfather, August, and my grandmother, Nyla. They're home."

I followed Landen as he stepped closer. His grandfather rose as he saw us approach his grandmother followed. Landen all but threw himself into his grandfather's arms; it was easy to see that he was closer to his grandfather than he was to Ashten.

"Willow, this is August and Nyla, my grandparents," Landen said, formally introducing me to them. I was quickly pulled into their joyful embrace, and from the dance floor I could hear applause.

"I'm proud of you," August said to Landen as he looked at me again. "We've been trying to get home for days. The storms were more difficult where we were...they haven't been giving you a hard time, now have they?"

"They're silent," Landen said in a frustrated tone as he pulled me closer, smiling down at me.

"I imagine that they are," August said, smiling at Landen. "I spoke with your father. You've certainly humbled him."

"Not intentionally," responded Landen.

"I left something for you at your house. You'd already left when we stopped by," August said.

Landen tilted his head curiously. August leaned in closer and whispered something to Landen, ending the conversation.

Couples filled the dance floor as dinner ended, and one had my full attention: Olivia and Chrispin; they seemed to glide across the floor. The smile across Olivia's face overshadowed her recent blindness, and no one dared to try and divide them. Landen and I were separated unintentionally. His grandfather, Brady, and others who names I had forgotten surrounded him. I was surrounded as well. The space between us was odd, yet bearable, being filled by people who I'd seen the least since being there.

I was nestled next to Rose as the conversations blossomed around us. I felt safe next to her, and understood. The uncomfortable separation brought Landen back to me, his followers were close behind, and then it was simple just to relax and feel the harmony.

Across the street, I watched as Libby and an older woman were talking. Libby then followed her into the store that they were standing in front of, almost certainly convincing the woman to give her a special treat. My eyes were growing heavy. Our day had been long and arduous. I laid my head on Landen's shoulder as he listened to one of August's stories of recent travels.

Kissing the top of my head, he thought, "You're not leaving me, are you?"

Before I could protest his thoughts, I felt Libby crawl across my lap and onto Landen's.

"Willow, I have something for you," she whispered.

"You do?" I said, genuinely surprised.

Libby reached into the pocket on her dress and brought out a small brown bag, trying to hide it from my parents' view, not caring that she had Landen and Rose's full attention.

"Tonight when you go see Hannah and Jessica, you'll need this," Libby said.

"What will I need it for?" The bag felt as if it were full of sand.

"When you see the mean monkey, throw this in his eyes, and he'll go away and not hurt you."

Landen reached for the bag and causally slid it into his pocket before anyone else noticed the exchange.

"What is it, sweetie?" asked Rose.

"Garlic salt," Libby said, covering her lips to let Rose know it was a secret.

The feeling of certainty coming from Libby was frightening. A mean monkey—what did she mean? A little girl with ivory skin and liquid blue eyes came over, beckoning Libby to play with her. Libby hugged me tightly and said, "Don't be scared. I've protected you."

As she ran across the dance floor, my heart sank and my breath left me. We had no power to protect her from what she saw; defenseless, she would witness the battle before it came to be.

The dread was coming from Landen as well, but we were both thankful that whatever we faced tonight would be mild. Libby had no fear; her certainty still lingered around us.

The celebration went on. Not wanting to appear ungrateful for the companionship, we stayed, half-heartedly listening to the many tales around us. Rose's distraction was apparent, as her laugh would be delayed when a story called for it. As the moon shifted, everyone's eyes seem to grow weary, and one-by-one the town began to empty of people. Hoping we'd served our purpose, Landen excused us.

Libby had fallen asleep in my mother's lap, and I hugged and kissed them both good night. Landen hugged August and Nyla. I looked for Rose, but I couldn't find her. My father made his way to us, and he kissed my forehead, telling me goodbye.

When we reached Landen's Jeep, we saw Rose leaning against the side of it, waiting patiently for us to reach her. She hesitated as a group of people passed by before she spoke.

"I know the last thing you want is someone else telling you what to do. That's not my intent, but I implore you to please tell me when you leave tonight," Rose said.

We weren't concerned with the 'monkeys' we were supposed to see that night, simply because Libby had no fear when she'd told us, assuring us we had no reason to be afraid. Rose's concern, though, was shaking the solid ground on which we stood. Our pause gave her reason to explain further. "If you're gone too long, or if you're afraid, I want to try and wake you. That monkey could be anywhere between here and those girls, and waking you might keep you safe."

Hearing her conclusion, we nodded slowly with eyes wide open, realizing the danger that she feared for the first time.

Rose's calm returned to her.

Landen was looking up the street, watching Ashten and his mother leave, waving bye to them.

"Willow, I think we should tell your father, his insight would make what Rose wants to do more efficient."

The sudden relief that came over me told him that I agreed. Looking now at Rose, Landen laid out a plan for her. "We're going to tell Jason so he can help you watch us. After we fall asleep, we'll come to the two of you before we leave."

The conversation was halted as Karsten and my parents approached. Rose coaxed my mother into letting her and Karsten take her and Libby home; sensing that I needed my father, she went hastily.

Landen opened the passenger door of the Jeep for my father to get in. Looking confused, he complied. I then climbed in the back, and we drove off to a more private place. Landen and my father talked casually about the celebration, August, and others that had come from so far to see all of us.

The lights of the town faded; now only the stars and moon, which was growing fuller each night, showed the way. We stopped at the edge of the driveway that led to my father's house, and Landen and I got out.

Slowly, my father made his way out, confusion coursing from him. I nodded in Landen's direction, encouraging him to start. He cleared his throat and said, "Jason, we need you to do us a favor." My father nodded, agreeing before he even knew what we wanted him to do. "Willow and I can control where we go when we sleep, and tonight we're going to see if the herb healed Hannah and Jessica."

"You can control it?"

"We taught ourselves last night," Landen said proudly.

"We came to see you," I added.

My father looked quickly at me. "Did you change my emotion?"

I nodded. I felt my father's amazement, mixed with pride.

"Jason, Libby told us we'd see mean monkeys tonight. She gave us garlic salt and told us to throw it in their eyes. Rose wants to wake us if we're scared. You'd be able to see if we were hurt," Landen said.

"How would my mother know if you were afraid?" my father asked, shaking his head, trying to understand what we were saying.

I glanced at Landen, and he looked back at me; we'd both forgotten that Rose had kept her insight a secret.

"She has the gift of emotion, too," I said, putting my hand on my father's shoulder. "She said her father told her that she should keep it to herself if she truly wanted to help people."

My father nodded. I felt his understanding.

"If you know there's going to be danger, why are you going?"

"It's just a precaution. Libby's not afraid of what we're going to see. Tonight will serve as a test. If we have a strong enough control over this, maybe we'll be able to get the star back without putting anyone in danger," Landen explained.

"I don't think it's a good idea for you to go into Esterious without your bodies. I'm more than sure that they'd be able to hurt you."

"How do you know that?" I asked, looking for more answers.

"The Priests were able to put Drake in that state. Obviously, they'd know how to hinder you," my father explained. He looked glanced between Landen and me. "How are you going to contact me? Should I stay at your house?"

"We'll stop here before we leave, try and get some rest," Landen answered.

"I'm going to get Rose to stay with us, so you only have to stop at one place. I'd think you'd be stronger just as you left...don't use all your energy finding us."

We agreed with my father. Landen drove him to his front door, then took us home.

Walking in our home, we almost looked over the small package lying just inside on the floor. August had told Landen that he'd left something for us. I reached down for the box. I was excited to see what was in it.

"Do you know what it is? What did August whisper to you?" I asked, handing it to Landen.

"He said it would keep us both safe."

When Landen opened the small brown box, something fell and hit the hardwood floor. It was two silver rings, which began circling in place. When they stopped, I reached down and grabbed them.

They were quite heavy for being so small. Within the band of the rings an eye was inscribed. Two long lashes stretched out from the bottom, and seven gold lines made a border along the base of the eye. Landen slid the smaller ring on my left hand, and I slid the larger one on his. As if they'd found their rightful place, the rings tingled our fingers upon first touch, and the silver seemed to brighten.

I slid the ring off again to look at the inscription; as I did, the silver dulled and the tingle left my hand in protest.

"Do you know what this means?" I asked, counting the seven gold lines. I'd seen this before—the night I picked out my tattoo. It was the eye of RA, and it meant "protection." My ankh meant "eternal life." I reasoned that if I had eternal life, I wouldn't need protection—that's why I chose the ankh.

"August told me a lot of stories. If I remember correctly, I think it's a watchful eye. I don't remember what culture or dimension he was referring to when he described it, though."

"Well, if it's the same as my tattoo, it came from Infante. It's Egyptian," I said, looking at my wrist and the uninvited star inside my loop.

"Egyptians, as you call them, are in a lot of dimensions and are a very advanced people," Landen said, sliding the ring on my finger again. The tingle came as the shine returned. "They're the only other people that we've discovered exploring the strings. They've settled across many dimensions."

"Seriously?" I asked, thinking he was just teasing me.

Smiling, he answered, "The string is energy. In theory, everyone should be able to see it. People have the power to change their perspective. They just get caught up in an endless cycle of foolish things that don't matter."

I looked down at my olive skin, matching my tone to Landen's and wondering if that culture was a part of me.

"Do you know what my tattoo means?" I asked Landen.

He smiled. "'Eternal life.' I remember when you got it. I thought you were trying to tell me something," he said, tracing the cross while avoiding the star in the loop.

"I think I was trying to tell myself something that I'd find you in this life or the next," I said, looking up at him and smiling shyly.

Landen kissed my lips softly causing my soul to seize with anticipation. "I always knew I'd find you," he swore.

I looked down at the rings again. It felt like I had seen them before, too, like they'd always been ours. "Did August tell you where he got these?"

"He really didn't have a chance. All he said was 'time is simply an illusion, and the gifted live on,'" Landen said, smiling. "August isn't like the others. He isn't quick to offer advice. He likes to watch your mind work." He laughed a little, tucking a piece of my hair behind my ear. "He said he needed to show us something in the morning."

"Is he going to tell us what the others are hiding?"

"I believe he will."

We changed out of our party clothes and into the all-black attire. We then laid in our bed in silence. Hoping we'd given Rose and my father time to rest, we drifted to sleep, almost simultaneously. Standing over our bodies, the addictive rush of excitement came over us again. Landen checked his pocket to make sure the garlic salt was with us then looked at me.

"Let's try this: think of your father's porch." He reached his arm around my waist and pressed his forehead to mine, concentrating on my father's porch.

"We did it," he thought. I opened my eyes to see that Landen was right. We were on the front steps. A rush of excitement came through us, more exhilarating than before. I gave him an alluring smile; this power was becoming less elusive.

I led the way through the door. All the lights were off, and I could sense peaceful sleep coming from five people. Karsten must have stayed there, too. Walking up the stairs, we stopped in the guest room. Rose was asleep in a chair with an open book resting on her lap. I was afraid to wake her and startle her. We went down the hall to my parents' room. When we opened the door, my father raised his head and whispered into the darkness. "Willow."

I walked over to him and pulled back his blanket, letting him know it was us, and a rush of excitement came over him as he watched the blanket move without seeing anyone. Landen found a note pad on my mother's side of the bed and wrote "wake Rose, we are on our way now."

Already dressed, my father slid on his shoes and walked to Rose's room.

"Do you want to see if we can make it to the hospital the same way?" I asked. Landen smiled, and we held each other again and focused on the roof that we'd been on earlier that day. A moment later, raindrops could be heard. When we opened our eyes, we were on the roof. It was an awful looking day; the sky was so dark, it was hard to tell that it was daylight. There was thunder in the distance with increasing wind.

Knowing the way, I took Landen's hand, and we walked in the door and down the steps. The hospital was quiet; not much was happening there, new births being the most exciting thing.

The maternity ward was on the fourth floor, and we passed that doorway on our way to the third floor.

We opened the door slowly, not knowing who might be standing close to it. At the end of the hallway, we could see two women standing outside one of the doors. As we approached them, I could see it was Chase's mom, and Gina, Dane's mom. We listened as they talked.

"It just doesn't make any sense, how did they get here so fast?" Gina said.

"At least they're safe. The search for Monica was called off yesterday...I don't think this town could bear losing another child," Chase's mom said in a sorrowful tone.

I looked at Landen. He felt my grief and put his arm around me.

"I wish someone could get a hold of Jason, or Grace, for that matter. Jason would know what was wrong. That man is the best doctor on this planet."

I felt a rush of pride all my own as they spoke of my parents.

"How is Dane anyway? I can't believe he ran off with Willow like that. I bet you're happy, aren't you?"

Landen was shaking his head and smiling. He wasn't angry or jealous. It was just odd how Dane and Clarissa had met.

"He's not with Willow. He's—he's seeing one of her friends, Clarissa," answered Gina, confused by her own words.

"Oh, I see. Do you know if Willow's okay? Chase said that Willow and Dane were really hung up on each other. That kid, Drake, made a move on Willow, and Dane showed up, saw it, and was furious. Chase said they had to stop Dane from tearing that guy apart."

"Remind me to tell Dane he's awesome when we get back," Landen thought.

"Willow is happy, too. Grace said she's in love with a really great guy, and Grace and Jason both seem to love him. They went to school with his parents, I think," Gina said, trying to curve the conversation.

"So tell me about Clarissa, what's she like?"

"Dane called a day or so ago. He's going to go to Paris, too. Right now, they're in New York. He said he'd come home before he went overseas."

"So Dane could ask Jason to come home, too?"

Before Gina could answer, the door they were standing in front of opened, and Olivia's aunt, came out, holding a pad of paper. Still studying the words on it, she looked tired and aged by the event.

"How's Hannah," Gina asked.

"She's asleep now. I don't know. She doesn't remember anything about getting on a boat or going to the Keys," Olivia's aunt said, leaning against the wall and staring at the notes.

"Do they know what happened to her voice or Jessica's hearing?"

"The doctor said the memory loss is due to trauma, but he thinks the girls will recover if they rest."

"What about Olivia? Does Hannah remember where she is?" asked Gina.

"Hannah can't even tell me if she was ever with them to begin with."

Feeling their agonizing grief and confusion, I shifted my way in front of Olivia's aunt. Landen took a protective step forward, bracing himself for anything that could happen.

As I reached for her shoulders, my trembling hands anticipated the rush. Staring into her eyes, I concentrated on peace. I remembered how happy Olivia looked dancing with Chrispin, hearing her laughter over the music. Her eyes closed slowly then opened again, looking past the room. Gina and Chase's mom started to yell her name, fearing she was passing out. My fingertips tingled. Just as I felt her emotion change to joy, a flash of light came across my face, causing me to lose my touch. The rush found Landen, and the sensation boomeranged between us, intensifying the high and energizing our spirit.

Olivia's aunt let out a gasp of air as Chase's mom and Gina both reached for her, blocking a potential fall. At first, I thought I'd done something wrong or hurt her somehow, but she just gasped again then smiled.

"She's fine. Olivia's happy, she's found her place."

"What?" Gina asked, looking behind her, halfway expecting Olivia to be standing there.

"I could see her, dancing and laughing. She's in love. It's in her eyes, a light I haven't seen ... since," Olivia's aunts words faded as tears surfaced in the corner of her eyes. She took a deep breath and stood up straight. Smiling, she still carried the joy I'd given her. "I think I need some coffee. Will you guys go with me?"

Gina and Chase's mom walked behind her, whispering and looking back through where we stood.

"What was that? Did it hurt you?" Landen reached down, examining my fingertips.

"No, it was amazing—exhilarating."

"Were you thinking of them dancing? Is that what she saw?"

"Yeah, I don't know how she saw them. I always think of something when I help. Did you see that light?"

Landen nodded.

"Where did it come from?"

"Her, well, the both of you. A light came from your fingers, then another burst from her chest."

The elevator door dinged, then opened. A nurse got off as Olivia's aunt and the others got on. We watched as the nurse checked a clipboard before going into the room across the hall. As we waited, we were hit hard with terror. Looking at each other, then to the room, we were sure where it was coming from.

Landen grabbed my hand before going into Hannah's room. It was dark. Only a little light came from the gray windows where rain sheeted across the pane. I could see Jessica's mother sleeping on a couch under the window. All of a sudden, the terror we were feeling seemed to double. Landen saw them first – the 'monkeys.'

Jessica and Hannah were in beds side-by-side, asleep, and on their chests sat small demonic animals that resembled monkeys. They had short red hair, and spikes made of reddish bone lined their spines. Horns crowned their head and black collars circled their small necks. Their feet were planted firmly on the girls' chests as they stared centimeters from their sleeping faces.

We stared, frozen with horror.

"We have to hide our fear," I thought, remembering that Rose would wake us before we'd be able to help if she felt it in our bodies.

We both pushed it aside and found anger instead. As we stared, not believing our eyes, we listened to the growling of the monkeys as they breathed. Landen reached in his pocket for the bag of garlic salt. He then opened it, grabbed a handful of it, and gave me a handful, too. We never took our eyes off the demons. The girls moaned as if they were in pain, and the chuckle of a growl filled the room.

The terror coming from the girls was growing stronger. Not knowing if the demons could see us, we stepped cautiously in their direction. All at once, the growling halted, and the one on Jessica looked slowly over its shoulder, its red eyes glowing in the dark room. The other one sensed us and turned as well. It was clear that they could see us. As they stepped off the two girls' chests, their terror faded as they turned restlessly. The demons sauntered toward us as the growls resumed and grew louder. Landen and I threw the handfuls of salt at them. They let out large growls as the salt hit their faces then leaping at us they suddenly vanished. Stunned, we looked slowly at each other, allowing the fear to come out.

A resilient pull came over us, and as we gasped for breath, we suddenly found ourselves back in our bed. My father was standing over me, and Rose was standing over Landen. They were shaking our shoulders. We jolted up, making sure we were both back. Landen dove across the bed and pulled me into his arms, burying his face in my neck. His fear was in rhythm with his heartbeat. He knew just like I did that those things had visited me often. The weight on my chest—that was them.

"Never again, Willow. He will never do that to you again. I swear I'll kill him—never again," Landen said through his teeth as he rocked me back and forth.

The fear in the room was overpowering. Rose and my father stood like statues, not sure what had happened.

"Olivia...Landen...Olivia," I said, pushing him back and holding his face so he would have to look at me through his rage.

Olivia was sleeping now. The demons could be tormenting her where she lay.

"Jason, where is Olivia?" shouted Landen, still staring at me.

"She's...uh...she's with Felicity. What's—"

My father was cut short as we rushed by him down the stairs, out the door, and into the Jeep. Landen didn't even use the road. He tore off across the field in the darkness. Just over the second hill, a house could be seen in the moonlight. Like the others, it was wrapped in porches. We stopped inches short of the front porch.

Landen charged open the door not caring how loud it banged back. He raced up the stairs two at a time. I ran to keep pace with him. At the top of the stairs, he took a quick left, opening the first door. The light flicked on, and Olivia lay, sleeping peacefully. I walked breathlessly to her side to wake her, and I could hear Brady charging down the hall with Felicity close behind.

"Olivia! Olivia, I need you to wake up!" I said, trying to catch my breath.

Landen stopped Brady at the door, and Felicity peered in under his arm as they stared, wide-eyed.

Startled awake, Olivia sat up defensively.

"Have you had a nightmare?" I said through the tears that were catching up with me, the demons' eyes staring through my memory.

"What? Willow, are you okay? What happened?"

"Have you had a nightmare!" I yelled.

"No, not since I was little—why?" she asked, reaching for me.

I pushed away before she could touch me, charging my way out of the room and back down the stairs. I needed air. I was gasping, not wanting to cry, not wanting to succumb to the terror that had chased me through childhood.

Landen was right behind me. He grabbed my arm and swung me into his arms as I reached the porch. I buried my face in his chest. Letting it all go, I cried breathlessly. The images that I'd helped, the pain I endured each time, the fear I'd overcome—it all flashed through my eyes.

I felt Rose and my father approach as the others looked out at us. Landen waved them all away and let me cry. Holding me tighter as the minutes passed the tears ran dry. Light was starting to peak over the hill. When the tears finally dried on my face we went in the house.

They were all in the living room; Felicity and Olivia had fallen asleep toe–to-toe on the couch, and Brady, Rose, and my father were sitting, tensely waiting for us.

Brady raised his hands to question what was going on; looking at my father and Rose, it was clear they hadn't told Brady about watching our bodies. Landen slid in one of the oversized chairs and nestled me against him. I laid on his chest, not wanting to make eye contact with anyone.

"We went to check on Hannah and Jessica. We..." Landen stopped, looking at my father, then down at me. "We saw these things, demonic monkey-looking things, sitting on their chests. They were being tortured with nightmares."

"Sitting?" my father repeated.

Landen nodded. "Like a heavy weight," he bit out. Anger coursed through him as he squeezed me tighter.

Brady stood, rubbing his arms nervously. As he began pacing the floor, fear and confusion overcame him. "Landen, are you serious? Demons—seriously!" he said in a harsh whisper, looking back to make sure Felicity was still sleeping.

Landen's angry blank stare told Brady we were very serious.

"What did you do? I mean, how do you come back from something like that?" asked Brady.

"Garlic salt," Rose said, realizing Libby had given us the weapon that saved us.

Brady raised his hands in the air protesting the foolishness he heard. "I don't think I want to know," he said, sitting back down. "Does Dad know?" he stood again, ready to defend Landen's point of view if his father came charging in the door. He looked at my father, trying to measure his perspective.

Landen shook his head. "Not yet. Libby told Rose, and we needed Jason to watch our bodies as we slept."

"What do you mean, 'bodies'?" Brady said, looking at Rose and Jason.

"We can control where we go when we sleep," Landen answered.

Brady sat back in his chair and stared blankly. I felt him arguing with his emotions; he wanted to be proud of us, but he was too terrified.

"What did you see?" Brady asked my father.

Landen and I looked curiously in his direction to see if he could see the rush we'd felt helping Connie.

"Their adrenaline levels rose repeatedly, elevating their heart-beats. We didn't start waking them until Rose could feel their fear," my father answered.

Brady looked awestruck at Rose; it seemed everyone would now know that she had always had the insight of emotion.

"I think we may know why Landen never had nightmares: this world can't be found that way either," Rose said.

Hearing her words, I sat up slowly, staring into Landen's eyes as relief came over him. He realized that Drake couldn't reach me there, that I was sheltered from the nightmares, but Jessica and Hannah now bore the horror that had tormented me for so many years. Landen's relief was only a small reward. I wouldn't rest until I stopped Drake from hurting anyone—not just the ones I cared for.

The phone rang, and Brady dove across the room, answering it on the first ring; it was my mother, looking for my father. My father took the phone, whispering and promising my mother that we were all safe. I wondered how many houses she'd called, looking for us, how many knew now what we could do.

Brady coaxed a sleepy Felicity to her room. As she glanced back at me, I whispered, "I'm sorry."

She smiled, understanding the chaos. Rose guided Olivia back to the guest room. My father went to speak. Not finding the words, his lips hesitated. Landen then answered the unasked question. "Tell him, and the others. Right now, our bodies need rest," he said, standing setting me on my feet. My father nodded and hugged me before we left, clearly relieved that Landen was cool with him telling his father about this night.

Chapter 15

L anden drove us home. Feeling the exhaustion come over us, we laid our bodies down, clinging to one another. Sleep came immediately. Rising in synch, we drifted onto the porch and rested on one of the couches as we watched the sun rise over the hill.

As the night's events raced over and over in our minds, we didn't speak. Landen played with my hands, studying my fingertips, and the ring that still gleamed as if it were brand new. I tried remembering how many times I'd concentrated on a memory to help others, wondering if they'd seen what I was thinking. The only difference I could find was the connection that Olivia had to her aunt.

Olivia was the mirror image of her mother. It was as if, for the first time, her aunt had let her sister go, passing the grief that she carried as she raised Olivia. Thinking of Olivia, I wondered, not doubting anything at that point, if Olivia's mother had somehow helped me that night...if she were the light that came out of Olivia's aunt.

We watched as Aubrey pulled up. She reached for a basket in the front seat of the car and made her way to the door. Aubrey then peered through the window, and not seeing anyone, she set the basket on the porch and turned to leave. She hesitated and looked slowly toward the couch where we were laying, and her eyes searched, not focusing on anything. She walked back on the porch toward us.

We glanced at each other, wondering if she could see us. Aubrey went to speak, and, holding her hand out, she hesitated, checking her words before she began. Smiling at herself, she then looked in our direction.

"Landen...I'm sorry. We both are. But you have to understand, you're our little boy...you're so much like your father, ready to risk your life everyday to bring someone else safely home." She smiled at herself, looking down the empty road.

"Truth is, I dreamed of Willow, too. I could see you with her. I remember keeping you awake at night so you could sleep through the day, to see her longer while she slept in her time...you needed to have a childhood...so did she...that was our intent. We failed to see that you never carried the soul of a child. You were born for the task before you, and the way you feel about Willow is not only your reward, but also your weapon. I don't want you to be upset. Being angry at the mistakes made by the heart will only leave you bitter. The time taken from you will be repaid beyond your imagination. Your father understands why you've built these walls, everyone does, I promise. He'll wait for you to come to him. No more lectures. You're a man now, and we're all waiting for you to teach us, to tell us how to help you fill your purpose." Aubrey looked down at her feet. I could feel her remorse.

"Please just forgive us, trust us," Aubrey said with tears pooling in her eyes.

Landen couldn't take another word. He woke himself up and ran down the stairs, almost tripping on the basket in the threshold. Running to her, he scooped her up, and happy tears flowed out of her pale green eyes. Giving him a moment, I woke and stayed in our bed, feeling him change her mood.

After a shower, I found my sketchbook. The first sketch I drew was of the room Olivia was in, struggling to call back every detail. Taking a deep breath, I faced my demons, literally. Landen came in the room, breakfast in hand; hesitating as he saw the outline of the hospital room, he didn't stop me. He simply sat down and calmly watched as the demons came to life in black and white.

August knocked softly on the front door; we felt him coming and were waiting for him. Landen led August to the kitchen table. He was carrying what looked to be a large scroll. I followed shyly behind them.

"Interesting night," he commented as he sat down. We both smiled warily and settled at the table with August.

"What is this?" Landen asked, looking at the scroll.

"This is what you haven't been told," August said, smiling widely. My stomach turned. Landen reached over to hold my hand.

August unrolled the scroll, revealing a large circle with lions, fish, rams, scales, twins and scorpions, there were other symbols that lined the outer edge as well. I couldn't conceive what they might be. Dots were arranged under strange symbols.

"Landen, this is your birth chart. Your sun is in Pisces." Landen nodded. "Your moon is in Virgo, that's what gives you your ability to see truth," August continued.

"I've heard that before," Landen commented. Grinning, he glanced at me.

August nodded, then rolled out a second scroll. "Willow, this is yours. Your sun is in Scorpio, and your moon is in Leo, which gives you a powerful impact on emotions, both yours and others."

My eyes widened. Moon...I'd never heard of a moon sign. "I don't understand, how do you know that?"

"When we're born, each planet is aligned in a position, and their positions outline our characteristics. The alignments are not re-peated exactly for 4,320,000 years. This means that there is not another person that shares your traits on Earth."

I noticed he still had two scrolls that he hadn't unrolled. August smiled, his excitement growing as he unrolled the last two. They were much older than the ones he'd just shown us; the cloth the charts were on was frail and faded.

He removed the vase from the table and arranged the four scrolls. The old ones were next to the new ones, and the markings were identical.

"How is that possible?" Landen asked, clearly understanding the charts more than I did.

"This is Aliyanna's," August said, pointing to the one that matched mine. "And this is Guardian's," he said, pointing to the one that mirrored Landen's. I still didn't understand. I looked at Landen, and his eyes were glazed over. His emotion was basked in disbelief, clearly denying whatever August was trying to tell us.

"Who are they again?" I asked.

"They were the first. Priests attempted to contain them, but in-stead they were pushed into the string."

"So, um, that's why we can do what they could do?" My voice was timid. August smiled, and his eyes encouraged me to move past my first impressions.

Landen closed his eyes and said, "You think we're them...that we're back?"

August smiled at Landen and moved his hand to his shoulder. "I do."

"Wait, four million years...were dinosaurs even around then? That makes no sense to me," I argued.

Landen leaned back in his chair and looked at August, wanting him to teach me. August smiled and placed his hand on mine, then stared into my eyes. "First of all, to think that time can be measured is unwise. Second, I can see how you perceive this, Willow. The dimension you were raised in is still in its infancy. Most dimensions are not divided into countries, nor have one specific leader. In fact, beyond Infante and Esterious, there is only one other. Esterious is thought to be one of the first, they had passed the prehistoric times before Infante was ever conceived."

"How can you not have a leader?" I asked.

"People lead people just like we live here. We can divide ourselves any way we wish, but we are still, in fact, a part of humanity. In most dimensions, one person doesn't have a say over many. That's seen as a form of judgment. "

Landen never looked in my direction. I felt a wall building between us, and I didn't understand why.

"What do you know about them? How do Drake and Perodine play into this?" asked Landen. August's eyes questioned why Landen had said Perodine's name.

"Willow dreamed of her, too," Landen offered.

August smiled at me. "That makes sense. She is, or was, your mother."

Landen buried his face in his hands, shaking his head. August went on, "Perodine is a strong woman, but in her younger years she was subservient to her husband, Donalt. Perodine turned to the universe. She planned her child by the planets. She then developed powers to protect her and her child, Aliyanna, and those powers unwittingly suspended her life."

August's eyes fell to the charm around my neck. He smiled warmly as he looked back in my eyes. "Perodine had a medallion made—a sun filled with black glass to represent the darkness the world was in. A crescent moon was carved in the center to represent the rebirth of life. The star was placed on the back to show that the supremacy of man would always fall behind the universe—God. All the power that Perodine had found was placed inside the charm.

"Aliyanna was promised to a man in the court, a man her father had chosen for her, but her heart loved another: Guardian, a man of the common people. Donalt instructed his priest to remove Aliyanna's power and to kill her and Guardian. The charm served its purpose, though, and protected both Aliyanna and Guardian," August explained.

"So, let me get this straight. You think that we're those people? That this whole scenario is being played out again? Are you saying that Drake has been chosen for me by Donalt?" I clarified.

I felt a deep rage and jealousy rise inside Landen. August could see it, too. He looked at Landen and put his hand on his shoulder. "I know that Drake has Donalt's favor," he said quietly. "I know lore can never be counted on to speak the entire truth, only the flavor of such."

My eyes raced back and forth as I tried to understand why any of this mattered. I wanted to take it all away, to undo what had been done then, but then I remembered my dream with Perodine. "When I dreamed of Perodine, she told me she couldn't undo what was done. What did she mean? Is that true, or can I fix this?" I asked.

Landen looked at me quickly. I had never told him the details of the dream.

August glanced in my direction. I could feel a deep respect inside of him. "Once a spell is spoken, it cannot be undone...it has to be resolved. I would say that she meant that whatever was said over you then still holds true today. The only prediction I know beyond your births is that 'the innocent will lead you, and you will lead the innocent,'" August answered.

My emotion moved to fear as Libby's face flashed before me, and Landen felt the same way. We had no way to protect her; we both felt helpless and lost.

"What happened after Guardian and Aliyanna landed in the string?" I asked, hoping that we'd done something to help Esterious.

August looked down and traced the grain in the wood table. He sighed, regretting his words as he spoke them. "Aliyanna had the power to go back, but..." August looked into my eyes. "You chose to stay, which left Esterious in the state it's in today according to some." His tone was sympathetic. Landen's anger grew as August spoke. He looked at August and said, "If Aliyanna had never met Guardian, would the people in Esterious be at peace now? Would the threat of war be the only way to bring them peace?"

I looked sharply at Landen. What was he saying—that he wished we'd never met? I felt my insides fall, and all the color left my face.

August leaned forward and put his hand on Landen's shoulder. "You were made for each other, don't let this story cause you to forget that. This a war of this plane, nothing compared to the war of the heavens," he said with deep concern in his voice. "The answers rest in you. Do not rely on the stories written by those who were not there."

Landen broke his gaze with August and stared at the table. "I need to know how to heal her friends and stop those demons," he said, standing, not wanting to look at the charts. "That's my problem now, not old myths and superstitions... of any world or plane."

August didn't seem surprised by Landen's obvious rebellion to what he was hearing. "The only difference between black magic and white magic is the intent. You're going to have to find the counterpart to what was spoken over them."

"Will these rings help, or the medallion?" Landen asked, staring out the window.

"Only you truly know the power of those rings; they belonged to you then."

"How serious is it that they have the star?" Landen asked.

"Willow is the power—the star has part of her energy from the past. Any part of Willow gives them a source of power that is undeserved."

I could feel people coming, our family, and so could Landen. Our time alone with August was coming to an end, and we still had so many questions.

"You will find your way and finish what you left undone. I'm sure of it," August said.

August saw Ashten through the window walking toward our home. He was across the field, and he wasn't alone; my father, Marc, Chrispin, Brady, Dane, and Clarissa were all with him. August smiled at Landen and bowed his head. We knew that this conversation was over, at least for now. August gathered the scrolls and moved the vase back to the table.

Landen walked over to where I sat, pulled me up, and wrapped his arms around my waist. He then leaned his head against mine. His eyes were closed; he was blocking them all out, putting us in our own world. August walked outside to meet the others, giving us our privacy.

"What do you want me to do?" he asked me.

"All I can see are the demons."

"Do you want me to bring your friends here for now?" he thought quietly.

I didn't answer Landen's thoughts. He kissed my forehead and pulled my hand toward the door.

"Let's go get them," he said under his breath.

We walked out to the porch where they were all waiting, and the quiet whispers stopped when they saw us. Landen looked at his dad first, then at each of them in the eye, one by one.

"We need to bring those girls back here until we can stop the demons. Does anyone have any objections to that?" Landen asked.

Ashten glanced at August, then they looked at my father. My father cleared his throat. "We've brought family here before. Olivia seems to be fine," he answered, looking up at Landen.

"What is he talking about?" I asked Landen.

"There's an old myth that you must be loved by someone who lives here to survive in Chara."

"You tell us what you need us to do," Ashten said.

"What's your plan?" Marc asked.

Landen looked down then out to the others. Their anticipation and excitement frightened him. He didn't want them involved in this at all. "Jason, we heard the mothers talk about you last night. They respect your medical opinion. Do you think you could convince them to let the girls come with you?"

"I'm sure I could think of something," my father said, certain of himself.

"Dane, your mother is expecting you any day now. I say we go to Franklin with Dane. Jason, you can run into one of the parents and convince them that you have to take them away somewhere," Landen planned out. The others nodded in agreement.

"All right then. We need to go, it's almost night time there," my dad said.

August decided to stay behind. I reasoned he didn't want to place himself between Ashten and Landen. We waited as Ashten and my father called home. Brady and Chrispin didn't have to go far to say goodbye to Felicity and Olivia. They were in the field by our house, picking flowers. Olivia's emotion elevated as she heard Chrispin's voice...the emotion was undeniable. "Has he told her yet?" I asked, knowing how they both felt about each other and that Olivia would never have the nerve to say it first.

Landen smiled as he watched them. "He's waiting. He thinks she needs to see his face," Landen answered. The smirk on his face made me smile, but we were both too stressed to find the energy to laugh.

In the string, I lingered near the back with Clarissa. I thought Landen needed space. I didn't feel comfortable with the way he was acting...he had changed since he'd seen the charts. He was aloof and trying desperately not to seem that way to me. Brady and Marc took the time to try and show Dane the passages. He was able to feel them, but the colors escaped him.

"So, do you think I am going to like Franklin?" Clarissa asked me.

Like any other time I'd seen Clarissa, she resembled a runway model: a unique beauty that could capture anyone's attention.

"I think Franklin is really going to like you," I muttered, smiling faintly.

Clarissa grinned, staring at Dane. "He never really talks about anyone from there, except you and his family."

I smiled, remembering how oddly Dane and I fit into Franklin. "For us, it was like a waiting room. We've always known that we were meant to be somewhere else," I offered as I realized that my soul seemed to know way more than my mind.

As Infante came into view, green passages illuminated the walls. Landen glanced back in my direction, smiled slightly, and then walked on. A moment later, the walls seemed to turn completely green, and you couldn't see one passage from another. Landen stopped and looked at the wall cautiously. The others watched him carefully. To them, it was solid white.

"What is it, Landen?" Ashten asked.

"I'm trying to remember which one is Willow's house. That's the best place we could all appear out of nowhere without being no- ticed," Landen said, debating now on one area of the wall.

The admiration coming from the others was intensified in the string. Landen held his hand up, telling us all to stay put then he stepped inside the haze. Everyone in the string tensed, expecting Landen to feel the burn as he walked through the wall. I saw Ashten look at my father and shake his head in disbelief.

Seconds passed, and Landen didn't come back. I felt my heart rate rise. Pain was seeping into my veins, the same way it did when he left me before. I held my breath, trying to block it out, but with each second that passed it intensified. I saw spots in my vision, and my head started to spin. I fell back without warning. Brady, who was standing beside me, caught me.

"Jason, what's going on here?" Brady yelled.

My father quickly turned and saw my condition. I felt his panic, along with everyone else's. It wasn't helping me at all—it was draining me.

"It's happening again. Their bodies can't be separated by the string," my father said, trying to remain calm. My head was so heavy it fell back.

"What do we do?" Brady said, picking me up. "Do I walk through the wall?"

Suddenly, I felt life come back into me—I felt Landen again.

"No," I heard Landen say.

He emerged several feet from where he'd disappeared, walked quickly to Brady, and took me from his arms. With his touch, the pain left, leaving a tingle in its wake. I was weak. It had taken my energy, but when Landen kissed my lips, it sent a rush of energy through me. He squeezed me in his arms, and it was as if nothing ever happened.

"I'm sorry. I wasn't thinking. Are you okay?" he thought.

I nodded. Hating that I looked weak. Feeling that emotion he slowly put me down.

"Is something wrong? Why didn't you come back?" Marc asked, ready for a fight.

"No, that goes to their house, but there are a ton of people there, cleaning up after the fire." I couldn't just disappear. I had to find another opening.

"Let me look at you," my father said. He circled Landen and me, shaking his head. "I don't understand why you can't be apart. I mean, you were apart for eighteen years."

"Maybe that's their bodies way of saying that they should have never been kept apart in the first place," Brady bit out, still upset with Ashten for hiding me from Landen.

Clarissa saw the potential disagreement and added a more positive note. "Or maybe it symbolizes that they are now joined forever," she said, glancing at Brady. "We can't change the past. We've all made mistakes in judgment."

Landen squeezed me tighter and kissed the top of my head. I could sense turmoil inside him. He didn't want his family to fight over any of this. My father nodded in Clarissa's direction and let the matter go.

The current in the string began to flow more aggressively, and the hum grew a little bit louder. Landen looked at my father. "You don't have long to convince them to come. The storm will pass here in less than six hours," he warned.

"I don't think it's going to be hard. Grace told me that both Jessica and Hannah's parents wanted the girls to go with Willow to Paris," my father said.

Landen held me tight and led us forward. Everyone lined up behind us, and we passed through the green wall together. The passage led to a wooded area just fifty yards from my house. I could still smell the smoke in the air.

We causally walked to the road, and in the distance I could hear hammers and saws. As we approached the house, trucks lined the street in front of the shell of a home that was left. People were rushing in every direction.

We walked into the front yard, and I looked up at the home in which I was raised, the one in which my mother was raised, the brick remained in place. The roof was gone, and so were all the windows.

It didn't take long for someone to notice us. On the front porch was Josh's father, Mr. Campbell. He owned a very successful construction company. Mr. Campbell saw my father and grinned from ear to ear.

"Well, now, I didn't expect to see you back so soon," he said to my father, once he reached our side.

"We're just passing through. Grace wanted me and Willow to see if there was anything that could be saved before we went overseas," my father said, clearly not comfortable lying.

"Now, Jason, I told you the night it burned that I was going to fix this for you, and I meant it," Mr. Campbell said looking over his shoulder, then back at my father, feeling proud of what he'd accomplished in such a short time.

"Really, it's not necessary," my father said, raising his hands.

"Look, Jason, I had doctor after doctor tell me I needed open heart surgery, but you took one look at me and told me how to heal myself. I vowed then to repay you. All these people here, they don't work for me. They're volunteers, your patients, Grace's friends, and Willow's friends. I've never known a man as good as you before, none of us have. This is our way of saying thank you."

"I really do appreciate this. This town will always be a part of me and Grace," my father said humbly.

"Well, there isn't a lot that can be salvaged. We have a few storage containers in the back of the house. Anything that we think you'd still want or use, we put in there," Mr. Campbell said, looking at all of the people my father had with him. His eyes landed on Dane.

"Son, your mother is going to be happy to see you." He then looked around at the trucks lining the street. "How did all of you get here?"

"Cab," my father said quickly. "We're actually on a layover, and we don't have very long before our next flight," he continued, getting better at lying.

Mr. Campbell nodded as my father talked; that was a trait about him that I'd always found funny. "Well, I'll tell you what," he said, pulling his keys out of his pocket. "Dane, take my truck go and introduce that pretty thing you have with you to your mother."

Clarissa blushed, not knowing how to respond to Mr. Campbell. Smiling, Dane took the keys then glanced back at Landen and me before he left; it was clear he was amused by how blunt Mr. Campbell was.

"I tell you what, Jason. They've been hoping you would show up. Seems two girls showed up at the hospital, and they don't know what to make of what's wrong with them," Mr. Campbell said.

"Are they still at the hospital?" my father asked.

"No, I believe they sent them home," Mr. Campbell answered, waving his son, Josh, over to us. Josh walked over to all of us and looked at Landen and Brady, confusion all over his face.

"Are you a doctor, too?" Mr. Campbell asked Ashten.

I felt my father's embarrassment as he looked back at us, realizing he hadn't introduced anyone. "I'm sorry. That was rude of me. This is Ashten. Yes, he's a doctor; he taught me everything I know," he said.

Mr. Campbell reached over and shook Ashten's hand. Everyone else was trying not to laugh at the idea of Ashten being a doctor.

"And these are his sons, Brady and Landen, and his nephews, Chrispin and Marc," my father said.

Mr. Campbell shook everyone's hands, saving Landen's for last. It was not hard to see that we were a couple. Since the pain in the string, Landen had made sure that one part of him was always touching me.

"You must be a lucky man," Mr. Campbell said to Landen. "I told my son Josh here that girls like Willow are rare." Mr. Campbell looked back at Josh, shaking his head in a teasing manner. "Maybe next time he'll listen to me."

Josh rolled his eyes at his father then nodded in Landen's direction, still confused.

"Josh, let Jason take your truck. He needs to go and check on those girls," Mr. Campbell said. Josh complied without complaint.

"I want to stay here to see what's in storage," I said to Landen and my father.

"Dad, just go with Jason. I'll stay here with them," Brady said to Ashten.

Mr. Campbell waved then turned to go back to the house. Josh looked at Landen one more time then followed his dad.

"Maybe your herb didn't work that well on him," I thought, Landen shrugged his shoulders, not really caring what Josh thought of him.

"We'll be back in a little bit," my father said over his shoulder.

Brady and Chrispin walked toward the house, and Mr. Campbell gave them hard hats before he allowed them in. Landen, Marc, and I walked around the house. Looking up at the damage, I felt an overwhelming grief. I wondered how many people I would bring destruction to before this conflict with Drake was over. I tried to hide my emotion from Landen, but he felt it.

"I'm sorry, Willow," he thought, filling with remorse.

Though we never lost touch, I could feel his mind drifting some-where else. If I could turn back time, I wouldn't have allowed him to look at those birth charts. They'd changed him.

We walked around the house along the fence. Volunteers had laid out paintings that could be saved. Most of them were mine, a few were my mother's. I walked by them slowly. Remembering the images, I wondered if I'd really helped them, or if I'd only sustained them for the moment.

"Are all of these yours?" Marc asked.

"The ones of the people are," I answered.

My mother was more of a still art painter. Marc leaned closer to get a better look. "I think I know this girl," he said, looking at one of the paintings. It was one I had done of a young girl almost a year ago. I remembered how lonely she felt.

"Landen, this looks like that girl we helped bring home a while back—for umm... what was his name? Austin, wasn't it?" Marc said, not feeling sure of himself.

Landen looked closer at the painting. "It does look like her," he said. "Was she lonely?" he asked me.

I nodded, astonished that it could be the same girl. "You know her?"

"Maybe. We've carried so many home, it's hard to say for sure. I only remember her because she had no family or belongings. Austin found her living in a shelter; a storm had taken everything from her. It was like she breathed for the first time when she stepped through the gates of Chara.

I smiled, hoping it was the same girl. I wanted all the people that I'd helped to be happy.

In the center of the backyard, there were two large containers. Inside them were more paintings, books, and small knick-knacks. I walked in and started going through the things, making a pile for us to carry home to my mother. I knew it would make her feel better.

The sun was setting, and the volunteers were leaving one by one. Brady and Chrispin came over to us. We all leaned against the fence, waiting for my father. Mr. Campbell waved at us as he climbed in the passenger seat of another truck. I was sure he was going to Gina's Diner to retrieve his truck. Josh and Chase came around the house with handfuls of bottled water, then they walked over and passed them out to us.

"Thank you," Landen said, taking two bottles, one for me and one for him.

Josh had yet to lose his confused expression. He must have said something to Chase because now they both looked confused. "It's Livingston, right?" Josh said to Landen. Marc and Chrispin were in mid-drink when they heard Josh. They both stopped and stared at him while Landen tilted his head and pulled his brows together, questioning Josh.

"Landen," Landen said finally. I could feel the tension building.

"Sorry. My fault," Josh said, glancing from Landen to Chase.

"Do you know a Livingston?" Chase asked Landen.

Landen's lips turned into a sinful smile. "I think I may have met one before. Why do you ask?"

Chase and Josh shook their heads and laughed at themselves. "It's nothing," Chase said.

"Chase," I said sternly, knowing that he knew something. Landen put his hand on my shoulder, trying to calm me down before I lost my temper.

"All right," Chase said, raising his hands, knowing that I'd rip him apart if he didn't come clean. "Remember your friend, Drake?" I rolled my eyes. "Yeah, anyway, he asked Josh and me if we'd ever seen a guy named Livingston with you or your dad. He said he was tall, dark, wavy hair and unmistakable dimples. We thought he was talking about an older man, but I don't know," Chase said, looking at Landen. "You kind of fit the profile. We just thought it was weird that you showed up after he said that."

Landen turned his head slightly to look at Marc and get his take on what Chase had said. Josh followed Landen's eyes to Marc. "Hey, do you know Drake?" he asked.

"Should I?" Marc asked, trying not to look baffled.

"I don't know. You just look like him," Josh said defensively.

Everyone turned and stared at Marc. It was clear the comparison made him uncomfortable. Josh had a point, though. Both Drake and Marc were built the same way, with a dominant profile I hadn't noticed before. I think it was the eyes that threw me off. Marc's are light brown with a sparkle in them, but Drake's are as dark as the night, with a degree of magnetism that pulls you in.

Headlights beamed around the side of the house, breaking the tension; it was Gina's truck. I could feel Clarissa and Dane. Landen held my hand and led us to the front of the house. Another van pulled in behind Gina's. I felt Hannah and Jessica with my father and Ashten. My father must have had success.

Dane and Clarissa got out of the truck and walked over to the van where the girls were. Olivia's aunt was driving, and my father was in the passenger seat. He rolled down the window. "Willow, I have good news for you," he said. "It seems Jessica and Hannah are in need of some relaxation to relieve some stress they're under, so

I invited them to come to Paris with us for a week." I smiled, not having to try hard to seem surprised. Olivia's aunt leaned forward, looking at all of us grinning, but her eyes hesitated on Chrispin for a moment. That's when I remembered showing her Olivia dancing with Chrispin.

Landen remembered, too, and he quickly stepped in front of Chrispin. "You guys split up. They're going to take us to the airport," my father said. Landen nodded, then turned and pushed Chrispin and Brady in the direction of Gina's truck. Chrispin looked back at Landen like he'd lost his mind. Landen nodded his head, telling Chrispin to go. Once out of sight, we climbed in the van with Jessica and Hannah. My father had given them something to help them relax, and it was clear it was already taking effect by the peace I felt within them and the smiles on their faces.

After we were dropped off at the airport, we waited for a few moments, then hailed a cab to take us back to the passages near my house. Inside the string, the current was flowing more aggressively than before, causing us to rush through the passage. Landen and I stayed on the outside, ready to pull everyone through if the storm erupted before we reached Chara.

Once home in Chara, we took Hannah and Jessica to my father's house. I could sense how nervous my father was about having them here. I'd never thought my father believed in myths, but then again, I never imagined that he was from another dimension either. It seemed everyone except Marc had someone to see, to tell that they were home safely. Marc, Dane, and Clarissa followed us back to our house, and we all gathered in the living room.

"You don't think I look like Drake, do you?" Marc asked Landen.

"Does it matter if you do?" Landen retorted, falling back into one of the large chairs and staring at the ceiling.

Marc was immediately irritated by Landen's short tone. Landen was being distant with everyone, but I'm sure it hurt me more than them.

"I just want to know how he knew Dad's name," Marc argued.

"He's always in Esterious," Clarissa answered, trying to give Landen a break from always having to have the answers.

"So am I. So are you. Did he say our name? No."

Landen sat up and looked at me, then at Marc.

"Where is your dad anyway?" Landen asked.

Marc stopped pacing and looked back at Landen; a singe of fear hit him. "I don't know. I haven't seen him since your celebration... Ashten said he went to Esterious to find a way in the palace."

"He should be back by now, don't you think?" Landen said.

Marc had been so distracted by everything that had happened that he hadn't noticed. Guilt came to him immediately.

"You know, you're right," Marc answered. Fear coursed through the room. Marc rushed to the kitchen to call Ashten.

Aubrey told him that he was already on his way to our house. We waited, watching Marc get more upset, pacing across the room.

Ashten and my father came through the back door at the same time. As they came into the room, their concern grew as they saw Marc in his freaked state.

"What's going on?" asked Ashten.

"Where's Dad? Shouldn't he back by now?"

"Well, not really. He was intent on staying until all this was worked out," answered Ashten.

"Did he go into the palace?" Marc asked as his anxiety grew.

"I don't think he'd try anything that would put himself in danger," Ashten promised.

I glanced in Landen's direction. I could tell Ashten didn't believe his own words.

"We need to get him, he needs to know what we know!" Marc yelled.

"What do we know? What did you guys figure out?" Ashten demanded realizing that they were missing something.

"Drake asked Willow's friends if they knew a Livingston," Landen explained.

My father and Ashten looked at each other. I clearly felt their confusion and frustration.

Ashten looked back at Marc. "I can see why that would bother you, but I'm sure there's a reason," Ashten stated in a forced calm tone as if he knew Marc was seconds away from doing something foolish.

"Yeah and I'm going to find out right now," Marc bit out, walking to the door.

Ashten moved to block Marc's exit. "You're not going to find him tonight. Curfew has already set in—he won't be out, and you're sure to be killed if they see you on the streets," he said as Marc's face fell. "Look, he's fine. We'll all go in the morning, well, Jason and I will go with you."

Ashten glanced in Landen's direction, then at me.

"We're not afraid of him. We're going to have to face him sooner or later," Landen said shortly.

"Later sounds better to me," retorted Clarissa, reminding Landen that this affected all of them, not just us.

Landen closed his eyes and shook his head, avoiding a sarcastic remark that he would regret as soon as he said it.

"Look, let's just argue about this tomorrow. You all need your rest, especially if we're going to Esterious tomorrow," Ashten said, defusing the situation.

Marc charged toward the door, anger coursing through him. He had every intent of going to Esterious that night.

"Marc," Landen said, halting him. "Rest...I know where you sleep."

Marc's face fell then he turned and walked slowly out the door. He knew we could see his intent, as well as the fact that if we wanted to we could watch him sleep without him ever seeing us.

The blunt prediction and threat that Landen had given left the room stunned; the power that we'd built using each other had escaped their attention until now.

"So, am I to presume that you two will not need me tonight?" my father asked.

"No, we'll stay here," Landen answered, staring at the ground.

Dane and Clarissa quietly walked out after Marc. Before leaving, my father walked over to where I sat and kissed my forehead. Ashten hesitated, then followed.

We were now completely alone, and for the first time in my life, that was something I didn't want. I could feel the tension between us. The pressure of everything that was happening to us made itself known.

Chapter 16

Landen stood and walked to the mantle. He was staring at my willow tree. His anguish hit me like a ton of bricks.

"Willow," he said solemnly, "we've made a big mistake." His words were a dagger in the heart.

"Excuse me?" I managed.

He stared at the floor with disdain. "If that lore is right...then or now...and you can help those people," he dropped his head. "That matters. It's important.

I stood. His emotions were a brick wall between us. I reached for his arm, but he shifted away. He wouldn't look at me. The rejection burned every part of me.

"You can't say that—"

"You haven't seen what I've seen, know what I know. Donalt's people— those people live a life that I wouldn't wish on my worst enemy."

"Landen—"

He raised his hand to stop me. "No, listen to me. It's a virtual hell. No color, they live in identical houses, inside and out, they eat the same food, wear the same clothes, work day in and day out. They're executed if they break the simplest law. No one smiles or laughs. It's dark, no life. No one has a will to live."

"How is that your or my fault?" I shouted.

He paced the floor, his hands on his head, his eyes closed.

"I stole your heart. You were supposed to stop all of that, but you fell in love with me and never looked back, and now look—how many people do you think have died because we were too selfish?"

"I am not selfish," I bit out.

Landen turned quickly and put his hands on my shoulders. His eyes were different. The blue had changed, it was darker.

"If you have to choose between me or saving those people. Save them."

I jerked his hands off me and stepped back, more angry than I'd ever been in my life.

"Are you insane? What are you saying? You—you want me to be with Drake!"

"Willow—"

"No. Don't 'Willow' me! One minute you're telling me that you love me and you're going to fix everything, and the next you're telling me to go to another man. How dare you!"

"I am not telling you to go to another man!"

"Yes, you are! Are you even listening to yourself?"

"Willow, I told you to save those people."

"Which means I have to be with Drake! How can you stand there and ask me to pay for something that was done millions of years ago?"

"Do you think this isn't killing me? Do you not feel how bad it hurts for me to tell you that? We have to fix what we've done wrong.

Chara will go to war with Esterious, they will never think twice about it. People will die, Willow. They have died because of us, and will die because of us."

"Do you happen to remember what happened four million years ago, because I sure don't. If you do, enlighten me. Tell me why I'm cold and selfish?"

"I didn't say you were cold."

"Basically, you did. I know that if those stupid charts are right and I'm back or whatever they mean, then I should be the same person, and I happen to know myself well: if I stayed here, I had a damn good reason."

"You loved me."

"And I still love you, and if that was my reason it was good enough then, and it's good enough now."

"Willow, neither one of us will let others suffer so we can be together."

"You've lost your mind!" I screamed.

He turned his back to me. I felt rage coursing through me. I took off the necklace with the charm and slid off the ring, then sat them on the table and walked to the front door.

"Don't leave," he said. "You just told me to be with Drake. To be a pawn in a game that I'm not playing," I said coldly as I opened the door.

"Willow—"

I stormed out of the front door and down the front steps. I couldn't find my breath, my chest hurt so badly. I ran through the field. I ran as if the demons themselves were on my heels. I didn't stop until my breath left me. I fell to my knees and looked up; the moon was almost full. I could see the outline.

I crawled the three feet between me and the base of the large windmill, then leaned my weak body against it and raised my head to the heavens. My breath was coming back slowly.

I don't know how long I sat there, questioning who I was, before I felt someone coming toward me. I glanced up to see a small figure on the hilltop. It was Rose. Her emotions were so peaceful that I felt that emotion seep into my soul. When she reached me, she sat down quietly by my side.

"How did you find me?" I asked.

"Libby called me. She said you were sad."

"Did you call Landen?"

"No, I could feel you. I knew you were alone."

I glanced to her.

"My home is right there." She pointed to the hill she had just walked over. I smiled at myself, realizing that I'd run almost all the way to her house. "Do you want to talk about it?"

"He wants me to be with Drake. There's nothing to talk about."

"You know that's not true," she said with a smirk.

"He told me to choose him."

"Willow, I'm sure you only heard what you wanted to hear."

"It's just not fair...it can't be that black and white."

"It's not."

"Then why is everyone telling me I have to choose?"

"Who is 'everyone'?"

"Perodine, Landen—"

"Did Perodine tell you to choose between Landen and Drake?"

"She just said that I had to choose again...obviously, I chose Landen last time, and Landen thinks it's our fault that the people in Esterious are suffering, that Monica is de-"

I couldn't even say the word before tears hit me like a flood. Rose wrapped her arms around me and let me cry, rocking me back and forth.

"It's not either of your faults. Everything has its reason, and you need to take this grief and use it as your weapon."

"Why am I being punished for the day I was born?" I asked, trying to dry my face.

"Why do you think you are?" Rose asked, genuinely surprised.

I sat up straight and shook my head in frustration. "Ever since I came to Chara, all I've heard about is the stars and moon alignments; it decides how you learn, what your insight is, and apparently dictates what your fate is. What is the purpose of living if it's already chosen for you?"

Rose let her shoulders droop; she understood why I was so angry. She shifted in front of me on her knees and gently placed her hands on my shoulders.

"You've misunderstood why Chara looks to the heavens," she said softly.

I looked up at her and brushed my hair out of my eyes.

"Chara's foundation is love. We learn about our planets to help us understand who we are. If you love yourself, then you can love others more powerfully."

"Then why am I asked to pay for something that was done so long ago?"

"You chose this path. You were chosen by this path," Rose said with certainty.

"Rose, you aren't making any sense," I said, lowering my head.

"Yes I am. You're just not listening to me," she said, a little louder than I expected.

I looked up at her quickly.

"At any moment, you can change your destiny. Your thoughts lead the way. Your soul is old, and you've chosen this path so often that it has now come to you at a younger age than ever before. So, it's natural for it to feel forced upon you."

"Are you telling me that it doesn't matter that August is walking around with a birth chart that says that I'm Aliyanna? That I selfishly left others behind to suffer?"

"I'm telling you that you are Willow Haywood, and Willow Haywood decides her fate, not the stars," Rose said, lowering her head and looking up at me. "Listen to me, you have the strength to do this."

"I have to have Landen. I don't care if he doesn't want me. That means I'm as selfish as he said I was."

Rose reached for my face and ran her hand across my cheek, then stared at me, smiling, pride coursing through her.

"You have the heart of a woman, and a woman's heart is the strongest thing in any dimension. We love without reason, and we can turn a heart of stone into water."

"What am I supposed to do?"

"You follow your heart. When you do that, everything will find its way. The woman who began this world knew that, and so do you."

"I didn't go back. I stayed here, and so many have suffered."

"Do you honestly believe that your soul didn't have a reason for staying in Chara at the start of time?"

I tilted my head and let my mind try to conceive what would have stopped me. Rose smiled as she felt me calm down.

"Today, you do not have one. Go back with Landen and right what is wronged, side by side."

"He doesn't want me. He wants me to be with Drake."

"Now, I doubt that," Rose said, standing. She smiled over her shoulder at me as she walked over the hill in front of her house. I sat stunned for a moment. What was my reason? A moment later, I felt a strong emotion of love and knew Landen was coming to find me, and he was coming fast.

In the distance, in the light of the moon, I could see Landen running in my direction.

I was so mad at him.

So freaking in love with him.

I ran to him.

I was running home, where I belonged.

When we reached each other, our bodies collided with powerful force. His lips found mine and as they moved with mine you would have thought it was the air we were breathing. He was holding me so tight, it almost hurt.

"I'm sorry, I didn't mean it. I love you, and I would die before I let you leave me for anyone. I love you, Willow. I've loved you from my first breath."

"I love you."

We fell to the ground, holding one another. In the field of beautiful flowers surrounded by darkness, under a moon that was nearly full, we loved each other. At that moment we owned the night. The flowers were our bed, the warmth of the summer air and the stars were our blankets, and the rhythm of our passion was serenaded by the distant sounds of nature.

I wanted to crawl inside of him and hide there for the rest of my life. I wanted to forget who I was, who I am, and what was still left to be done.

Once back at our house, in our room, Landen reached in his pocket and pulled out my necklace and ring. He clasped the necklace around my neck. I felt a tingle as the medallion touched my chest. He gently reached for my hand and slid the silver ring on. It hummed and brightened as it rested on my skin. He looked deeply into my eyes; my window to his soul was opened again, and the blue was breathtaking. I lost myself. If it were possible, I think I fell deeper in love with him.

"We'll do this together, me and you," he said softly.

I wrapped my arms around him and closed my eyes, knowing that I'd never choose anyone above him. I wouldn't let any one get hurt because of us either.

After drifting to sleep, Landen made good on his promise, and we went to Marc's house. We found him pacing the floor in his room, wanting to go, daring to see if he would be able to get away with it. Landen walked over to his bed pulled back the covers, and Marc jumped with a startle. I reached for the light and turned it off. He walked slowly to his bed and laid down stiffly. We sat against the wall and watched him stare at the ceiling.

"I still feel her," Marc said into the room. "I'm not crazy. I will find her one day," he finished.

I could feel the words hit Landen like a ton of bricks. "Why is Marc alone?" I thought.

Landen stared at Marc with compassion. "The urge to look doesn't come until at least the age of twenty, but for some it comes much later. Some say it's because those have a purpose to fill," Landen explained.

"You think he hasn't looked because he's still looking for his mother?"

"He remembers her more clearly than Chrispin. I can see how his search for her would cloud over the urge to want to find his soul mate."

"Doesn't he realize when he finds her that she'll make him stronger?"

Landen glanced at me letting that sinful grin emerge before wrapping his arms around me. "He knows we're not meant to be alone. He just needs his time."

After Marc drifted to sleep, we made our way to my father's house to check on Jessica and Hannah. They were both in the guest room, sound asleep. There were no demons; our plan to protect them had worked.

Before leaving, we checked in on our little princess, Libby. Her eyes were closed as they fluttered back and forth. I pulled the blanket up over her shoulder. Just as we went to leave, she said, "How many?" We looked quickly at her to see her still sleeping. "What color?" she said, a little louder.

We passed a curious look, careful not to move or wake her. "What do I say?" Libby said turning in her bed.

"Will Willow come home with Landen?" Her face squinted together, then she lay silent.

Stunned, we didn't move, waiting for her to say anything to answer the questions she'd asked.

Libby never moved again, but we rested our souls in her window seat, watching her sleep, waiting for her to say or do something, knowing she could very well hold the key to every question we'd ever had.

At daybreak, a knock on our front door woke us. We heard footsteps coming in the hall and up the steps; we knew it was Marc.

Landen grudgingly pulled the covers over us, letting our bodies wake up before arguing with him.

"Ahh...so how does it feel having someone come in your room and scare the hell out of you?" Marc said as he walked in our bedroom door.

Landen threw a pillow at him. "It was for your own good, and you know it," he said, wiping the sleep out of his eyes.

"Look, as I was lying there last night, I realized something," Marc said.

"What? That I was right?" Landen said.

"No," Marc said, throwing the pillow back at Landen. "You said you could control where you go, right?" Landen nodded, squinting at Marc through the sunlight. "So you could beam yourself right into that palace and take that star back, couldn't you?"

"Jason thinks they'd be able to hurt us," Landen corrected.

Marc's enthusiasm faded as he walked over and sat on the edge of the bed.

"Hey, do you mind? Can we have a minute here?" Landen said, pushing Marc off the bed with his foot. Marc looked at me and blushed a little before leaving the room, giving us a chance to get dressed. Landen looked at me and shook his head in disbelief.

"The best part about getting through this is the idea of having you all to myself."

Even though I knew he meant it, I still laughed at his new observation.

Downstairs, Marc had laid out breakfast for us, and he stared at Landen and me as we ate. Every once in awhile, he would start to say something, then hesitate and look out the window.

"Say it," Landen said as he finished his breakfast and pushed his plate away from him.

"This doesn't freak you out?" Marc said with a burst of air coming from him.

"What part?" I asked, making light of his perspective.

"I just think, Landen, you and I have seen a lot of crazy stuff over the years, but nothing like this, like the two of you," Marc said.

Landen shifted in his seat, giving Marc a stern look and a sideways glance at me before he answered.

"I don't know why you're so surprised. I've known you my whole life. You knew about the dreams and the intent I could see."

"That doesn't mean that I knew that you were really out walking around with Willow somewhere. Where did you guys meet anyway?"

We glanced at each other; we'd never even tried to figure out where we went.

"We don't know," Landen said as he stared into my eyes.

"We've been to a lot of places, you've never seen the place awake once?" Marc pushed.

Landen leaned back in his chair and stared forward as the memories danced across his eyes. I felt him remembering all the places that had brought him joy.

"I've never been there awake. I'm sure of it," he said finally, staring at me again.

"Are you ready for this? I've watched that world tear my father apart," Marc said, calling Landen's attention back to him.

"It doesn't matter if we're ready or not, it's here," Landen answered, reaching over and squeezing my hand.

Marc leaned back in his seat, seeing that he wasn't going to talk us down from whatever we faced. "You're my purpose," he said.

"What?" Landen said, surprised.

"My purpose...is to keep you safe," Marc said in a hushed voice.

"Marc—"

"No, Landen. Seriously, I know what I'm talking about. I remember when you were born, looking at you and knowing that I was supposed to protect you."

"You were just being a good 'brother'...you feel the same for Chrispin."

"No, that's just it. Chrispin is my baby brother, and yes, if I was there and he needed me, I'd keep him safe, but with you I feel like I'm supposed to make sure that I'm there to protect you," Marc argued.

Landen sighed deeply and shook his head as Marc finished his explanation. "Listen, I want you to put what you just told me aside and clear your head...find that feeling and follow it. We all need someone, you aren't meant to be alone."

"I know that. I just have to do this first, so if you're ready, then bring it on," Marc said with an uncanny boyish grin.

Through the kitchen window, I saw Libby in the valley; she was picking flowers, and she had a basket almost too large for her to carry. As I focused on her, I could feel her urgency. Landen followed my stare, and so did Marc. "I wonder what she's doing out so early," Marc muttered.

"Something's wrong," I said to Landen, pushing back from the table, not losing sight of her. As Landen and Marc followed me, my quick walk turned into a sprint. "Libby, what's wrong? Libby? What's wrong?" I screamed. Libby jumped as she heard me, and relief filled her eyes.

"Willow, help me find the blue and green ones," she ordered.

"What?"

"Willow, hurry—blue and green, I need lots." Libby was now frantically searching the ground, looking at all the flowers.

"Find blue and green ones, hurry!" I yelled at Landen and Marc as they approached, and the three of us searched the ground frantically with Libby. Once her basket was full, she took off in a sprint toward her house, and we all followed her.

As we approached the house, I counted the emotions around me; beyond us, I could only feel two. I ran past Libby up the stairs to Hannah and Jessica's room. My stomach dropped before the door even opened. There was something wrong. The room was without emotion. Libby pushed past me and opened the door.

From the doorway, I could see the blue tint of their skin as they lay in the same place we'd seen them last night. Marc took one look, then ran down the hall, screaming my father's name.

Libby sat the basket on the floor between the beds and began pulling the petals off the flowers and putting them on Hannah's chest. I looked at Landen, and we both rushed to her side to help her.

"Put them everywhere, Willow," Libby ordered.

My father and Marc came crashing into the room; just like Landen, I could feel my father's dread when his eyes fell on Hannah and Jessica's bodies. We all knew that they weren't breathing, and my father knew more. The basket was empty now, and the girls were covered in blue and green petals. Libby looked over them once, picking up a few loose petals and putting them on the girls' chests.

"Okay, say this with me: land and will, will and land," Libby said to Landen and me.

In a sacred trance, we did as she ordered and said, "Land and will, will and land," in unison with Libby, repeating it over and over.

Seconds later, I felt a burst of energy coming from Hannah and Jessica at the same time, and my ring and necklace warmed against my skin. I closed my eyes, and a numbing emotion swept through my body. As it passed, a dizzy feeling caused me to open my eyes, gaining balance. I looked at Landen and could see he felt it, too.

As Landen and I stood paralyzed by each other's stare, my father rushed to the girls' sides. We didn't notice Libby dancing in place, my mother rushing in at the last moment, or even the overwhelming fear coming from Marc and my father as they looked back at us from the girls' bedside.

Hannah and Jessica's chests began to rise and fall, but their eyes never opened, and they didn't move.

"Jason, what happened?" my mother demanded, taking into account that the girls were covered in flowers. My father kept his stunned look, staring at Landen and me.

"Jason? Willow? Somebody talk to me!" my mother shouted.

"They were sleeping too far away. The flowers helped Willow and Landen bring them back to the right sleep," Libby answered, giggling.

"Libby, sweetie, why don't you go and get some breakfast. I'll be there in just one minute, okay?" my mother said, pushing Libby out of the room.

"Dad, are they okay? Look, are they okay!" I demanded, trying to get his attention away from Landen and me.

He slowly turned to look at Hannah and Jessica, shaking his head as he took a second look. "They're fine, for now," he said quietly.

"Were they...? Were they...?" I tried to ask if they were dead.

"Yes...for a while," he answered in a low tone.

"What is this? Why flowers? Why did you say that?" my mother asked frantically.

"Libby told us to. We saw her picking flowers; she only wanted blue and green. Is that myth true? Did we hurt them by bringing them here?" I asked, feeling sick to my stomach.

"I don't know if it's our world, or if it's something that was spoken over them. They're fine now," my father said, looking over Landen and me again.

"Are you sure?" I asked, looking at Hannah and Jessica.

"Their hearts are weak. Somehow they started to beat again, but they aren't beating the way they're meant to; it's like they're on life support."

"The flowers," Landen whispered. My father looked at Landen and nodded.

"So we have two choices? We take them home and let demons dance across their chests, or we leave them here barely alive?" I said through my teeth.

"They are very alive, and they shouldn't be—you brought them back," my mother said calmly.

"Did you know you could do that?" Marc asked.

"We have no idea what we can do," Landen answered, pulling me to him.

News travels fast with an energetic little girl proud of her morning's accomplishments. Rose and August came to my mother's house first. My mother was frantically fixing breakfast, trying to keep her mind busy. The only sound in the kitchen was the clanging of pans and plates

Brady, not hearing the news of the morning's events, strolled in the back door, beaming with excitement and slapping Marc on the back as he smiled proudly at him. "You guys aren't going to believe what happened," he announced to the room, but his words fell on deaf ears, so to speak.

His frustration grew with our blank expressions. "Did you guys hear me? I have good news, not just good news, amazing news." While he spoke, Felicity slid in behind him, giving way to Chrispin and Olivia.

When Olivia came in the room, her eyes met each of ours for the first time, and we knew she had her sight back. She then ran to me and hugged me tightly, laughing out loud.

"Oh my God—how—what happened?" I stuttered.

"It's amazing...this whole place is so beautiful," Olivia said, not hearing my questions. We all stared in shock, looking at a grinning Chrispin, waiting for an explanation.

"You told her, didn't you?" Landen asked.

Chrispin grinned, then walked over and pulled a stunned Landen into a bear hug. "You were right. I was stupid for waiting. I told her as soon as we got back, and this morning when she woke up, her sight was back...it's amazing."

"What did you say to him?"

"That he was an idiot," Landen thought, with a smirk.

"Well, this is certainly uplifting compared to the morning that's transpired," August commented.

"What happened?" Brady said as his smile fell.

The room fell silent. Felicity eased over out of Brady's way and started helping my mother cook breakfast. Chrispin and Olivia stared with the shell of a smile on their faces.

"The girls are sick," my father said finally.

"What do you mean?" Chrispin asked.

"We don't know if it's Chara or something that was said over them in Esterious, but right now they're on the edge of life," my father said.

"So we take them back," Chrispin said blankly. As the words left his lips, the demons flashed before my eyes, and fear suddenly filled me. Landen and Rose looked at me simultaneously.

"You don't know what we saw. If you did, those words would have never left your lips," Landen said kindly, looking at me with all the compassion his body possessed. Chrispin's regret was immediate. Olivia's emotion fell, and her tears followed.

"After breakfast, I'm going to call Ashten, and we're going to look for Livingston. Whoever wants to come is more than welcome," my father said, looking at Landen and me.

At the gates of the string, we all stood dressed in black. The only traveler to stay behind was Rose. The string was calm by our home, but as we walked on the current changed to the point that you had to push forward with each step. The hum was so deep; you could feel it in your soul. Just before the passage, Clarissa whispered instructions to Dane. Landen used our gift to prepare me.

"You can't smile, not even your eyes, and we can't touch. You and Clarissa must lead. It's illegal for a man to walk before a woman, it's the only respect the women in this world have."

I wanted to ask why, but I was too busy burning his simple instructions into my memory.

"Keep your left hand in your pocket—rings are forbidden here."

"Then I'll take it off."

"No, it's protecting you. That and the necklace are the only reasons you are not feeling my anxiety about having you here."

I did as he said, not wanting for one instant to feel his pain; it was almost as bad as being separated from him.

"Keep pace with Clarissa. She's going to lead us to the courtyard. Today is the day that Donalt speaks to the people of Esterious. If Livingston is here, he'll be in that crowd. We have to leave after that. It'll be too easy for them to see us as out of place."

Before stepping into the passage, I turned to Landen.

"I love you," I thought.

"You're mine, Willow. I will always love you."

Chapter 17

I warily grinned up at Landen then took my place at Clarissa's side as we stepped through after my father. The passage led into a large building. I could smell oil burning, and the room was sweltering. My father led us up a metal staircase encased in rust. Once at the top, he knocked twice quickly, hesitated then knocked again. A moment later, you could hear someone unlocking chains on the other side, then the thick metal door opened.

Standing in front of us was a man. His years were near my father's, yet his brown eyes were older. He was dressed in a long black cloak shambled with dust and holes. He looked down the stairs at the large group my father had brought with him. I could feel his fear as he stared at Landen then me.

"Jason, I do believe that you're premature. The moon is not yet full," the man said.

Ashten and my father gave each other a cautious look then slowly shook their head 'no' to the man. Landen looked crossly at our fathers, then to August for an explanation. The only response he received was smiling eyes and an emotion of pride.

"We're only searching for Livingston. Have you seen him?" my father asked.

"Yes, he was mistaken for another and was assigned duties in the fields. His time is over today. He should, like everyone else, be in the courtyard."

The man's eyes never left mine as he spoke to my father.

"Am I allowed a formal introduction?" the man asked.

"My apologies," my father said.

"This is my daughter, Willow. Willow, this is Patrick, an honored friend of Esterious."

Patrick smiled at me and bowed his head slightly. He then extended his arm, inviting us through the doorway. The room was dark. You could see a simple table, bed, and desk aligned on one wall and a fireplace on another. The floor was made of wood, and there was no color to the walls. At one time, they may have been white, but now they were a dull gray. Patrick pulled the long thick gray curtains shut and lit a row of candles that lined the mantel over the fireplace.

"And who might this young man be?" Patrick asked as he glanced over his shoulder at Dane.

"This is Dane. He and Clarissa are one now," Ashten answered.

"Ah, and he's here because...?" Patrick asked.

"Dane has a gift as well. The string is visible to him," Ashten replied.

Patrick was either unaware of how sensitive my gift was or simply didn't care if he was revealing. He was astonished as his eyes danced across each of us. The uneasy feeling coming from Ashten and my father was making itself known.

Patrick walked by us one by one, looking up and down. As he reached Landen, and me he stopped and stared into my eyes. A smile then came across his aged face, and his eyes seemed to lose a few years.

"Have you brought something to cover the color in your eyes? Especially Willow's? I would dare say even an old man like Donalt could see them in a crowd," Patrick stated humbly.

I took an uneasy breath and leaned back into Landen, too afraid not show my fear. Landen put his hands on my shoulders and kissed my head softly, taking my fears away and filling my soul with calming warmth.

"People here only have brown eyes. We have to wear a film over our eyes to change the color," Landen explained.

"Like a contact lens?" I asked.

"Yeah, just like that. It doesn't hurt."

My father pulled a box out of his pocket and passed out the lens to change our natural color to a stone black. Patrick walked over to a small closet and pulled out a long black scarf.

"You'll want to cover that sovereign gem upon your neck, unless you're seeking attention I'm not aware of," Patrick said to me.

"Should I put it in my pocket? Isn't it hot? I'll stand out in a long coat and scarf."

"No," Landen and the others said in unison. It was easy to feel that they all thought it was protecting me, or at least feared it would be lost as well. August took the scarf from Patrick, walked over to me and explained, "It is always cool here. The sun doesn't shine. The sky, like everything, is gray."

A loud chime could be heard outside Patrick's home. Anxiety filled the room. The only one who still had his peace was August.

"Ah, it is time. Shall we?" Patrick said as he blew out the candles.

Clarissa and I left the home first. I didn't look to see who followed behind us or how closely. I only concentrated on the one that I knew was Landen and walked forward. There was no grass, plants, or trees to be seen, and the birds didn't sing. The silence was screaming at all of us.

I kept my pace shoulder to shoulder with Clarissa. Several others, all dressed in black, were walking in the same direction that we were. From most, I could feel the sorrow they had, and from others a void that was as real as it was when Drake was at my side.

Like in my dreams, the buildings were all the same. On the street level, there were what looked like food and clothing stations, and above them the rest of the buildings were tall with gray, perfectly spaced windows. As a river would flow, the people streamed toward the palace. My eyes were held straight, not touching anyone but Clarissa.

To my right, I saw Ashten and my father flank off, and to my left, Brady and Marc did the same, leaving Dane, Landen, and August behind us. At the end of the alley, a large wall could be seen. Men dressed in black cloaks lined the top of it, facing a much higher structure.

This structure was indeed the palace. It was over a mile wide, eight stories high, and solid gray. Windows were sporadic, and wide diamond-shaped balconies were on every level.

Along the rooftop, a line of men stood, staring out into the crowd with daring composure. We halted just past the gate. As we stared forward, I couldn't imagine how we'd find Livingston in this crowd of solid black. I could feel my father and Ashten widening their path further away from us, and Brady and Marc mirrored them.

The air filled with the chime of a large bell that rang three times, and the crowd grew still. On the fourth balcony, the doors opened. From the darkness emerged two figures. One was undeniably Drake; he was dressed in a black suit. It was easy to feel that the females in the crowd were attracted to him. He smiled, and I heard a few breaths let loose from the women. I wondered if they even cared how dark he was. He brought new meaning to fatal attraction.

Beside him, a much older man stood. I was sure it was Donalt. He was smaller than Drake and had long white hair. His face held no expression; neither of them held any emotion that I could feel. The bells chimed again as they stepped closer to the edge. I had expected the crowd to roar at their approach, but the silence rained on. It was then that I felt someone staring at me. They were in the palace, and my eyes searched from window to window, balcony-to-balcony.

In the window above the fourth balcony, I saw a small figure. Squinting my eyes, I saw him smile at me. He was the little boy with blue eyes in my nightmare, the one that only needed to be loved. He smiled and waved his little hand. Air wheezed through my lips as the dream came rushing back to me. My emotion didn't go unnoticed.

"What is it, Willow?"

"I've seen that boy before. He's called me, and I helped him."

"What boy?"

"The one on the fifth floor."

As I thought the words, the boy stepped back into the darkness, not to be seen again. Donalt had been speaking the entire time, and for the first time As Donalt's speech ended, the crowed turned, and the faces before me all seemed familiar.

Dream by dream, my eyes landed on person after person. My mouth fell open, and every part of my body froze as each and every nightmare came back to me. The fear within me was uncontrollable, so strong that even Clarissa could sense it. She hooked her shoulder behind me and urged me to turn. Wide-eyed and in a trance, my body was led by Clarissa out of the courtyard. Keeping a fast pace, we reached Patrick's house, where she went to lead me in. Before I took the step off the street, I hesitated, looking for Landen's emotion behind me.

"I'm here."

Taking my last step in the door, Clarissa briskly opened the metal door that led to the passage. Still in an absent trance, Clarissa grabbed my hand and pulled me down the stairs. At the bottom, I felt my feet leave the ground as Landen picked me up and carried me through the passages. The only ones that I knew were safe were Landen and Clarissa.

As Landen all but ran to our home, the string's passages flew past me. As the green fields came into view, I found my clarity.

"Is everyone here?" I thought.

"What's wrong with Willow?" Marc asked.

"We're all here."

"I'm fine," I said aloud, defusing the concern I felt coming from everyone.

I looked behind me and saw Livingston pass through the passage; he frantically looked at us one by one, anger engulfing him. "Why did you do that?" he yelled. "You should have never brought them there! Do you have any idea what could have happened?" He halted when his eyes found August.

"You shouldn't have stayed that long not with all that's going on!" yelled Marc.

"That's exactly why I needed to be there because of what's going on!"

"Let's just calm down," Chrispin said, stepping in to squash his father and brother's feud.

"Let's go. I'm done," Landen thought as he pulled my hand toward him.

We walked away from them, still feeling their frustration and hearing their arguments. I don't think our absence was noticed until we'd already reached our house. Once inside, Landen pulled the drapes and pushed a chair against the door that had no locks. He then led me back into the den and fell into one of the large chairs, pulling me with him.

Landen held me tightly, frustrated and angry. Not forcing thoughts or words from me as I laid with him, I listened to his heartbeat rising and falling with his chest. Time passed and the sun that had glowed behind the drapes faded into night.

As my eyes grew heavy, I thought, "Can we go to our place?" Landen stood with me in his arms and carried me to our bed. Lying side by side with him, I stared into his eyes, losing myself somewhere inside him. He kissed me just as softly as he had the first time, only now warmth accompanied the love that rushed from him. This was the only place where what I was made sense, and it was easy to feel that my feelings weren't alone.

Now the rush that had become so addictive was called again, and we were immersed with a feeling of love that was incomparable to anything on earth. We'd both missed our place, the place where we'd met each night in our dreams throughout our childhood; it was even more beautiful than the world where Landen was raised. Everything was bright, full of life. The only element it needed was sound. Though we could see the birds, their song was absent to our ears, and the water that flowed through the gentle stream did so in silence.

We glided hand in hand as we'd done since we were children. I watched Landen's eyes search each new horizon that came into view. We both felt safe there but had our bodies on high alert as they lay in our bed.

"Do you know where this is?" I thought, wanting to assure myself that now that he stood there again, he'd only been there with me.

"I'm surer now than I've ever been," Landen thought, pulling me to him and kissing me tenderly.

Our path had led us to a place we'd always loved to go: a small waterfall. Beneath the fall was an indentation that wasn't affected by the light mist that surrounded it. Inside, as we nestled, we looked through the water at the soft warm sun.

"How many did you see today?" Landen thought, drawing me against him.

I called the memories forward. "It was like they all were there."

His eyes closed as he pushed his rage down.

"Landen, something is...something is off about that little boy."

"What do you mean?"

"When I helped him, he was dirty, and he was in the town like the others. How do you think he got to be in the palace?"

"Are you sure it was the same one?"

"He looked right at me and smiled, like he knew me. Why were there children in there?"

"Donalt has a court: his blood line, the women he spends his time with, the priests and their families live in the walls."

"I just feel like I've been set up. I really thought that that boy was neglected."

"Neglected?"

"Yeah. He was dirty and sitting alone outside as his parents argued inside the building."

"You were set up. Did you not notice how the people didn't speak?"

"Yeah" I thought, baffled.

"They aren't allowed to speak above a whisper. If a couple were screaming at each other, they'd have been put to death, and the child wouldn't have been outside alone."

"So what did Drake do? Stage it all for me?"

"Maybe he was testing your sensitivities. Were they all children that called you?" Landen asked.

"No, they were all ages, in all different places."

Landen leaned back on his arms, judging his words before he thought them. "How crazy do you think it would be to go through that passage you made inside the palace?" I felt his anxiety and regret for saying the words.

"I've been waiting for you to bring it up. I thought you might be angry with me for making such a dangerous suggestion," I thought, reassuring him that no matter how dangerous it was, we had to save the girls.

"It is dangerous, but I can't think of a faster way to prevent Hannah and Jessica from dying."

"I can't lose anyone else," I thought in a heavy tone.

Landen took in my words and held me tightly. We slept on until late in the next day, hiding from it all.

Through the kitchen window, we could see Felicity, Olivia, and Libby picking the flowers. Their sorrow was very sobering. Walking to them, it was easy to see that the once full field of flowers was growing more and more barren.

Libby smiled when she saw us coming. She then set her basket down and ran into Landen's arms, giggling as he lifted her over his head. Olivia smiled at me; the sight of her had never been more beautiful to me. I'd known her for so many years, and yet to see her happy, at peace, all of her grief gone—she was a new person.

"Landen?" Felicity said in a solemn voice. "Brady wanted me to ask you to come and see him. He's at Marc's."

"Where's Livingston?" Landen asked already knowing the answer.

"He went back to Esterious. Marc stayed at our house last night; he left early this morning. Brady thought he was going to go to Esterious and followed him. Brady called just before we came out here and said that they were at Marc's and to tell you if you came out."

Landen passed a wary look to me. "What about Jason and Dad?"

"They went back to Esterious. No one has really said much since yesterday. They're waiting for you to tell them what to do."

Landen closed his eyes, wishing this burden away, just as any noble leader would want to do when lives were at stake.

"Landen, go. I'm going to go see the girls and check on my mom."

"Is that safe?" Olivia asked.

"Marc's is only a half mile away, we just can't let the string separate us," Landen explained. He then kissed me and hugged me tightly before he left. Even though it didn't hurt as I watched him walk over the hill, the longing to have him close made me uneasy.

"Should I help you pick? I saw some closer to my house," I asked Felicity.

"We have to be careful. They only work when they're alive, so we only pick what we need. I think we have enough for now," Felicity answered.

Walking toward my mother's house, I could feel her. Her excitement was gone, her emotions were full of dread.

We went up to Hannah and Jessica's room. The room was full of a beautiful floral scent. The flowers on their chests had wilted, and one by one we pulled them off and replaced them with new ones. They lay still, not moving; their beauty was remarkable. They deserved more than this. I wanted them to have the same joy Olivia had.

Feeling Olivia's guilt, I placed my hands on her shoulders, smiling and showing her how happy she was. As I pushed the power of love through her, her face lit up as she slowly looked at me.

"Thanks, Willow."

Felicity was watching our exchange, and her excitement filled the room.

"It's coming easier to you now."

"A little bit. I think I'm going to try and help my mom now. I've never seen her like this before."

Felicity's smile lessened a little. "Willow, imagine how you'd feel if you knew that your child had been chosen to fight a battle that they didn't start, and it didn't matter what sacrifices you made, you couldn't prevent it from coming to pass," she said, caressing her stomach and choking on her tears.

I hugged her tightly, showing her how happy she'd made me the first time I'd met her and how much life she'd brought to this family.

The baby kicked, and I felt it through her skin. Felicity laughed, and her bliss was back.

"Looks like she already loves her Aunt Willow."

"She?" I questioned.

"Women's intuition," she said, smiling. "I'll take Libby to my house and let you spend some time with your mother."

My mother was on her back porch, staring at a blank canvas. She was still, more still than I'd ever seen her. I put my hands on her shoulders and remembered all the energy she used to put off, how all my friends thought I had the coolest, most vibrant mother. I remembered her inspiring people to follow their dreams, not to be afraid of what they were capable of.

She smiled and turned slowly. "I told so many to follow their dreams, and yet I kept my own daughter hidden from hers."

"Mom, did you know?"

"We never knew for sure. Your father had a fear, an instinct...he never really told me why he wanted to stay there, but I know he had the best intentions."

She looked into my eyes for a few seconds before standing and putting her hands on my shoulders. "Willow, I just need you to promise me that you'll be the daughter I raised you to be and listen to your heart in every battle you face. Don't let anyone tell you your truth. Every story has countless sides to be told."

I smiled, promising her I would.

My father shuffled his feet across the floor; his sorrow was heavy, and when I turned to look at him, his now brown eyes made me sigh deeply.

"Where have you been?" I asked him.

"We went to look for Livingston. We can't find him anywhere."

"He went back to get the star, didn't he?"

"I don't know..."

"Has he told you anything that I need to know, Dad?"

"You know what we know. He kept Landen from going into that world and just wants more than anything to keep the two of you out of anything that has to do with that star, those rings, the whole deal. He thinks it's all his fault, and for the life of me, I can't figure out why."

"Dad, don't worry about it. We'll figure this out."

"I should be the one telling you that. Listen, we're going to have to think of something quick. When we run out of blue and green flowers, we're going to have to act fast. They may need to go home until they grow back or we figure something else out."

"Dad, you just don't know what those things look like, how painful it is."

"Willow, we're going to have to make a choice for them. To live, they're going to have to be in pain."

I closed my eyes, feeling the burden on my shoulders, knowing that regardless of what choice I made, Jessica and Hannah would pay a price.

"I think I'm going to go home. Landen should be back soon."

"Willow, don't do anything foolish. The two of you can't face this on your own."

I smiled warily at my father then walked past him.

Landen was waiting for me on the front porch; when he saw me coming, he walked toward me. The sun was setting, and the sky was a deep orange. Landen's silhouette was breathtaking; his broad shoulders gave way to his long, strong arms. My breath left me as he gathered me in his arms and kissed me. We'd only been apart for a few hours, yet the reunion seemed so much sweeter. I could not get over how the sight of him would make my heart pound.

"Did you bring peace?" I asked.

"Did you?"

"A little. Is Marc okay?"

"He's just mad at Livingston."

"He's not going after him, is he?"

"I made him promise to wait for us, and he said he would."

Landen's eyes were staring past me as he saw someone. Suddenly, I felt Libby's excitement and turned to see her standing on the hill between our homes, waving her little arms, trying wildly to get our attention. We smiled at each other and started walking toward her, sure that she was happy and at peace. Libby danced in place as she waited for us to get closer.

"Willow, hurry! Mom is going to call my name."

"What is it, baby?"

"Willow, you need a page."

"A page?"

"It's on a long table with red flowers."

"Where's the table?"

"You know, Willow."

Landen and I looked at each other quickly then back at Libby.

"Why do I need it?"

"Because it has words to make Hannah and Jessica all better."

"Libby, do we need the star, too?" Landen asked.

"I don't know. My friend said that you only needed the page."

"Who is your friend?" I asked. Libby shrugged her shoulders.

"Where did you see your friend?" Landen asked.

"I see him when I sleep."

"Libby, does he scare you?"

"No. He showed me the flowers. They're so pretty."

The front door to my mother's house opened, and she stepped out. "Libby, it's time to eat say goodnight to Willow." Libby drooped her little shoulders, then shuffled toward us and hugged us.

"Love you, Willow."

"Love you, too."

We walked slowly to our house. Not turning on any lights, we passed into the living room and settled into the couch, watching the last light fall into the horizon.

"Do you think the passage is still there, the one that leads to the altar?" I asked.

We both knew Libby was talking about the room where we'd found the girls, the one that the priests and Drake were in.

"I don't know why it wouldn't be."

"What do you think we should do?"

"I think that place was a temple, which means during the day it will be full of people."

"What about at night?"

"I don't know."

"Should we go?"

"I like the idea of finding a cure without having to get the star back," he muttered.

"Are we going to let him keep it?"

"I didn't say that. I just don't want to play games with Drake while those girls are clinging to life."

"Dad said when we run out of flowers, we have to take them back if we want them to live," my voice cracked as I reached for my chest, remembering the pain of the nightmares.

Landen closed his eyes and sighed deeply. "We should go tonight," he said after a moment.

"Awake or asleep?" I asked.

"Awake. I don't want our souls trapped there."

"We're going alone, aren't we?" I said under my breath.

Landen nodded. Neither of us wanted anyone there with us; we knew we'd be walking into the heart of Donalt's palace. We agreed to wait until the night so no one would know that we'd left.

Chapter 18

Just before opening the door, we hesitated, staring at each other, both pushing the fear as far away from us as possible. Landen cradled my face with his hand, his blue eyes searching deep in mine.

"Are you sure?" he asked.

I nodded.

He leaned in; let his lips brush against mine, I sighed on contact and leaned up so our lips would meld together. "We've already won," I whispered as our kiss broke.

Beside the string, Brady and Marc stood, waiting for us in the full moon light.

"You're not going with us," Landen said as we approached them.

Their resolve was apparent, and we knew their intent was to leave with us no matter what we said to discourage them.

"We're supposed to go," Marc said, crossing his arms with a stubborn expression across his face.

"Libby told us," Brady said, stepping closer to the string to lead us in. His overwhelming calm was unsettling.

"Libby told you what?" I asked, wondering what part we were all about to play.

"She came to me, and then Marc, and said we needed to go to the string and wait for you," Brady explained as he put his hand on my shoulder. "She seemed calm. I think we'll all be okay."

Landen reached for my waist and pulled me to him, and Brady lost his touch. He stared at Landen as if he had no choice but to go with us, but Landen looked at Brady and shook his head no.

"This has nothing to do with you, Brady. Go home. Felicity needs you." Landen moved his attention to Marc, and I could feel him becoming consumed with gratitude and sympathy. "Marc, you're wrong. You need to find the one made for you."

"We are going with you," Brady said calmly.

Landen looked at the ground. "Where does Felicity think you are?"

"She thinks I'm helping someone, now can we please go?" Brady bit out.

"No one else knows, you're sure?" Landen clarified, looking at Brady.

"We didn't tell anyone," Brady assured Landen by letting him hear the truth in his words.

Brady made his way to the string opening, and Marc followed. Landen sighed deeply as his eyes made their way to the full moon that seemed to engulf the sky. I gently pulled his hand, and we stepped in the string.

Landen took the lead, turning into the passage with the waterfall, hoping that when they saw that we were walking directly into the palace, they'd hear our pleas to go home. Once past the waterfall, we stepped cautiously into the dark forest. Brady and Marc kept their resolve, and no fear came from them.

Landen turned and looked at them. "Listen, I don't know what's in there or who could be waiting. Our purpose is to pull the page from the book on the altar, which has the words that will heal Hannah and Jessica," Landen explained.

"How are you going to know what page? Why not take the whole book?" Marc protested.

"Libby said the page. If we can take the book, we will," Landen said.

"What about the star?" Marc asked.

"For another day. Tonight, we need to find the cure for the girls," Landen said, looking at both of them. "This is your last chance to turn around, this is not your fight."

"Show us the way, Landen. We're going with you," Brady said as his eyes searched the darkness, looking for my passage.

Landen's sorrow was immediate, but he knew that Brady would follow him one way or another, and he'd rather have him by his side.

The passage that I'd made to rescue the girls was still there. Landen gave one more pleading look to Brady before reaching to lead them in with us. When the string passed darkness surrounded us. As our eyes adjusted the moon gave light through an open ceiling. Cold, damp stones made the floor and walls. The wind was the only thing that could be heard.

The altar was in the center of the room, and three velvet red stairs led to the stage upon which it set. It was covered in a black cloth, and blood red roses were centered on the table. In front of them, the book was lying open. Along the back wall, eight planets were carved into the stonewall. Shadows from a candle lit at the bottom of each one gave definitions to the carvings.

A massive stone fireplace lined the wall to the right. Above it, a large portrait hung; it was of Perodine. On the opposite wall, a long, beautiful wood box laid, a bright light shining from the top. Marc's curiosity took him there as Brady made his way to the wall to look more closely at Perodine's portrait. I looked cautiously up at Landen before we stepped forward to the altar to take the page that would save my friends.

When I stepped on the first step I felt a spike of fear that caused me to hesitate. Looking to the source, Marc. I saw him standing over the long wooden box, covering his mouth and trying to hide his disbelief.

"What is it?" Landen whispered harshly.

"It's Adonia," Marc answered.

Landen quickly looked around the room, searching for another coffin, one that might hold Marc's mother, Beth, wanting to shield him from such a pain. Not finding one, we slowly walked to his side. The box was sealed with a glass top, and inside laid a beautiful young woman frozen in time. Dressed in a white gown, her hair was long and dark and decorated with diamonds, and her olive skin lay against silk sheets. Marc stepped back, slowly shaking his head in disbelief as grief filled him along with the memory of his mother.

"What is this? How is this possible?" Brady said leaning closer to make sure it really was her. He was just a small child when she went missing.

"This must be preserving her somehow," Landen said, running his hands along the coffin and examining it.

"Why would they preserve her?" I asked, not understanding why someone would hold on so tightly to someone who had left this world so long ago.

"She was Alamos' daughter. Maybe he's trying to bring her back somehow," Landen said.

I remembered the story my father had told me before—Alamos was Donalt's most powerful priest. I felt my stomach drop, my hands began to sweat, and my heart was pounding through my chest. I couldn't help my unexplained panic. Landen glanced at me just as we heard someone laughing.

Drake had appeared out of nowhere and was now walking across the room, dressed in a black suit.

I swallowed hard and tried to control the adrenaline that was coursing through my veins.

Landen took the first protective step, pushing me behind him. Brady then stepped in front of Landen as Marc stood in front of us all. Stopping in the center of the room and looking over Marc carefully, Drake said, "Ah, you must be Marc." Half-circling him, looking him up and down with his coal black eyes, Marc didn't answer. Stepping closer, he dared Drake to make a move, anger coursing through him. Drake shook his head as a boyish grin spread across his face; he then turned and walked to the altar, and as he climbed the steps, he glanced in my direction. Catching me peeking around Landen, he winked then placed his hands on the book. "I've waited for this," Drake said to the room.

He snapped his fingers, and the candles that lined the walls all lit, giving the room an eerie glow. Growls could be heard at once, and now standing at his feet were the demons. Drake turned in my direction and smiled through Landen at me. I felt Landen reach the point of wrath. "Hey, fair is fair, Willow. You brought your friends, so I thought I'd bring some of mine." He stepped down and walked toward us, weaving his head and trying to pull me into a stare, ignoring Landen and Brady.

Marc held his ground.

"Willow, can you see his intent?"

"No."

"He's trying to get you alone. He can't do what he wants with me this close to you."

"I have to get the page."

"Okay, we're going to ease our way over there. Stay behind me."

We took two steps sideways toward the altar. Drake then took a dominant step toward us, and Marc charged him. As he did, a demon jumped from the stairs onto Marc's chest. Brady rushed to help defend Marc when another smaller one jumped from the stairs onto him. Marc and his demon rolled across the floor, crashing into the fireplace.

Landen reached back to ensure himself that I was still safely behind him. Drake walked without fear to Landen and stared him down.

"Get the page, Willow."

I closed my eyes, hearing Landen's request, not wanting to leave his shield. I hoped he was using his gift of intent and knew I would be safe. I stepped out from behind him. Drake and Landen were now face–to-face, glaring at each other with their shoulders back, waiting for someone to make a move. I kept my eyes on Drake, ready to dash back to Landen if he even attempted to come near me.

A blood-curdling scream went out, but Landen and Drake never broke eye contact. I looked to the fireplace and saw that Marc had taken a poker and stabbed the demon in the heart. As he did, the one on Brady squealed then they both vanished. Marc was enraged and charged across the room with the intent of killing Drake, then out of nowhere a woman screamed out and threw herself at Drake's back.

"Marc, no!" she screamed.

Marc froze as he stared at the older woman dressed in a black gown. Her hair was decorated with jewels, and tears streamed down her beautiful face. Drake turned his back to Landen and glared at Marc over the woman's head. Landen stepped in my direction, staring in disbelief.

"That's Beth."

"Are you sure?"

"She looks just like her pictures, only her eyes have aged."

I could feel the woman's grief, and Marc's emotions were out of control. "Why are you here?" Marc asked breathlessly, not believing his eyes.

"Where else would she be, but with her son?" Drake said as he grabbed the poker that was pressing against the woman's heart from a stunned Marc. Now standing side by side, the resemblance between Marc and Drake was undeniable.

"What kind of game are you playing here?" Brady asked, looking at Beth, not sure if she was real.

Beth stared forward into the darkness, past the room, then gasped as tears fell from her eyes. We followed her gaze across the stone room and saw Livingston walking into the room, holding the hand of the little boy from my nightmare.

"And now let me introduce you to my father," Drake said harshly to Marc, watching his words burn at their touch.

"What's going on? If you knew you're one of us then why are you still here? Why are you playing the part of the devil?" Landen said harshly, looking at Drake with absolute disgust.

Drake turned toward Landen, sinfully grinning. "Me? I would dare say that you are the devil, my friend," he said confidently.

Brady and Marc advanced as Drake waved his hand, sending an invisible force that knocked them down. Beth screamed in terror as she saw them hit the ground.

"Drake," Livingston said.

Drake raised his hand and pointed at Livingston. "I allow you to be here for her, not me. Your words mean nothing. Willow belongs to me, and I shall have her." His tone was definite.

Landen's wrath filled the room, and mine met his as we passed the point of rage. Livingston let the little boy run across the room to Beth.

"Drake, Landen was born five minutes after you...they're only using you...this is not your place, it's Landen's," Livingston said, walking slowly toward Drake.

I edged backwards, getting closer to the altar and watching everyone in the room, hoping this turn of events would serve as a distraction. My heel found the bottom step, and I began to climb the stairs backwards. I felt the little boy's fear grow, and I looked in his direction and saw Beth holding him back from me.

Drake raised his hand to Livingston and flung his body across the room, sending him crashing into the stonewall. Then a rush of energy took the ground from me, and the poorly lit room was replaced by a white glow, much like the string. There was no current or hum, just utter silence. Every single gift that I possessed—including my most precious one, Landen—was stripped from me. I knew that Drake had seen his intent through. He stepped out of the white glow, smiling cunningly at me.

"Now then...for the first time, I have you all alone."

"Drake, take me back!"

"But, my love, we've never left." His voice was warm, alluring, calling me closer to him.

I let my anger rise to defend me. "Drake!"

"Now, now, my love, you must listen to me. If we're ever to leave here, you are the way out, not me." Drake gracefully walked over to where I stood frozen and stopped inches from me, staring down as I stared forward, pulsing with anger. He put his hands on my shoulders, and his touch sent an addictive, blissful, warm sensation coursing through me.

"See? I'm not so bad," he whispered as he moved his left hand down my side and his right hand to my face, tracing my cheekbone and leaving a warm tingle where his touch once was. I let out a quiet breath, and he smiled as he saw the effect he was having on my body. "You really shouldn't listen to all the bad things you hear people say. It's wrong to judge someone," he whispered into my ear.

I let another quiet breath loose as I felt his lips near my skin. I was losing my sense of reality.

"I haven't listened to anyone. I've seen with my own eyes," I answered, searching for clarity.

"What have you seen?" he said, now tracing my eyes with his fingers, then letting his lips dance across my cheek. I was losing control of my body and mind, and I couldn't find a way to grasp the sensation he gave me.

"You're the reason Monica is dead," I sneered, pulling myself back into reality.

Drake hesitated, leaned back then pulled his brow together, questioning my words. Now holding my face with both of his hands, he sent my head into a spin, and I struggled to stay focused.

"She followed you there...she drowned," I said, more sure of myself.

"Ah, now, my love, that would be fate, not my fault," he said, grinning with relief.

"You took them...why?

Drake tilted his head, and his eyes slowly moved across my face, then settled on my eyes. His brow drew together as if he'd been through a great pain. I almost felt sorry for him.

"I needed your attention. I couldn't have you running off and hiding in that ghastly dimension, now could I?" he asked innocently.

"Chara is where I belong, and if you're Beth and Livingston's' son, then you belong there. You need to find the one you're meant to be with and leave me alone. Are you some kind of fool, playing with demons?"

Taking in my rejection, his jaw tightened, but he recovered and laughed casually, then pulled my face to his chest and pressed himself against me. As the warm vibration touched the front of my body, I closed my eyes, and for the moment my body was winning the battle with the help of my mind. I was having a difficult time remaining angry with him, but finding strength, I slowly pushed away and gasped for air.

"You are meant for me. This is not the first time we've loved one another," Drake said, regaining his touch, holding my face, and sending the head-spinning vibration through me again.

"I don't love you," I said, astonished at his words.

He stared in my eyes, looking at someone I was sure didn't exist. "Your memories of me may be gone, but mine are so vivid. You are the same woman I've always loved," Drake said in a voice that almost trembled.

"Your memories are toying with you. I belong to Landen. I always have, and I always will."

It was as if I could see his heart break, but I didn't understand why. I barely knew him. It was my power, not my heart that he wanted.

"I want you to think, Willow, for one minute—how are you so sure?" he asked in a quiet, desperate tone. His eyes captured mine, and I stared back, trying to understand who he was. When I couldn't find the answer I was looking for, clarity came back to me. Nature had proved more than once that Landen and I could not psychically be apart, meaning we were one and that no one could part us. If Drake knew this, he'd know his efforts were in vain.

As if he had read my thoughts, Drake said, "We can be together, if you choose to take another vessel." His eyes were searching mine for understanding.

Now Adonia's body had a purpose.

I was disgusted by his words and scowled at him. "My soul is his—not this vessel."

I looked away from his eyes, trying to break the pull he had on me. "Willow, we have a destiny to fill. You chose this, and you have to let go of your foolish misconceptions." His eyes chased mine, trying to catch my gaze.

"I will never let him go," I said, locking stares with him.

"Never say never, my love. Tonight, you have a choice to make, and your choice will not only impact you, but the entire universe."

Drake pulled my chin up slowly and kissed my lips tenderly. The warm sensation was so heavy, I couldn't move. He slowly pulled away and smiled at me. "If you will be my queen, I will give you the universe as a canvas. You can bring all the flowers and color you want here, you can move their emotions to happiness." Drake moved beside me, draping his arm around my shoulder. Before us, the solid white room opened up, and faces rushed by covered in smiles.

Color was everywhere, birds were singing, and the crowds were cheering. I saw Libby playing in a field, and my mother and father walking hand in hand, smiling. Franklin came into view, and I saw all my friends, happy. I watched as Monica waved eagerly in my direction, full of life. As the sickening grief set in, a tear streamed down my face I wanted to run to her, but I knew she was only an illusion. My eyes searched the room and saw Olivia at the theater, then I could see Dane helping his mother at her Diner. Their loneliness reached through to me as my eyes found their way back to Monica. "I can take it all back to the way it was, and I can give you the power to bring the color you crave for this world, all you have to do is say you will have me and only me."

"Do you take me for a fool? I know that this is not the whole story. What do you get out of having me?" I said, closing my eyes and hiding from the illusions.

"This is the truth I have shown you before remember, my love," he whispered just before kissing my neck softly.

Through the sensation, I found a way to remember the nightmare I'd had in the car: the crowds cheering, the absence of my tattoo, my gift of emotion, and Libby—all vanished.

"Together, and only together, we could rule the universe. Alone, we are but mere mortals," he said, quietly studying my face for compliance.

I breathed in and closed my eyes, trying to find control over my own body. "It is not my place to rule over anyone, and it's not yours either." I stepped away from Drake, causing him to lose his touch. As he did, the numbing feeling left me, and as clarity came back, the anger rose.

"Do you not love your family?" he said, tilting his head and questioning my resolve.

"Do you not love yours?" I retorted quickly. He shook his head as he laughed at my newfound comfort with him.

"I cannot help the cards that I was dealt. If Donalt is to die, he wishes his will to live on through me, for him to have a final say in eternity. And Alamos, well, Alamos only wants to give his daughter's body life again. They are my true fathers."

"If you let his will live on, you are just as evil as he, all the more reason for me not to love your dark heart." I couldn't feel him, but I think my words hurt him. Pain was in those obscure eyes of his.

"Once we are joined, it will be our choice, not theirs. You cannot fight the way you feel about me. I know that you love me. I've seen it, my touch is real."

Drake walked slowly to me and pulled me to him, kissing me softly and sending his numbing sensation through every part of my body; the high was pulling me up and away from my body. He then stopped and cradled my face with his hands.

"For you to bring back your friend and save this dimension, you must leave this body, join Adonia, and be one with me as we rule the universe."

His eyes smiled, and his expression softened. I was so dizzy, I had to close my eyes, and when I did I saw Monica's face, Hannah and Jessica laughing out loud, and color in the gray world that had haunted me my whole life. I felt Drake's lips touch mine, and my balance came into question. Then, Landen's blue eyes finally surfaced above all the images in my mind, giving me the strength I needed. I pushed Drake away, looking at him intently.

"I love Landen."

Drake sighed deeply and wrapped his arms around my limp body. Holding me tightly, he hesitated before he spoke. "Do you love him more than Libby?"

I gasped, pushing away from him and breaking the spell he had on me again. The room opened, but this time the images were of Libby dirty, crying, and alone. The graves of my parents and all my friends slid through the room. The gray world had grown darker. I covered my mouth, stopping the scream that wanted to come out.

"Do you?" Drake said as he stepped in front of the images, blocking my view.

"How could you! How do expect me to believe that someone as cruel as you could ever love someone?"

A sardonic smile echoed on his lips. I had the strangest sense of déjà-vu; it was as if I'd seen him smile that way at me somewhere else in time.

"There you go judging me again," he said under his breath.

"You can't force me to love you," I said through my teeth.

Drake's grin lessened abruptly, and he looked down and slowly back up at me. "I shouldn't have to, love. I never have before," he said finally. I looked at him with utter confusion. Was he insane? He didn't even know me.

"I am giving you the chance to not only rule a dimension, but an entire universe. Wherever you go, you will be honored, the most beautiful and powerful woman to ever take a breath. You can be as kind or as cruel to your followers as you desire," Drake said as if he were painting a beautiful portrait.

Libby's image danced across the room, her laughter echoing around me. Drake's eyes followed her.

"Would you put your comfort before hers? Yours before billions?"

He'd managed to put his hands on my face again, and my clarity left me. My head fell back, and his lips touched my neck. I felt the ring on my finger burn, and the necklace responded.

"I love Landen. I always have, and I always will."

As I said the words, the white glow vanished, and we were back in the dark room. I felt someone jerk me away, and I fell to the ground. Opening my eyes wide, I saw Landen and Drake on the ground, fighting. Beth and Marc crouched over Livingston's body, which was lying at the base of the stonewall. I looked to see that it was Brady that was holding me, and I struggled to stand, halfway pulling him up with me.

"Landen, tell me you love me—tell Drake that's how I got away."

Landen stood, and Drake followed. As they glared at each other, Landen said, "I love Willow, she loves me. What you have done will be undone, today and every day that follows."

Silence fell on the room. Beth stood and slowly walked toward Drake. The rings that we were wearing were drawn to each other, putting me in Landen's arms. Wind turned in the room. Electricity could be felt coursing through us, and a stunning white light came from our hands then bolted toward Drake. Beth dove in front of him, screaming. Suddenly, she vanished and so did Drake.

On the stonewall, the candle under the moon ignited into a flame that burned the entire wall. Brady raced to the altar, fearing that the book would be next. "I've got the page. Do you want to look for the star?" Brady yelled, running to us and handing Landen the page.

"It's gone," Landen said in a whisper.

"What?"

"I'm sure that's where his power came from, it's still with him," Landen said, stunned.

"Is he dead?" Marc asked, not looking up from Livingston's body.

"We don't know where he is," Landen said, looking at Marc with remorse.

Sorrow and grief hit Landen and me with a force that wiped our energy away. I looked to my side and saw Livingston. The absence of emotion told us he was gone. I walked slowly to Marc, pulling every single happy memory that I'd ever had forward. He saw me coming and stood and opened his arms. I hugged him tightly and thought the words 'everything happens for a reason' over and over, and I finally felt Marc's emotion break. He was at peace, at least for the moment.

"We should go," Brady said with a heavy heart. He leaned down and picked up Livingston's body and carried it to the string. I turned and went for the book on the altar. When I went to pick it up, a force repelled my hands. Landen then reached for the book, only to be repelled as well.

"You have the page. Let's go," Brady said.

We looked at each other, knowing that this was not over, and walked toward the passage. I then remembered the little boy and searched for him in the darkness. Landen and I felt his grief and followed it to one of the dark corners, where he was huddled in a small ball. Landen reached down and picked him up, checking to see if he'd been hurt.

"What's your name?" I asked softly.

"Preston"

"Preston, are you okay?"

"Where did my mommy go?"

We looked quickly to Marc to see the blank, fearful expression on his face.

"She had to leave for now. Where's your father?" Landen asked.

Preston reached his arm out and pointed at Brady holding Livingston.

"He's sleeping now," Preston said in an innocent voice.

Brady stepped through the passage, taking Livingston out of sight. Marc walked over to Landen and reached his arms out for Preston.

"We're going to take you home now. You're safe," Marc promised the little boy.

Marc walked to the opening in the string, shielding Preston. Landen and I followed. Just as we reached the string, I heard, "Aliyanna—Guardian," in a comfortingly familiar voice.

I turned to see Perodine walking from the shadows toward us. Marc's fear spiked, but Landen reached his hand back to tell him that we were safe. She had the intent of helping us, we could feel love coming from her.

"It's not over, is it?" I asked her.

Perodine closed her green eyes and shook her head no. She then walked closer, stopping just before us. Landen wrapped his arms around my waist. Perodine smiled kindly at him, bowed her head, and said, "Your task has only just begun. There are eight beyond the sun and the moon, and they will all test your love."

"Is Drake gone now?" I asked with an ache in my voice.

"Alamos will bring Drake back. Alamos has given Drake a power unique to himself, but for any man to see the universe the way he desires it to be, he must have your heart."

"I will always choose Landen."

"It was my wish then, as it is now."

"You aren't angry with me, for what I did, for not coming back?"

Perodine smiled warmly at both of us. "It was impossible for you to return then." Perodine waved her arm, and the smoke from candles on the altar began to take the shapes of images—images of me, of a life I could not remember. Landen and I were in this room, and men in cloaks pushed a light toward us, then we vanished. The scene changed to a beautiful field of wildflowers, and my body changed, too—I was carrying a baby. Time then shifted forward, and Landen and I were playing in a field with Libby.

"She was ours," Landen thought as I felt a deep compassion rise inside of him.

Perodine smiled as she saw me and Landen take in our past. The guilt we had for not returning was washed away. Libby was our reason.

"Today, everything has moved. You can be the souls I dreamed you to be."

I felt Perodine and Landen's fear rise and heard footsteps coming closer. Perodine leaned in and kissed my cheek, then smiled up at Landen and said, "Go. Quickly."

Hastily I hugged her, then Landen pulled me into the string. Marc was holding Preston, and when he was sure that we were okay, he led us home. Landen and I followed. We had it all wrong: we weren't selfish. We had no choice. Knowing that lightened our hearts and brought us closer. We stared forward, wide-eyed, trying to conceive how Preston was Livingston's son. In the string, it was clear that little Preston had no problem seeing. He looked over Marc's shoulder at me and smiled. "Do I get to play with Libby now that I'm going home?"

I smiled and nodded, too stunned to ask how he knew her name.

Chapter 19

It was daybreak when we reached our home, and for the first time I saw the rain fall in Chara. Brady had vanished into the dawn with Livingston's body. Marc, still carrying Preston, followed us to my parents' home. The porch light was on, and upstairs we could see Libby sitting in her window seat, patiently waiting for us. We saw her in a new way. It was clear why her insight centered on us. We loved her even more deeply now.

Libby ran outside to meet us, and we knelt down and scooped her up into our embrace. Both of us had tears in our eyes. We couldn't ever leave her, no one could.

"I knew you'd come back to me. I just knew it, love you," she whispered in our neck.

"We love you..." Landen whispered.

Libby let go, then ran to Preston and hugged him. My father was on the steps, confused and scared when he saw us so early with a little boy. We walked past him, keeping our eyes down.

Landen and I walked up the stairs to Hannah and Jessica's room. The girls were lying in the same positions when we'd left them.

We knelt down between their beds, laying the page on the floor between us. We then joined hands and touched the girls. Landen held Jessica's hand as I held Hannah's. We looked at each other one last time then to the page to read the words scrolled on it.

"Speak pure, hear love, sleep only to dream, dream only pure, dream only love, be no more...leave this now."

Beneath our left hands, a pure white light glowed and a mesmerizing hum centered in my soul and sent a sensation throughout my body. I looked to Landen to see if he could feel it, too; in his eyes, I saw a beautiful glow. He smiled at me. Locked in our stare, we didn't notice Hannah and Jessica wake from their sleep.

"Where are we?" Hannah said.

"I don't remember," Jessica answered.

They looked at each other, realizing that they'd they been healed then threw themselves in each other's arms.

Landen's eyes were still locked into mine. As he leaned slowly forward and kissed me, the room disappeared. I realized how easy it would have been to succumb to Drake's touch, and I was amazed at my will power and thankful that Landen's love was strong enough to carry me through.

Walking down the stairs, we could hear Libby and Preston giggling in the kitchen. My mother was waiting for us, wide-eyed, not understanding what had happened through the night.

"We need to talk, but we can't do it here," I whispered to my mother, looking at Preston.

At that moment, Olivia stepped in the back door. We could feel her grief, and we knew she'd seen Brady.

"Um...I can watch Libby if you guys need to go to Willow's for a little bit," Olivia said to my mother. "Did...did the page work?" she asked, bracing for our answer.

Hannah and Jessica trailed into the kitchen, answering her question. My mother let out a few happy tears as she witnessed our reunion.

Brady had gathered his parents, Chrispin, Felicity, Dane and Clarissa at our house. Landen made a call to August and Rose's home, telling them that there had been an event.

We sat in silence, waiting for the others to arrive, feeling the heavy weight of grief coming from those who knew. In rain-drenched clothes, one by one people filled our house. Brady looked to Landen to explain, knowing that Marc wouldn't be able to find the words. Marc went to Chrispin's side as Landen stood in the front of the fireplace.

"We left last night," Landen began. Sighs filled the room, and anger came over Ashten and my father. Landen continued, "Libby told us we needed a page to heal the girls – and she also told Brady and Marc. We didn't leave you out of this to be spiteful; we only had your safety in mind." Landen's eyes shifted between Ashten and Chrispin then he continued, "Once there ... once we were there, we saw Adonia's body."

Aubrey put her head in her lap, trying not faint.

"Livingston was there," Landen said.

My father and Ashten sat at full attention, feeling less nervous to know that he'd been at our side to help us.

"Um...you may know this," Landen said, looking at his father, Ashten, "but it seems that Beth was alive and well. Drake is her and Livingston's son, not Adonia's."

Astonishment filled the room. It seemed Livingston had managed to keep his secret close to him. Chrispin stood, raging with anger as Marc pulled him back down. Landen took an uneasy breath and continued, "Livingston tried to talk Drake down, but he didn't listen, and with the power of the star...he flung him across the room, knocking him into a stone wall."

"Where is he now?" my father said as he stood, wanting to deliver any medical attention he could.

Landen swallowed hard and looked at Chrispin, who was still being held back by Marc.

"We brought his body home," Brady said, helping Landen.

A chilling silence came over the room. I walked to Landen's side, embracing him, trying to give him peace.

"Where is Beth?" Rose asked.

"We faced Drake, and when it was over, a light came from us, then pushed toward him. Beth jumped in front of it, and she and Drake disappeared. We don't know where they are."

"Who is that little boy?" my mother asked.

"His name is Preston. He told us that Livingston was his father and Beth was his mother. He helped us; somehow, he told Libby through a dream about the page and the flowers," I answered.

August had been staring out the front window, watching the rain. He was calm, at peace, and proud of all of us. Landen could feel it, too; it was the only comfort we had at that point.

"Did it work—the page?" asked Felicity.

"They are completely healed, but we need to take them home soon. I can't tell you that this world will not reject them again," my father said, consumed with grief and dread and holding his eyes down.

My mother rubbed his shoulders, calming him with her touch. Aubrey raised her head and looked at Ashten, then at Marc and Chrispin.

"I, um, Marc...I know you have a lot to take in right now, but I want you to know that I'd be honored to raise your baby brother—and give you time." Aubrey walked over to hug the boys that she'd raised in Beth's absence, and Marc and Chrispin let out the grief that couldn't be held back as she held them. Ashten went to help Aubrey comfort them.

August was still standing silently in the back of the living room, listening to our explanation of the night's events. He cleared his throat, then crossed the room and offered his condolences to Chrispin and Marc. Though he had lost his son, Livingston, I could feel how at peace he was. Reaching into his jacket, he pulled out three envelopes, then handed one to Chrispin and one to Marc; turning to the rest of us, he opened the third.

"Just before Livingston returned to Esterious for the final time, he came to my home and spoke the words that I've always known in my heart to be true. He asked that if he didn't return and we were certain that his life here was over, to read this to all of you – especially the two of you," August said, glancing to Landen and me.

As if the letter had already been read to us, a surge of adrenaline rushed through our souls. The room was still and silent, waiting for the last message left for us by Livingston.

"The letter reads:

If these words are being read to you, you may very well already know what has been left unspoken for so many years. Donalt was seeking a bloodline, my bloodline. Donalt knew I was a direct descendant of Guardian, and he believed that Beth and I would bear

Guardian. I was allowed to go home only to defuse any turmoil. Donalt knew my love for Beth would call me back day after day. Years later, Beth was with child, and we knew that the love of our son would keep us prisoners of Donalt's for the rest of our lives, and we would bear that burden.

Donalt knew he only had half of the prediction; you see, a man is never whole without the heart of the one he loves, this heart would be the power to move so many. The girl was to come from Chara as well; eight months and three days from the birth of the son, Aliyanna would return as well. Willow was the only girl born in that eleventh month.

I asked Jason to keep her hidden, knowing that if she were brought home Donalt would know exactly where she was. I did not realize it was Landen, not Drake, who was born with the power to love Willow until Landen showed us his gift six years later. I planned to take my son and Beth and come home as soon as Donalt had found the fault in his stars. That day never came.

Last November, Drake and I seemed to see eye-to-eye for the first time. I told Drake that soul mates did not need anyone to guide them to one another. If Willow were the one to complete his soul, he would find her without the help of Alamos. He was confident that Willow was meant for him. Drake refused to allow Alamos to invoke the dreams. Beth and I were proud of him; we were both sure that he would find the one he was really meant to be with and leave Willow alone.

With the last new moon, Drake once again refused to dream. The following morning, Donalt and Alamos came to him. They told him before he gave his reign to another man he should first see where my alliances were held. Drake followed me that night to Chara. He saw me in the field with Landen and Marc. He ran to Beth to tell her I had another life. Beth told Drake that it was he that was the secret – not his family in Chara. The next night, he submitted to the desires of Donalt and Alamos and allowed the dreams.

All I could think to do was make sure Willow was safe in Chara. I sent Ashten to warn Jason, but by then it was too late; Willow had been marked, a star that will always serve as a beacon for Drake.

You must know that the priests helping Drake are powerful. My son's sole ambition is to win Willow's heart. Donalt believes that Preston, my fourth son, is the innocent one meant to lead Drake, a prediction that was made with Landen and Willow's birth. Preston is just a child and spoke of Libby days before I knew who she was. Bring him home if you have not already; he and Libby are an undeniable part of this and have a power equal to that of Landen and Willow's. I love all of you, and though you may never see it, somewhere deep in the soul of Drake is the love that Beth and I gave him."

August folded the letter and put it in his pocket. The room seemed to stand still. No one knew what to say or do.

Landen looked down at me and pulled my wrist into his view. This star was a brand; for the rest of my life, each time I saw it Drake's face would pass through my thoughts. From the time I told Landen that Drake had placed that star on my wrist, he had avoided touching it.

Landen stared deep in my eyes. As he gently raised my wrist to his lips, I felt a rush soar through me. He was telling me, and everyone else, that he would never let Drake take me from him.

My father made his way to the front porch and stood silently, watching the rain. Rose left to make arrangements for Livingston. Felicity took a weary Brady home. My mother took an uneasy breath before she stood, and as I hugged her goodbye she whispered, "Thank you for being the daughter I raised you to be."

Aubrey followed my mother to meet Preston.

The room was quiet. We were waiting for an explanation, for someone to explain it all further.

"We didn't know," Ashten said as my father was walking back into the living room. "I mean, he was different after Beth went missing. He never talked about what had happened, and we never pushed him to."

"You didn't know about Drake?" Chrispin snapped, raging with anger.

"No. Livingston did everything in his power to protect Landen and Willow. Landen, if you'd followed Drake into that dimension, you wouldn't have survived," Ashten said. Trying to clear Livingston's name even further than the letter had. I shuttered at the thought of Landen being hurt. Landen pulled me close to him.

"He loved all of you. I'm sure if Drake was his son, he loved him, too. He only wanted peace," Ashten finished.

Landen settled onto the couch, making room for me next to him. We were both tired and weak, but we weren't leaving there until we understood everything.

Landen looked at his father. "Why did you keep me from her?" he asked in a solemn voice.

"I didn't think you were strong enough to protect her," Ashten said as regret coursed through him.

"And exactly when were you planning on deeming me strong enough?" Landen said in a harsh, hushed tone.

"When your fate would not seem forced upon you," Ashten said quietly.

"What does the time that I was born have to do with this?" Landen asked.

"Everything in the universe moves minute by minute, even twins don't have the same alignment...a moment would have changed everything," Ashten answered.

"Is Drake dead? Is this over?" Chrispin asked, standing ready to find him at any cost.

"Perodine told us they'd bring him back," I answered.

"You saw her?" August asked, smiling.

"She only wants to help us. We can do today what we couldn't do then," I answered.

August smiled widely and knelt before us. "Do you know now why you chose to stay and not return?" he asked.

I looked up at Landen and felt his bliss. "We do, a child, our child," Landen said, looking intently at me. The emotion between us was moving everyone in the room.

"We couldn't leave her behind, and she couldn't come with us," Landen continued.

"Her?" Ashten asked.

"Libby," I whispered, still staring at Landen.

The room was still, and all at once they understood Libby's bond with us.

"Is it over now?" Clarissa asked.

"No. She said that there are eight beyond the sun and moon, and that there are more trials ahead," Landen answered.

I closed my eyes and lay on Landen's chest, too tired to worry about the next time that I or we would be tempted. I felt the others find their way to their feet, wanting to move past this revealing morning.

"Ashten and I are going to take the girls home. You all need your rest," my father said.

"I'll go, too. Olivia wants to say goodbye to her family," Chrispin said.

"We're going, too. I want to see my family," Dane said.

They all left silently one by one. I felt Landen carry me up the stairs, and thunder clapped as he laid me on our bed. I opened my eyes as he settled next to me. Quietly, we lay side by side, staring at each other. Lost for words, we drifted to our place, hiding from the grief that awaited us when we woke. Landen never asked what happened when I was alone with Drake. It would have been too painful for the both of us.

In our waking hours, the next few days went by in a haze as mourners flocked to say goodbye to Livingston. My parents, along with Landen, and me went to Infante to mourn Monica's loss with my friends. Everyone was given the space they needed to digest all that we'd been through.

Today, Chrispin and Olivia are to return home to be celebrated. My mother hosted this celebration, letting Aubrey ease into her life with a new little boy. Landen spent the day with Marc and Brady, and I helped Felicity and my mother set up the party. As I critiqued the bouquet I'd just made, my thoughts took me away to the dark images that Drake had shown me, and a shiver ran down my back as I wondered where he might be. My mother must have been watching me; I felt her concern as she put her hands on my shoulder to comfort me.

"Willow, I want you to understand that love is the most powerful thing in this universe, and it will be what you're going to have to call on again and again, but you're going to see your way through this."

I hugged my mother tightly and buried the dark images deep in my memory, only to be used as a weapon against Drake's touch. I stared at her for a moment, taking in everything I'd learned since I found Landen.

"I just don't understand it all. Doesn't it bother you about Libby? I mean, I just can't comprehend it," I said, almost to myself, wanting to remember something about another life just to make this all make sense.

"Willow, take comfort in knowing that no matter what life you live, you'll always have the ones you love the most near you. That's how I see it," my mother said, smiling.

I breathed in and wondered what other roles she'd played in my life.

I dressed for the party at my mother's, remembering how nervous I was going to my own celebration, not knowing my family.

The minutes passed by too slowly. When I walked down the stairs at the end of the banister; I saw Landen was waiting for me. His smile went through me, bringing a unique light to my eyes, and I fell in his arms, welcoming him after a day of absence.

We took our place in the crowd and cheered as Olivia and Chrispin were introduced as one. We raised our glasses, soaking in the harmony that this dimension had bore. Landen took my hand and escorted me to the dance floor, where we danced, lost in each other, thankful that for the first time, the spotlight on our love had dimmed and given way to a new one.

Across the floor, I smiled as I watched Chrispin and Olivia. Brady took Felicity's hand, and Dane and Clarissa swirled past us all. Watching and smiling were my parents, alongside Rose and Karsten.

Above everyone in the room, we could feel an overpowering peace. Looking to the source, we saw August standing with Ashten and Marc. We approached them, grinning. Seeing our attention being taken, others surrounded August. He looked across at each of us, then down to Libby and Preston.

"Libby and Preston asked me to bring them something. At first, like a fool, I doubted their words, but I listened to my heart and brought you this little one," August said, staring down at Libby.

She smiled proudly up at him, jumping in place. August then opened his bag and uncovered a long branch with light green and pink blossoms and handed it to Libby.

"This branch comes from a beautiful Willow tree that's now in Donalt's center court," August announced.

The crowd gasped, then everyone leaned in to look closer at all the color the branch had on it.

"It seems it grew overnight, and each time they cut it down, it grows just as tall and faster than before," August proclaimed.

Landen's arms were around me. As I closed my eyes, he kissed my hair, and I imagined color in the gray world; the first mark I'd left on this universe, a victory that could be looked to for inspiration long after my days on Earth.

The attention of the crowd quickly returned to Chrispin and Olivia, but Landen and I stayed locked in a stare with August, waiting for him to tell us something. He searched our eyes wildly with a profound amount of bliss and said, "The moon on the wall burned that night, did it not?" We nodded. "Then that was indeed the end of the first trial."

"What's the significance of the moon?" Landen asked.

August wrapped his arm around Landen and me and guided us away from the crowd. In the darkness under the stars, he gazed at the heavens for a moment. "The moon is in the fourth house, the house of home and family. It represents your conscious mind, the emotional energy. We all find our own contentment with the moon." He stepped forward and turned to face us. He then looked at Landen and me and smiled in absolute wonderment.

He continued, "It is true that we choose our life, but it's also true that we can choose at any moment to change our path. Within the passing of this moon, you found each other, as well as your home and family. You were given a choice. You were tested." August looked in Landen's eyes. "You could have surrendered to the turmoil, given away what you desire the most for a chance to change Esterious." August looked at me. "You could have believed that the only way to protect the ones that you loved was to surrender your soul." His eyes drifted back to the heavens above us. "You both chose love. Love is prevailing. I can only wonder where every dimension would be if they followed your lead."

"Did we make the right choice? Are those people going to suffer on because of us?" Landen asked, tightening his jaw, unsure if he wanted to know the answer.

August chuckled a little under his breath, then put his hand on Landen's shoulder and looked deep inside him. "The people in Esterious are no different from any others. They have a choice, and for now they've chosen the fate they live," he answered.

"I don't understand," Landen said in a low tone.

"It is true that there are times we all need to be inspired to change, but it's foolish to assume that you have the power to think the thoughts of another. Live in your bliss, and you give others permission to find theirs," August said, smiling widely.

"What are we supposed to do now? How do we inspire?" Landen asked, glancing at me, then back at August.

"Love one another. The stronger your love grows, the more powerful you become. In fact, Jason has a theory," August said in a delighted tone.

I looked quickly back to the party to see my father and Ashten looking in our direction, full of peace and harmony. My father raised his glass and nodded in our direction. I turned back to August.

"Each time you part, your bodies are damaged. Each time you help another soul as one, your bodies rejuvenate. In theory, if you continue to 'help,' then you'll never age or grow ill. Having immortality in one form will grow undesirable to you one day, but for now enjoy your youth," August said, laughing under his breath.

I stared at Landen, wide-eyed. He tilted his head and grinned impishly at me. The feeling we received when we joined as one was extraordinary; knowing that it suspended us in our youth was breathtaking.

Laughing, August patted Landen on the back, then turned and walked into the darkness, gazing at the sky. The peace we always felt from him seemed to grow stronger.

The music from the party shifted to a soft lullaby. Landen reached his arm slowly around my waist and pulled me to him. In the darkness, under a diamond blanket of stars, we swayed. Our eyes fell into one another. We both felt overwhelmed with gratitude. He was real...I was real. We had loved each other across time. He reached down and kissed my lips softly and thought, "I love you, Willow...I always have." I pulled him closer, thinking, "I love you...I always will."